DELIBERATE MALICE

LOIS

AWARD WINNING AUTHOR

CURRAN

Cover Design – Jaycee DeLorenzo
Publishing Coordinator – Sharon Kizziah-Holmes

Paperback-Press
an imprint of A & S Publishing
Paperback Press, LLC.

ISBN -13: 978-1-960499-61-5

DEDICATION

To my three sons, Kenny, Lon, and Jason Waterman. I love you guys to the moon and back.

And, to a special friend, Jason Hacker, who never fails to encourage me.

ACKNOWLEDGMENTS

I never want to fail to thank God for always walking beside me.

Shirley McCann is the greatest proofreader a writer can have. She rocks.

A special shout out to Jaycee DeLorenzo at Sweet 'N Spicy Designs, who makes my book covers express exactly what I want to reveal. She is amazing.

And finally, I want to acknowledge my publishing coordinator, Sharon Kizziah-Holmes. Thank you for believing in me and for gently pushing me to become the best I can be.

PROLOGUE

The street was deserted. It was so quiet she heard the digital clock on the dashboard tick to 12:17 a.m.

She eased the car to the curb and parked on the north side of the community healthcare center. The red brick building, nestled in the middle of a residential area, looked eerie under the streetlights. Flanked by ancient, gnarled oak and walnut trees, it stretched out for nearly a block.

So, what are you waiting for? Get going.

She wiped a moist palm across her jeans then grabbed her bag and the LED flashlight from the passenger seat. Clutching them to her chest with one hand, she used the other to pull a Cardinals baseball cap low on her forehead and climbed out of the Toyota, eased the door shut, and left it unlocked.

The air was humid and smelled like rain. Clouds had clustered in and gobbled up the moon like a crazed Pac-Man. A perfect night for sabotage.

Her footsteps pounded the pavement, echoing like a jackhammer in her ears as she raced across the street. She ducked behind the large black dumpster sitting on its concrete pad and studied the parking lot. Empty. Security lights tucked under the eaves of the one-story structure made a yellowish halo. It gave her a clear view of the rear entrance.

Lightning flashed in the distance. The thunderstorm watch for Lester County might turn into a full-fledged tornado warning. August in central Missouri was ripe for producing storms.

By morning, she suspected she'd be able to hear the city sirens screaming their warning to take cover.

She liked storms, enjoyed the thrill of wind-driven rain blowing hard across dark skies, whipping sheets of water against her plate-glass windows while the branches of the oak trees in front of her house bent in the wind, genuflecting to a higher power.

Scanning the lot in one final sweep, she drew in a dose of oxygen then shot from behind the dumpster. She sprinted across the asphalt then skidded to a halt at the back door. She eased her key into the lock, twisted it open, and slipped inside the building.

The heavy metal door thumped shut behind her, wiping out all traces of light. The stabbing darkness conjured terrible shadows from childhood nightmares. For a nanosecond, she was twelve again.

She gulped hard and tamped the urge to reach for the light switch. Couldn't risk it. Instead, she aimed her flashlight down the hall and followed the beam to a long, narrow room—an entrance at both ends. The room had no windows, so she closed both doors, flipped on the ceiling light, and set her tote bag on the counter.

In a few swift movements, she raked the merchandise from the shelf and crammed the goods into her bag. She yanked the zipper closed and hoisted the bulging carryall over her shoulder. Leaving the room as she'd found it, she headed for the exit.

She pushed the back door open a few inches and peeked through the opening. Her ears caught the grating rhythm of cicadas, but the parking lot remained empty.

Silent lightning bugs, black with red and yellow spots,

flashed on and off, on and off, into the sultry Missouri air. One curious little guy hovered a few inches in front of her.

"You won't tell on me, will you, little bug?" she whispered and gave the insect a wink. "This will be our little secret."

She stepped outside and locked the door.

The indifferent bug faded into the night.

So would she.

CHAPTER ONE

Lacey Bookman, armed and caffeinated, was ready for Monday morning.

A mug of steaming coffee in hand, she headed down the hall. As she circled the clerical area, the fax machine beeped and spewed out mounds of paper. She snatched the pages from the gray plastic tray, went to her office, and tossed the documents on her desk.

Lacey liked the first thirty minutes or so of alone time at the health department. It gave her time to prepare for the day. Also, a chance for a quick check on Facebook if she was in the mood. Usually, she was.

She settled into the swivel chair and took a sip of coffee. Stifling a yawn, she thumbed through the faxes. The first was an advertisement from an insurance company promising superb rates if she'd choose their agency.

Yeah, right.

She wadded it up and tossed it overhand into the trash can.

The next one was Salmonella. A couple of cases had been reported last week. She'd have to make sure there wasn't a common denominator. She tucked the report to the back. The one after that was a Hepatitis C.

Lacey raked a hand through her hair and hit the start button on her PC. No Facebook this morning. All communicable diseases—CDs—in the county were faxed to the health department for follow-up investigations. Not a difficult job but frequently time-consuming.

She flipped to the last fax.

And froze.

Panic hovered beneath her skin, burning to the surface. Fear threatened to overpower her. She sat paralyzed for a moment.

The urge to move resulted in her jumping up so quickly she knocked over her coffee. She yanked a handful of tissues from the box beside her phone, sopped up the mess with her free hand, and righted the cup. Then she looked again at the disease case report clutched tightly in her other fist.

Oh, my Lord in Heaven. This can't be right.

Polio.

A disease no one should have. Not in this generation where inactivated polio vaccine—IPV—protected against such a frightening illness.

Lacey tossed the soggy tissues in the trash can, shot through her door, and burst into the clerical office. She cranked the handle and slid open the vast ceiling-to-floor filing cabinet that housed the immunization records, shuffled through the Cs, and located Holly Collier. The birth date matched. She snatched it from the shelf and scanned the documented shots.

This child was up to date on all her immunizations.

She raced back to her office. With trembling fingers, she scrolled through her phone. Who to call first? She rubbed her temples. Pulled in a long breath. Only 7:30 a.m. Why did it feel an eternity had passed?

Too early for anyone to be in their office.

Lacey shoved the phone aside and pulled her laminated directory of after-hours names and numbers from her desk organizer. A sudden chill slipped up her spine. She never thought she'd ever have to use the emergency call-down list.

She scanned the roster and stopped at Darrell Parker, the Missouri State Chief Epidemiologist. His office was housed in Jefferson City, ninety miles north of her small town. She'd start with him. Darrell had a level head.

With a sense of foreboding, she punched in the chief's cell number. He answered on the second ring.

"This is Lacey Bookman, Director of Nursing at Lester County Health Department."

"What's the problem?"

"It's crazy, Darrell. I hope you're sitting down."

"I'm in my car. Can the dramatics and get to the point, would you?"

"We have a confirmed case of polio."

"What? Did you say polio?"

"Yes. I just got the fax a few minutes ago."

"No way!" Disbelief cut his voice.

"I know. It's unbelievable."

"Seriously, Lacey, it can't be polio. Polio hasn't been around since—"

"It is! I'm telling you."

"Are you sure?"

"I'm looking at the report right now."

Darrell fell silent for a moment, then she heard him blow out a breath. "Lab confirmed?"

"Yes."

"Which lab?"

Lacey pulled the lab sheet. "St. Luke's Regional in Springfield. That's the lab our local hospital generally uses."

"Okay, read me what you've got."

"Holly Collier, six-year-old white female, was admitted to the hospital with a high-grade temperature on October 11. Acute onset of flaccid paralysis on lower appendages with decreased tendon reflexes in the limbs. No apparent cause. No sensory or cognitive loss." Pepsin tumbled in Lacey's stomach like towels in a dryer. Reading the report aloud made it feel ominous. She paused for a breath then added, "The test results came back early this morning, positive for Type I Poliomyelitis."

"What's her immunization status?"

"Letter perfect." Lacey rattled off dates of each IPV the child had received, the last one only fourteen months ago. "The child was adequately protected."

"The first thing you need to do is find out onset of symptoms. I'm talking early ones," he said. "We need to identify the incubation period as well as the period of communicability."

"My nurses will be here in a few minutes. We'll get right on the investigation."

"Enter what you have in the database. I'll call the CDC and let them know it's coming."

Not only were the counties linked with the state computer system, they were linked to the Centers for Disease Control in Atlanta. Lacey had been on the CDC site many times. For research. For statistics. For a dozen different reasons. But nothing even remotely close to reporting a case of polio.

"I'm on it." Lacey palmed the mouse, clicked to the state page, and typed in her password.

"Oh, and, Lacey," Darrell said. "Check with the hospital and make sure they sent a sample to the state public health lab. After Jefferson City does the confirmation tests, they'll send the isolate to the CDC polio lab for additional sequencing of the entire poliovirus."

"Okay." Lacey scribbled *state lab, and CDC isolate* on a Post-it note.

"I'm pulling into the office now. Fax me everything you've got on the case. Everything! Make sure you don't leave out anything. We've got to get a handle on this."

Darrell sounded as flustered as Lacey felt.

She hung up, a slight measure of relief taking root. The heads at the state level were working on this.

Still, she was uneasy at some deep, intuitive level as her fingers tapped the keyboard. She felt like she'd stepped into a bad dream. Polio was a terrible illness she'd read about in nursing school. A disease from the past. Certainly nothing she should have to deal with in her lifetime.

It took under fifteen minutes to enter the basics on Holly. Then Lacey faxed Darrell the hard copy and made a quick trip to the break room for another cup of coffee.

As she plopped back down at her desk, she felt a drumming in her head. She ignored it and checked her watch. Eight ten a.m. Even Joan, her chronically late nurse, would be here by now.

Lacey headed to the nursing station and cornered her three RNs. She pulled them into her office and told them the gruesome news. Shock blazed across their faces, and they stared at her with wide eyes.

"What?" Joan's posture transformed from relaxed to rapt in a heartbeat. Joan Hightower was short and sassy, plump as the Pillsbury Dough Boy, and wore plain blue scrubs with no-nonsense rubber-soled white nurse's shoes. "Are you sure?"

Lacey nodded and swallowed hard. Still difficult to wrap her head around this bizarre situation. If a well-immunized child was susceptible to polio, then no one was safe.

"This is insane." Disbelief flickered across Joan's features. "It has to be some other viral infection that's mimicking polio."

Did the woman honestly think Lacey would risk a panic without evidence? She couldn't keep the frustration out of her voice. "I know this seems crazy, but it's been lab confirmed. The state office is already involved. We have a lot of work to do, but communicable disease investigations are nothing new to us. We'll figure this out."

"Was Holly behind on her shots?" Betty Gann, the youngest of the three, asked. She leaned against the wall with her arms crossed. Her shoulder-length, bleached-blonde hair had been gathered loosely with a gold clip that matched the SpongeBob cartoons on her scrubs top.

"If she wasn't current," Joan said, "she wouldn't have been allowed to enter school."

"Unless her parents signed an exemption form," Betty said.

"She was right on schedule." Lacey held up the canary-yellow immunization card. "Had her final polio booster before she started kindergarten last year."

"Well." Ann Taylor tapped her foot as her large, cobalt-blue eyes pinned Lacey with her characteristic *I-know-it-all* look. "No immunization is one hundred percent effective. There's always that small percent that aren't protected."

Yeah, one percent. That's pretty good odds for the kids. Lacey bit back a sarcastic reply. She didn't have time to play Ann's nonstop power games. Ann was a couple of years younger than her but never hesitated to point out she'd worked at the health department longer than any of the nurses, Lacey included. Ann did know her CDs and Lacey depended on her, ignored her tenure arrogance...most of the time.

"Vaccine viability aside, we're talking *polio* here," Lacey said. "We shouldn't have even one case in our country."

"You've got that right," Betty said. "There hasn't been a case in the United States in forever."

"Well, apparently there's a case now." Ann blew off Betty with a wave of her hand. "We'll have to deal with it."

Betty bit her lip and shot Ann a look that could melt ice. Betty wasn't as sassy as Joan or as brazen as Ann, but in the eighteen months she'd been at the health department, she'd proven she could hold her own. No longer the insecure graduate, she'd shed her student-nurse cocoon and morphed into a full-blown, confident public health butterfly who didn't take guff from anyone.

Lacey pinched the bridge of her nose. She wished Ann would stop fidgeting. Why was she so edgy all of a sudden? Her constant toe-tapping was taking a toll on Lacey's already frayed nerves.

"Ann," Lacey said, "get in touch with Holly's mom or dad. They'll be at the hospital, but there's a cell number for them on the report. Find out Holly's symptoms, where she's been for the past month, and who she's had close contact with."

"Do the parents know...I mean, that it's actually polio?" Ann asked.

"Good grief." Betty shook her head. "I sure hope so."

"Me too." Ann never missed a beat with the muffled *whop-whop* of her shoe. "I'd hate to be the first to break the news to them."

Lacey remembered the time she had called a young man to follow up on a measles case. He had been home from the hospital for two days before the lab results confirmed rubeola. He'd left the hospital after being told he had a "rash-like illness of unknown origin." Lacey had definitely felt uncomfortable explaining why she'd received the news before he had. She couldn't imagine being the one to deliver the news of polio.

"They know they have one sick child, and I imagine the doctor's talked with them by now." Lacey glanced at her watch. She knew hospital protocol well enough to know that with something as serious as polio, the doctor would have been called in stat. Most likely had arrived before Lacey had made it to work this morning.

"Betty, you and Joan need to follow up on the contacts as soon as Ann gets a list compiled," Lacey said. "Every adult that has been around Holly for the past month will need a polio booster. Find out if she's been around any infants that haven't started their immunizations yet, and let me know ASAP. Talk to the school nurse; make sure everyone in Holly's school is right on target. Also, get a list of any child that wasn't immunized because of an exemption."

"I think the homeschoolers will be the ones that aren't vaccinated," Betty said. "How are we going to locate them?"

"Put out a news release if we have to." Lacey pushed a stray strand of hair off her forehead. "But let's wait a couple days on that."

As the team hurried out, Lacey picked up the phone and called Susan Gregory, the infection prevention nurse at the local hospital. They'd worked together on communicable disease cases many times over the years, but never on anything like this.

Susan's voice was laced with fatigue when she answered.

"Hey, Susan, this is Lacey. What can you tell me about the polio case that wasn't included in the faxed report?"

"Not a lot," Susan said. "Holly was put in isolation on admission because she came in with a temperature of 102.6. She had no visitors, other than her mom and dad, so we haven't had a lot of exposure."

"That's good. We need to keep this as confined as possible."

"I hear that."

"I assume the doctor has been contacted."

"Yes. As soon as the lab confirmed polio, they notified the physician, and he called me in."

"What time was that?"

"Six this morning. As soon as I got here, I gave Holly's parents, and the hospital staff who'd had direct contact with Holly, an IPV booster."

Lacey rubbed the back of her neck where a knot threatened. "Have you sent the culture to the state lab?"

"Yes. It went out by courier and should arrive within the hour."

Lacey crossed *state lab* off her list.

"What's the status on Holly at this point?"

"Her condition is critical."

"Poor little girl."

"I can't believe we actually have a case of polio," Susan said.

"Me either. Feels surreal." Lacey switched the phone to her right ear. The left ear was warm and tingly. "Will she be transported to Springfield?"

"No. She's scheduled to be transferred to Children's Hospital in Columbia as soon as arrangements can be made. I'll let you know when she's on her way."

"Thanks. Talk to you later."

Columbia is a teaching hospital, Lacey thought as

she hung up. *They'll take good care of Holly.*

Lacey's aching head demanded attention. She swallowed two aspirins with cold coffee then called Joe Phelps, an epidemiology specialist. He was her immediate CD contact in the Springfield office. She briefed him on Holly's condition while entering the new information into the database. Joe ended the call with a promise to do some research and check back with her later that day.

The rest of the morning sped by in a blur of phone calls and paperwork. Just before noon, Ann shot into Lacey's office. "I've got it," she said. "I know where Holly contracted polio."

Lacey snapped to attention. "Where?" She felt a tingle of dread but chased it away.

"Holly and her parents were in Lagos, Nigeria. Holly's uncle is a missionary in Lagos and the family spent two weeks with him. They just got back on October sixth."

Lacey typed *Nigeria* into the computer. "I'll check but I'm sure polio is prevalent there. Anyone else in the family sick?"

"No. Just Holly. Her mom and dad got an IPV booster two months before the trip. The doctor looked over Holly's immunization record and said she didn't need one."

"He was right, she didn't," Lacey said.

So why would she be the only one in her family that contracted the disease? Why weren't the parents susceptible?

"Okay, here we go." Lacey stared at her computer screen. "Nigeria is one of four countries that remain polio endemic."

"So now we know where she got it," Ann said.

"But the big question is why."

"One of the less than one percent that didn't

respond to the vaccine, I suppose." Ann shot her an *I-told-you-so* smirk.

Lacey rolled her eyes. "Or maybe her immune system is compromised."

"Yeah?" Ann hitched up a shoulder. "And no one's picked up on it yet?"

"I know it's a long shot, but Susan said the lab is running tests for any immunosuppressive diseases."

Lacey rubbed her temples. She fretted about the other children in Holly's class. What was the likelihood of another child in the county not responding to the vaccine? Slim to none. Or two kids in the same class with a faulty immune system? Zilch.

Tears threatened as she thought of her friend's little girl, Suzie, who attended Holly's school. If something were to happen to that child...

Shards of fear pierced her heart at the thought of any child contracting that paralytic, even life-threatening disease. She swallowed her panic and tried to focus. *Dear Lord, help me not to expect the worst.*

Lacey pulled in a long breath then blew it out. "What's the status on Holly's contacts?"

"Betty's working with the adults in Holly's extended family, encouraging them to come in for a polio booster. The kids at Hoover are up to date with all their immunizations. All the kids had three IPVs, properly spaced and on time, before they entered school."

"No children without vaccines because of an exemption?"

"Nope."

"Providing the vaccine is viable, the school should be okay. But Holly should have been okay, too." Lacey ran the tip of her tongue across a dry lower lip. "If the kids stand a chance of not being protected, then let's pray another booster will raise their immunity. If not, we could be in real trouble."

"We knew the students would be up to date before we started checking." A sardonic edge cut Ann's tone. "If you ask me, it was a big waste of time. If those kids hadn't been current with their immunizations, they wouldn't be in school. You know it as well as I do."

Lacey leveled a look at Ann and couldn't bite back the rebuke. "We're going to confirm everything. It doesn't matter how trivial it seems to you. Got it?"

"Got it." Anger flared in Ann's eyes and died out a moment later. She crossed her arms and said, "Betty asked the school nurse to let the staff know they need to get a polio booster ASAP. And she's sending a letter home with the students today to recommend another booster for the kids."

"Good." Lacey pushed her hair back from her face. "Check our IPV stock, make sure we have plenty. We'll be giving a lot more polio shots in the next few days."

"I've already put in an order." Ann headed to the door. "It should be here tomorrow."

Lacey nodded and turned back to her computer. More data to enter and she had a full-blown headache. The aspirin she downed earlier only caused her stomach to burn more.

And that nagging feeling of foreboding hung on.

CHAPTER TWO

Jacob Bookman strode across the parking lot and unlocked his car. As he scooted behind the wheel, he spied Kimberly Ames walking toward her fire-red Mustang. He sucked in a breath. The 'Stang fit her personality. Hot. Red hot.

Kimberly opened the door with her fob and had one hand on the handle when she spotted Jake. She smiled and headed toward his vehicle.

"I thought you'd be on your way home by now." She placed hands on her slim, but curvy-in-the-right-places hips. "You must have worked late, too."

"Uh-huh. I got tied up in a meeting with the boss. And you know how that goes."

"Oh yeah." She laughed. The rumbling sound in her throat was pleasing. "Brad never knows when to wrap things up."

"What about you?" He gave her trim figure a quick appreciative sweep. *Perfect* was a good word for it. "Why are you here so late?"

"I had a report I wanted to finish typing. Brad wants it ready for his signature first thing in the morning." She smiled, showing straight, white teeth. "I'd rather stay late than come in early."

Jake nodded. "Yeah, I'm not a morning person, either."

She cocked her head to the side and lifted one brow. "I wonder what else we have in common."

Jake had been wondering the same thing for six weeks, ever since she'd joined the workforce. He met her gaze and his stomach clenched, warning him to rein in his imagination.

"I've been meaning to ask you if you'd give me a few pointers on the accountant test. You know it's my final exam." She leaned down and rested both arms on the window frame. "I'm scheduled to take it next month, and I want to nail it the first time."

Her scent, something fresh and slightly fruity, made his pulse kick up a beat.

"Sure. Come by my office tomorrow and—"

"Huh-uh. The office is too noisy. I couldn't concentrate," she said and wrinkled her nose. "Maybe we could go somewhere a little more private."

His heart jerked. As tempting as it sounded, he couldn't spend time alone with Kimberly. Definitely not a good idea. It was one thing to flirt at the office. But be alone with her? No way.

"Well?" Kimberly stood and straightened the bottom of her navy-blue jacket. Jake couldn't help but notice how nicely she filled out her silky beige blouse. "What about it? I could sure use your input."

The word *No* formed on his tongue then dissolved as his cell phone rang. He glanced at the name on the screen. *Lacey Bookman.* "Gotta take this." He winked. "It's the wife."

Kimberly rolled her eyes but gave him a grin. She tossed her hair over her shoulder then trekked to her car. The swing in her hips seemed a little exaggerated even for her.

Nice though. Jake hitched in a breath and swiped a

thumb across the phone. "Hi, honey."

"Hey, Jake. Are you headed home yet?"

"Just getting ready to leave the parking lot. I had a meeting that ran over but I'm on my way now."

Kimberly's year-old Mustang thundered by, and she tossed him a wave. Jake threw up a hand as she hit the street and veered left down Adams Avenue.

"Dinner's gonna be late." Dismay nipped Lacey's words. "Again."

"Sorry, babe." Jake pulled his brows together and fired up the engine. "Couldn't be helped."

"Okay. I'll see you in a few minutes."

"Sure thing."

Jake hit *End Call* and backed out of the parking space. Kimberly was long gone. He smiled as he thought about her scent, her full pouty lips, her curvy body. She couldn't be much over twenty-two, twenty-three at the most. Brad had hired her as a secretary with the promise of a promotion when she passed the final accountant test. With just Brad and him as CPAs in the small business, they could use some assistance. She was good at her job and her coy persona livened up the office. Her flirty presence made Jake feel young, sexy.

Like he used to feel around his wife.

He sighed. What did he expect? He and Lacey had been married seventeen years. It was normal for the excitement to die down after almost two decades. Wasn't it? He loved her, would never do anything that would hurt her.

This thing with Kimberly was nothing. He turned into his drive and pulled into the two-car garage. Completely innocent, he assured himself as he stepped from the vehicle. He pushed through the back door and set his briefcase on the kitchen counter.

Lacey stood in front of the sink in faded orange

sweats, drying her hands on a kitchen towel. She turned and arched an eyebrow.

"Well, well." She tossed the dish towel at him. "It's about time."

He caught the towel. "Aw, don't be mad." He put his arm around her waist and pulled her close.

A slow smile tipped up the corners of her mouth. She stood on tiptoes and brushed her lips across his.

"Do I have time for a quick shower?" he asked.

"I suppose. But make it quick. The kids are starved."

"You, too, huh?" He glanced at the half-eaten twelve-ounce bag of M&Ms on the counter. It amazed him that she kept her size six shape considering the way she could put away food.

She shot him a look that said *don't even go there* and he stifled a grin.

The other half of the M&Ms will be gone by the time I get back. He raced upstairs, taking the steps two at a time.

Fifteen minutes later, he slid into a chair at the kitchen table. His hair was damp, and he'd changed into a red T-shirt and worn Levis. He eyed the meatloaf and potatoes and his stomach growled. He was hungrier than he'd thought. "Everything looks great."

"Thanks." Lacey scooped a spoonful of mashed potatoes onto her plate. "How come you have to work late so often? I thought the new girl was going to cut down on the overtime."

"She will, after she passes the boards and can actually take some of our cases."

"Are you happy with her? Kimberly, isn't it?"

Jake nodded. "Oh, she's doing great." He groped for his glass and took a long swallow of cold mint tea. "Just great."

LOIS CURRAN

Lacey was uncharacteristically quiet throughout the rest of dinner. Tight lines around her full lips revealed tension. As she sipped her iced tea, Jake wondered if she was irritated with him for being late.

At thirty-eight, she still looked as good as the day he'd met her, maybe better. Short, light-brown hair streaked with blonde highlights framed a heart-shaped face. She looked like one of the delicate porcelain dolls she collected. A fraction over five-five, she was shorter than Kimberly but carried her curvy frame well. Her chronic yo-yo dieting coupled with workouts kept her slim and toned.

What more could a guy ask for?

She smiled when she caught his gaze. Her blue eyes fringed with long, thick lashes could still melt his heart on any given day. He chided himself for even comparing her to Kimberly.

"So can I, Dad?" Todd asked.

Jake looked at his oldest son, wondering what he'd missed. "Can you what?"

"The car!" Impatience flicked across his face, and he sighed as only a teenager could. "I wanna drive my car to school."

"I don't know..." Jake shook his head. He'd helped Todd purchase a used Escort last week but wasn't comfortable giving him free rein just yet.

"I could drop Brian off at his school and we wouldn't have to take the bus. You know how I hate riding that stupid bus."

"Yeah," Brian said. "Me, too."

"You've only had your license a couple months, honey," Lacey said. Concern creased her forehead.

"Yeah. But I drove six months before that with my permit."

Lacey shrugged and tossed Jake a *the-ball's-in-your-court* look.

20

"Do you think you're up to fighting all that traffic?" Jake had seen the madhouse at the high school parking lot before and after school. Bumper-to-bumper cars loaded with teenagers vying for a parking spot in the morning. The afternoon was even worse— hyped-up kids anxious to hit the road after the final bell.

Todd rolled his eyes. "It's not that bad."

"Come on, Dad." Brian pleaded his brother's case clearly for his own motives. "Let him. All the other kids get to."

"All the other kids get to," Jake said in a falsetto voice and tousled his youngest son's hair. "You're just wanting off that bus."

Brian's face brightened. "No. Well, yeah, that, too. But you know Todd's a good driver." He ran a hand over his hair to push it back in place.

Jake glanced at Todd's expectant face. He knew his son was a responsible sixteen-year-old, and he'd have to trust his proficiency at some point. *Might as well be now.* He looked at his wife and she gave him a green-light nod.

"Okay. But you be careful. And absolutely no speeding."

"Gotcha." Todd flashed his brother a crooked grin, picked up his plate, and popped up from his seat. "I'm your new ride."

"All right." Brian high-fived him then shoveled the last bite of potatoes into his mouth as he scooted his chair back and headed for the door.

"Hey," Lacey said. "Take your plate to the sink."

"Oh yeah." He backtracked to scoop up his dishes. "You guys are pretty cool," he called over his shoulder as he bolted through the door right behind his brother.

"We were doing cool before you were born," Jake

said, and laughed.

Lacey chuckled and gave him a playful swat. But he noticed the troubled look in her eyes.

"Don't worry, honey. You know Todd'll be careful with the car."

"I know." She inhaled deeply then stood and headed toward the dishwasher.

Jake pushed back from the table and took his plate to the sink. He touched Lacey's arm. "Hey, are you okay? You seem down."

"I am a little." She lifted a shoulder. "It's work."

"Bad day, huh?"

"The worst." Lacey pulled her lips taut. "We got a case report of polio today."

"Polio?" He blinked. "People still get that?"

"They shouldn't." She sighed, opened the dishwasher, and maneuvered a plate into the wire rack.

Jake picked up the M&M's bag, popped the last two morsels into his mouth, and tossed the container in the trash. He grabbed a dishrag and wiped the table with wide circles. "I know you can't tell me a lot about it..."

Lacey gnawed her lower lip. Tension rippled off his wife in waves. He walked to the sink and leaned on the counter.

"It's a little girl who's up to date on her shots," she said. "None of us can figure out why she would've contracted polio."

"Even you, Lace? You don't have a gut feeling?"

Lacey was good at her job and worked by instinct a lot of the time. But she shook her head.

"The only feeling I'm getting is that something's not right," she said.

He leveled a look at her. "This is serious, isn't it?"

"Yes. Very serious."

"Why is this worse than the meningitis cases you've worked?" He flashed to the overtime she'd put in a few months back when two bacterial meningitis cases had popped up in the county and consumed her time for a solid weekend.

"Because polio has been eradicated in the United States. And most of the world." She shook her head. "This could mean we're not as protected as we thought."

Jake could practically taste her fear. Safety for the community was a big deal for her. He raked fingers through his hair and glanced toward the driveway where the boys were shooting baskets. "Any reason to worry about our kids?"

She hitched up a shoulder. "No. I don't think so. They are up to date on all their shots and they don't have any health issues. I'm sure there's nothing to worry about."

Her mouth said one thing but her eyes spoke differently. She was really spooked.

"Lacey, you'd tell me if I needed to—"

"I'd tell you," she said. "I promise."

Jake nodded. He trusted her medical sixth sense. She was a good nurse and a good mother. She'd let him know if the kids were at risk.

Lacey closed the dishwasher and pushed the start button. "I need to call Mom and see how she's doing with housebreaking the new puppy."

Jake smiled thinking about the stray pup Margaret had taken in. Lacey was a lot like her mother. They were both softies. Always willing to step in and help out anyone or anything, like that poor helpless dog someone dumped on Margaret's street.

"I'm going to go over some notes before the news comes on," Jake said. He stepped into the family room and scooted up to the desk nestled at the far corner.

As he opened his briefcase and pulled out the audit he'd been struggling over, laughter drifted in from the kitchen. Maybe Lacey's mom could cheer her up.

After refining his notes for much longer than he'd intended, the report was ready to turn over to his boss in the morning. He slid the audit in his valise and noticed a small envelope tucked into the elastic pocket. He popped open the seal and recognized Kimberly's superb penmanship.

Hi, handsome. Here's a little note to brighten your day, or night, depending on when you find it. Think of me when you read this because I will be thinking of you. In fact, I find myself thinking of you quite often these days. ☺Kimberly.

He returned the note to its hiding place, wondering when Kimberly could have planted it. Lacey couldn't find such a note from another woman. Although it was innocent—wasn't it?—it could easily be misinterpreted.

Jake was surprised by the heat that inched up his neck when he thought of the note. She was something else. So, she had been thinking about him, too. *Well, this could get interesting,* he thought then quickly reminded himself that Kimberly was off-limits. He closed the briefcase and tried to ignore the thoughts that raced through his mind.

Get a grip, Jacob. You know you'd never cheat on Lacey.

CHAPTER THREE

Tuesday morning, Lacey settled into her desk chair and sipped coffee as she filled out the monthly nursing schedule. When the phone rang, she picked up the receiver and said, "Hello. This is Lacey."

"Lacey, we have a problem." Susan sounded grim.

"What now?" Lacey snatched a pen and pad of paper from her top drawer.

"Another possible polio."

"Oh no." Her stomach turned over. A dozen things she'd need to do twirled through her mind like a kaleidoscope reflecting symmetrical images.

"Okay," Lacey said, "fill me in."

"Yesterday afternoon, a little boy came through the ED with the same symptoms as the previous polio case. Dr. Johnson transferred him to Columbia Children's. The infection control called this morning, and the child is being treated as presumptive polio."

"How old is he?"

"Six."

"Same age as Holly," she said, while she tried to organize her thoughts.

"Yes. Same age. Same grade."

Lacey massaged the bridge of her nose. She

couldn't wait for a verified diagnosis. Not with a second case. She'd call it confirmed. "Send me the information. We'll start the investigation immediately."

"I just faxed it to you. It should be there by now."

"I have a bad feeling about this," Lacey said.

"You and me both." Worry flattened the nurse's tone. "Everyone's freaking out over here."

Lacey gripped the phone tight. A knot formed in her throat making it hard to swallow. What was going on with these kids? Why, of all the long-ago eradicated diseases, would polio pop up?

They ended the call and Lacey retrieved the fax. She pulled the child's immunization card and flipped through the record. Michael Browning received his polio shots right here at the health department. Just like Holly. Up to date. Just like Holly.

Her jaw ached as she chewed on the information.

Lacey plunked down in her chair, flipped open Michael's record, and highlighted the lot number of the last polio vaccine then did the same with Holly's record.

She punched in Darrell's number and gave him the latest information while she logged into the state website.

He cleared his throat. "Okay, send me what you've got."

"I'm getting ready to enter the basics." She blew out her cheeks then released the air. "You'll have them in a few minutes."

"Did you check the lot numbers on the vaccine?"

"Uh-huh. Michael's lot number was different from Holly's. We can't blame this on a bad batch."

"Lacey, are you sure both of the kids were up to date on their shots?"

"Of course, I am." She couldn't keep the agitation

from her voice. Did he seriously doubt her ability as a communicable disease nurse?

Silence.

"That's the first thing I looked at," she said.

"I know. Sorry. I'm completely baffled. You know as well as I do these kids shouldn't be getting polio. Unless..."

"Unless what?" A sudden chill lifted the hairs on the back of her neck.

"Well, what if this is a new strain of polio?"

Lacey rolled the question around in her mind. She massaged her temple, trying to erase the headache that was attempting to take up residence. "But the lab confirmed Type I polio on Holly."

"True. But it could be Type I and mutated just enough to change the strain. That wouldn't be identifiable on the preliminary testing."

"If it's a different strain," she said and shuddered, "then our polio vaccine would be useless. We could have a nationwide outbreak on our hands."

"Yeah. But I'm probably overthinking this."

"Let's hope." Lacey twisted her pen. She struggled to focus. A case of polio in the United States was unheard of. *Now we have two.* "Something weird is going on. Good grief, polio doesn't evolve for no reason."

"I agree." A hint of anxiety radiated in Darrell's tone. He was usually calm and in control. Not much shook him. But dealing with a case of polio was reason enough to shake anyone's world.

"So, what next? Should I be doing anything else on this end?"

"We keep digging."

"How?" Lacey asked. "I mean, what else can we do?"

"I don't know. I've had a number of infectious

disease consults and CDC is on top of it. Hang in there, we will get to the bottom of this. We've got to."

"Thanks, Darrell."

Lacey ended the call and pondered over the information, trying to make sense of a no-sense situation.

Ann stepped through the doorway. She clutched a piece of paper in one hand, her lips pressed together like a vise.

Lacey pulled in a breath. *What now?*

"Just got a fax from St. Luke's." Ann shifted her weight from one leg to the other. "A sixteen-year-old boy who lives in our county died early this morning. And get this. Diagnosis, tetanus."

"Tetanus!" Lacey's voice shot up an octave. She reached for the report and stared in disbelief. "For pity's sake, what's going on here?"

She scanned the data and didn't like what she read. Gregory Morris, same age as her oldest son, Todd. She'd bet money Todd knew him.

What if it had been Todd?

Lacey chased away the what-ifs and chided herself for even going there.

"I received more bad news this morning," she told Ann.

"What?"

"I'm afraid we have another case of polio."

"You're kidding!"

"Well, presumable at this point, but it looks like it's going to be confirmed."

"Any link to Holly?"

"Yes." Lacey popped up from her chair. Her nerves were unraveling like a runaway ball of yarn.

She picked up the polio case report and passed it to Ann.

Ann drummed her fingers on the desk as she

looked it over. "We know his class is okay. The entire school is up to date with all their vaccines."

"That's right." Lacey waved Michael's immunization card. "This child was up to date, too. So was Holly. Up to date isn't cutting it anymore."

Ann aimed a flinty look at her. "What are you thinking, Lacey?"

"I don't know." She shrugged. "This is crazy. For no apparent reason, we have two kids with polio and a death from tetanus. I don't know what to think at this point. And what frustrates me is I have no idea what to do."

"I'll pull Gregory's immunization card. Uh, that is— if he had his shots here." Ann's hand trembled as she pushed a stray strand of hair behind her ear. She bolted out of the office.

Her CD nurse was shaken, but who could blame her?

Lacey's own hands weren't all that steady as she finished perusing the tetanus report.

In a few minutes, Ann returned and placed Gregory's immunization record on the desk. One glance told Lacey what she'd suspected. He was current with his immunizations.

"He got a tetanus shot two years ago," Ann said. "Right on schedule for his ten-year booster."

Lacey nodded. "Doesn't surprise me."

"Me, either. Now what?"

"Go ahead and start the investigation on Michael. We can't wait for the confirmation. I'll enter the data on Gregory, but first I'm going to run this information by Robert."

Robert Baker, the Administrator of Lester County Health Department, had been out of town at a meeting yesterday when the first polio case was reported. Lacey had called him on his cell to give him a heads-up. Though he gave her complete control of the nursing department, he didn't want to be left out of the loop.

Lacey tapped on Robert's open door and stepped inside. He looked up from his stack of mail, smiled, then pointed to a chair across from his desk.

Lacey blew out a long breath as she slipped into the seat.

He raised a brow. "What? More bad news?"

"Uh-huh." She updated him as quickly as possible then added, "The press is going to be all over this as soon as it gets out. And I'm sure it won't be long."

"I can handle the press." He waved a large hand in the air as if he were shooing a fly.

Oh yes. Robert owned the face that loved to go before the public. He was trim, muscular, and though his sideburns were graying a bit, he still looked good.

"Get a press release ready and fax it to the media," he said. "It's best they hear this from us first. Have the girls send all calls from the media to me."

"Thanks." That was one less thing she'd have to deal with.

"No problem. Glad I can help."

"I'll need everyone's help keeping the panic under control." She lowered her voice and met his gaze. "And you do realize there will be panic. Polio has been eradicated for years."

Robert tilted his head.

Lacey continued. "Even simple illnesses cause our residents to freak out. Can you imagine what this will be like?"

"Oh yeah. I can. I may not be a nurse, but I know what's going to come down. Two cases of polio is definitely a crisis. And now a fatal tetanus." He raked fingers through his hair. "We're in for major hysteria."

That's for sure, Lacey thought as she pushed up

30

from her chair.

"Thanks for calling me yesterday," he said. "I appreciate it."

She nodded and left. Staffers filled the aisle between the nursing station and the clerical office. The group was restless, with low talk and nervous laughter. They fell silent and gazed at Lacey.

"Robert is going to be the liaison with the press," she said. "I'm going to type up a press release and give everyone a copy. We want our information to be consistent."

She faced the clerical staff. "You guys will be the first line of communication. You're going to be bombarded with questions. People will be frightened, and they'll lash out at whoever is on the other end of the line. You know how crazy it gets with a case of meningitis? Well, this will be a lot worse. Just stay calm and try to keep the clients calm. Assure them we are aware of the situation and are doing everything we possibly can. Let them know the State Health Department and the CDC are working closely with us."

The clerks stood rock still, eyes wide as they stared at her. Kind of reminded her of the statues she'd seen at the St. Louis Historical Museum two weekends ago when she and Jake had gone away for a mini vacation.

"Don't worry," Lacey said. "You'll do fine. If you get a question that you aren't comfortable answering, transfer the call to one of the nurses."

The three nodded in unison. They were unnerved having this suddenly shoved in their laps, but Lacey had faith in them. They were used to dealing with the public and could handle the clients.

The youngest of the trio cracked her knuckles, one finger at a time. *Pop. Pop. Pop.* Her face reddened and she slipped her hands behind her back. "Could we be on the verge of an epidemic?"

"I hope and pray not." A shiver racked Lacey from shoulders to toes. She didn't want to go there. This had to stop. *Now.* But something in her gut told her this was only the beginning.

She finished instructions to the office clerks and headed to the fax machine. After faxing the press release to the media and passing out copies to the staff, Lacey slid into her desk chair. She scanned the tetanus report and entered the data into the computer. Though not a communicable disease, because of the serious consequences, a case of tetanus was reportable and required an investigation.

Lacey took a sip of coffee and set the mug down, scooting it aside. *Eeew, cold.* A bitter taste bit her tongue and she pressed her lips together.

She picked up the polio cases and fanned them across her desk, reread every word, one page at a time, and searched for something that would give her some insight. She pulled out her Communicable Disease Investigation Manual and paged to polio. She perused the information, though nothing new jumped out at her. She slid the book back into the drawer and leaned her head onto splayed fingers.

Lacey looked up when Ann sank into a chair opposite her desk.

"I talked to Michael's mother," Ann said. "She said the doctor is certain the child has polio. He's just waiting on the lab results to confirm the diagnosis. Needless to say, both parents are overwhelmed with worry."

"I can only imagine what they are going through." Lacey rubbed her forehead and pretended she could keep some measure of professional distance if this hit any closer to home.

"Yeah. I kept it short. Got the info I needed and let

the poor woman go."

"Any leads?" Lacey flicked at a hangnail that had been annoying her all morning.

"None." Ann shook her head and handed Lacey the completed investigation form. "His only possible contact is Holly. The family hasn't been out of the state, much less the country."

Lacey thumbed through the report. "Okay. We're reasonably sure Holly contracted polio in Nigeria. Then she brings it back to the States and Michael must have gotten it from her. The time frame is right."

"Looks like it to me," Ann said. "The incubation period is three to thirty-five days."

"That still doesn't explain why either of the children would have been susceptible in the first place. Both had their shots, so both should have been protected. I just can't understand it."

"Two kids didn't respond to the vaccine?"

"I don't know." Lacey picked up her pen and rotated it between her thumb and fingers. "Just doesn't fit. And now this case of tetanus. None of this makes sense."

Ann narrowed her eyes. "Not everything in life makes sense."

"Well, I'm not okay with that."

CHAPTER FOUR

Jake glanced at the wall clock. Almost five p.m. He stretched and scooted back from his desk then slid the Krueger report he'd worked on all afternoon into his briefcase.

The *plink-plink-plink* of spike heels clicking down the tiled hall caught his attention. Before he actually saw her, he picked up a slight whiff of Kimberly's musky scent.

"Here's the Jenson account." She bounced through the door, gave him a smile with her full, red lips, and laid the folder on his desk. "All typed and ready for your signature."

"Good girl." He scrawled his name at the bottom. No need to proofread it. He trusted her.

She pushed her hair back with nails that had been filed straight across and painted to match her lips. "You know, Jake, I'm always a good girl."

"Very good." Jake met her gaze. The dark-green flecks in her eyes gave him a warm rush. "And always ahead of schedule."

"I like to be a step-up on everything." Kimberly's voice echoed with mischief and she arched a brow. "Especially with my boss."

"Technically, Brad's your boss. But I'm glad I've got you fooled."

"You have me fooled?" She stood with arms akimbo and pulled her lips into a pout. "That hurts."

"Yeah, right." Jake laughed. He enjoyed the light banter with Kimberly. Maybe a little too much.

"Well, anyway, I'm glad I caught you before you left," she said in that flippant way she had. "We didn't get a chance to talk about you helping me study for the test."

Kimberly looked good standing there with a sultry grin. His resolve started to melt. He shifted in his chair. "I told you I'd help—"

"You did. And I told you it's too noisy here to concentrate. And way too many interruptions." She tipped her head to the side and narrowed her eyes. "Then when we're finished with the study session, I'll treat you to an espresso."

"I never mix business with pleasure." Jake kept his voice light and continued the jesting. A meeting away from the office would not be a good idea. Not with the embers of emotion she ignited in him.

"Why not?" She walked around his desk and stood inches behind him. One hand settled on his shoulder. "You can have both, you know."

Kimberly had never touched him before. Her palm felt warm, soft, even through his shirt. His flesh tingled.

She leaned down, her face so close he felt the heat from her breath on his cheek. He caught a whiff of cherry Life Savers.

"You have a nice night now," she whispered. "I'll see you tomorrow. And don't worry, we'll figure something out."

Kimberly gave his shoulder a squeeze before she headed across the room. She turned and met his gaze, held it, and winked. Then she walked through the doorway.

Jake puffed out the breath he'd been holding. Suddenly, it was warm in his office. Too warm. He pulled at his collar, loosened his tie, and opened the top button on his shirt. He massaged moist temples with his fingertips. Kimberly's lingering fragrance flooded his senses, filling his mind with unspeakable fantasies.

Don't go there. You're going to get in big trouble, the rational part of his brain whispered.

What's wrong with a little harmless flirtation? the other side countered.

Jake grabbed his jacket from the coatrack, hooked it over his shoulder with one finger, and headed to the parking lot. He slid behind the wheel of his car and pulled into the street, trying to shake off thoughts of the alluring Miss Ames.

But for the life of him, he couldn't.

A few minutes later, Jake walked into his kitchen. He set his briefcase on the counter, gave Lacey a quick kiss, and glanced at his boys.

His two sons had shot up in the past few months. Tall and lanky, they were about to catch him in height.

"What's up?" Jake asked.

"We're trying to decide what to have for dinner," Lacey said. "So far, we have two for leftovers and one for spaghetti. What's your vote?"

"I vote for leftovers." Meatloaf sandwiches and chips sounded good to him. And less work for Lacey.

"Leftovers it is, then." Lacey opened the refrigerator.

Jake glanced at Brian, the spaghetti nominator, who threw him a look of pure teenage attitude.

"You lose, buddy. You're outvoted."

Brian shrugged then slouched against the barstool.

"So, what else is new?"

Lacey smiled at her youngest son as she retrieved a bag of chips from the cabinet. "I'll fix spaghetti one night this week."

"Sheesh." Todd rolled his eyes. "He'd live without having his stinkin' spaghetti. And if you ask me, we have it way too much anyway."

"Who's asking you?" Making his famous loser sign, Brian tapped his index finger and thumb on his forehead then shot from the room. Todd was hot on his trail, threatening to slug him.

"Hey! No scuffling in the house. You'll break something!" Jake called. Pounding shoes on the stairs told him they hadn't heard a word he'd said.

Jake chuckled and shook his head. He was proud of his sons.

Todd, a junior, had made the varsity football team this year as a running back. He'd worked hard to develop lower body power and game-breaking speed and hoped it would pay off so he'd qualify for a college scholarship next year.

Brian talked a lot about football, too, which had been his passion since grade school. Only two years younger than Todd, he looked up to his big brother and, although he'd rather skip a spaghetti dinner than admit it, he admired Todd and tried to act just like him.

Jake swallowed a lump in his throat. "They're growing up, huh?"

"Too fast." Lacey sighed. "Sometimes I wish I could turn back the clock."

"Yeah, me, too."

It didn't seem that long ago that the boys had been toddlers. They'd run to the front door when he came home from work and wrap chubby arms around his legs. At bedtime, he'd bounce them on his knee, tuck them in bed, then read the little guys a story until droopy eyes could no longer stay open. They had grown a lot since those days. Turned into handsome young men.

Lacey gave him a nudge. "Better take your shower if you're going to before dinner. It won't take me long to put the sandwiches together."

"I'm on it." Jake headed to the bathroom.

He was in and out of the shower and back in the kitchen in record time. The meatloaf on wheat hoagies, piled high with lettuce and tomato and slathered with mayo, hit the spot. So did the together time with his family.

A pang of recrimination heated his face at the memory of earlier feelings he'd had at the office. He'd never jeopardize his marriage. There was no way he'd ever do anything that would hurt his wife and sons. They meant the world to him. They *were* his world.

After dinner, Lacey joined him in the family room. Her eyes were troubled, and her mouth formed an unsmiling line as she nestled in the overstuffed recliner like a mother hen. Jake muted the sports commentator's comments on the Chiefs' victory and focused on his wife.

"Okay," he said. "How did things go at work today?"

Lacey's face pulled tight. She scooted to the edge of the chair and replayed her day step-by-step. The worry in her voice and the self-blame in her expression didn't escape him. She hated not being in control, unable to methodically work through any given situation.

"This isn't your fault, you know," he said.

"Yeah, I know."

Jake didn't buy it. She wouldn't give herself a break until the cases were solved.

"I'm really bumming out," she said.

"I know."

"Can't help it."

"I know."

"I'm to the point I'm wondering if something, you know, something devious is going on."

"Like what?"

"I don't know. But something's off about all of this."

"I don't understand..."

"I'm probably overreacting," she said and attempted a half-hearted laugh. "Just ignore me."

"You sure?"

"Yep."

"So, what now?"

"I don't have a clue."

Jake wished there was something he could do to assist his wife. Other than letting her vent, he wasn't sure anything could help at this point.

After a few more minutes of hashing over her dilemma, Lacey threw a palm over her mouth. A wide yawn spread across her face.

"Let's go to bed." Jake stood and extended a hand. "You're exhausted."

"I am." Lacey took his hand and he boosted her up. "Jake, remember we're having a picnic after church Sunday. I really wish you'd come. Everyone misses you."

He closed his eyes. A frown tugged at his mouth. He hadn't been going to church much lately and he wasn't in the mood for a lecture. "I don't know—"

"What's going on with you?" Lacey's voice turned sharp. A new expression flickered over her face, merging anger and disappointment. "You never used to have a problem doing things with your family. What is wrong?"

Jake shrugged.

"I hate going without you, you know." Her tone softened.

A worm of guilt turned in his stomach, reminding him how slack he'd been in the domestic field for some time.

"Aw, don't be mad, babe." Jake pulled her to him. "I don't know what's wrong with me. I just can't get into the church thing anymore."

"Why don't you talk to Pastor David? He'd be happy to see you."

Jake met Lacey's gaze but didn't respond. He wondered how talking with the pastor could possibly change anything. True, he had been in a funk lately, but he'd pull himself out of it eventually.

"Let's get to sleep," he said. "I'm beat tonight, too."

Her brows knitted together, but she kept quiet.

He hitched one shoulder up and looked at his feet. Lacey had a way that made him feel guilty even when there was no reason.

CHAPTER FIVE

At 5:30 Wednesday morning, Lacey tugged on her gray and red Fila sweats then sat on the edge of the bed. She wiggled her toes into her white, black, and silver leather Reeboks and pulled the laces tight.

Jake was still sleeping. His mouth parted slightly to pull in slow, even breaths. She smiled. She'd be back from her run before he even stirred. He worked out in the mornings, too, but his workday started an hour later than hers did. That was good because Jake wasn't a morning person, never had been.

Careful not to wake him, she gently pushed back strands of dark, wavy hair from his forehead. He'd changed little over the years. She still thought he was the most handsome man she'd ever laid eyes on. Only a quarter Italian, but with his dark good looks, he could pass for full-blooded. She bent down and kissed his brow, catching the familiar scent of soap and aftershave that made her feel warm and safe.

Lacey grabbed her keys from the dresser then bounced down the stairs. She jumped into her car and five minutes later pulled into the park.

She dropped her tote on a bench, did a few stretches then started out at a nice, easy jog. Deeply inhaling the cool morning air, she allowed it to fill her lungs as she pounded the trail that butted up against the woods behind the Civic Center.

As her muscles loosened, she lengthened her steps. Several fellow joggers waved or greeted her. She waved back but never broke stride. Then she increased her speed, pumping her arms, enjoying the freedom and the release from physical effort. She ran completely around the perimeter of the park then turned toward the interior, zigzagging around benches. Her heart pounded and the wind hissed by her ears.

After jogging four miles, she slowed and walked for a couple of minutes to cool down. Her breathing had returned to normal by the time she flopped down on a bench. She wiped her face and neck with a towel then opened her water bottle and took a long drink.

Running always helped her focus and think through problems. Lord knew she had plenty of those at work. However, this morning, her mind had drifted to Jake. She couldn't put her finger on it, but he seemed different lately, almost unhappy. And he'd become so anti-church. She missed him at the services but especially at the family functions.

Like the upcoming Sunday picnic. Everyone would ask where he was, why he hadn't come. That wouldn't be easy to answer; she didn't have a clue. He just seemed so...well, so lackadaisical most of the time, especially about family things. And he refused to talk to their pastor no matter how much she prodded. She didn't want to be the proverbial nagging wife, but she had on more than one occasion practically insisted he talk to Reverend David. Lot of good that had done. He'd just blown her off.

She took another pull from the bottle and screwed on the cap. She sighed and wondered if she should just skip the picnic.

~ ~ ~ ~ ~

Forty-five minutes later she was freshly showered and dressed in Mickey Mouse scrubs over a ribbed long-john top. She scooted up to her desk and clipped her photo ID badge to her collar.

She pored over Holly and Michael's case files again. Line by line. Reading and rereading every word. Nothing new jumped out at her. She leaned back and tipped up her mug, took a gulp of coffee. There wasn't one single thing to indicate why those children contracted polio.

She paced back and forth in her small office, wondering why Holly and Michael had been attacked with an eradicated disease. When her cell phone rang, she smiled. It had to be Jake wondering where he'd left something. He wasn't the most organized person in the world. He was so haphazard with the work he dragged home. She dug her phone from her bag and looked at the caller ID.

Susan.

Oh no. The hospital's infection prevention nurse rarely called Lacey's cell. When she did, it was never good news.

"What's going on?" Dread clawed at Lacey's spine, setting off alarm bells in her head.

"For starters, we've got another case of polio."

"That makes three now." Lacey let out a moan and wondered if this was ever going to stop. "Are you at the hospital?"

"Yeah. I got called in early this morning when the case came in."

"Same age as the other two?"

"Yes. And it only gets worse. Right after I got here,

a seventeen-year-old boy was brought into the ED by ambulance. His body was in spasms. I've never seen anything like it. Never in all my years of nursing." Susan paused, the silence stretching for several beats. "The doctor's diagnosis is tetanus."

"Is he sure?"

"Yeah. As sure as he can be."

Lacey chewed the inside of her cheek. There is no specific test available to confirm tetanus—the diagnosis is strictly clinical.

"He died a few minutes ago..." Raw emotion bit Susan's voice. She cleared her throat while her words hit Lacey like a slap. "His parents are hysterical. They said he was fine when he went to his room last night. He'd complained earlier of a stiff jaw, but they chalked that up to the wisdom tooth he was cutting. They heard him thrashing around in his bed early this morning and rushed into his room. It appeared he was having a seizure. They called 911 because they were afraid to move him."

"Oh Lord." Lacey's stomach turned over. She flashed on a sterile hospital, full of antiseptic scents and death. Struggling for composure, she asked, "Do they have anyone there with them?"

"The hospital chaplain. Their pastor is on the way over, probably already here by now."

"My heart goes out to them." Lacey choked back a surge of fear. How would she ever cope if she lost one of her own boys?

"Losing a child has to be the worst," Susan whispered as if she'd heard Lacey's contemplation. "I don't think I could deal with it."

"I know I couldn't." Lacey shuddered and tossed off the unspeakable thought then asked, "How's the child with polio?"

"Stable. He was transferred to Columbia. I'll fax

you everything as soon as the ED sends up the records."

"Thanks."

Lacey hit *End Call* and shoved her phone into her purse. She waited the few minutes for the fax from Susan then picked up the office phone and punched in Darrell's number. Again. Would this ever end?

"Lacey, what's going on?" he asked. She could hear the apprehension in his voice. She'd talked to him more in the last three days than she had in her eight years at the health department.

"We have another case of polio and another fatal tetanus case."

"Good grief! You've got to be kidding!"

"Wish I was."

"Okay, give it to me."

She did, and he didn't interrupt. From the other end of the phone came the clicking of a computer keyboard.

"I'm checking the CDC site," he said.

"Anything new?"

"Still no results from the autopsy on the first tetanus case."

Lacey wished they'd hurry up and come up with something. Anything.

"What about the polio labs?"

"Hold on," Darrell said, and Lacey waited while he searched.

"The mutant strain theory has been ruled out. It's typical Type I Polio. Same strain that killed and crippled thousands before the polio vaccine was developed."

Lacey cringed. Was that going to happen here? *Please, God, no.*

Parkdale was just a small town, barely over fifteen thousand. Nothing bad ever happened here, until these diseases had invaded their peaceful burg. Suddenly her entire community was shaken, scared that they, or their loved ones, would get a crippling disease or worse, die.

"You're going to need some help with this investigation," Darrell said. "It's really getting out of hand."

"Don't I know it."

"I'll contact Joe Phelps and see if he and Linda are available to assist."

Joe, an epidemiology specialist, was Lacey's immediate CD contact in the Springfield office. Linda was right under him in the chain of command. Joe was up on Lester County's dilemma.

"It'll be good to have their expertise assistance," she said.

"I'll get it set up and have them at your office this afternoon."

"What about the school?" Lacey knew the answer before the question slid across her tongue. "It's time to close it, right?"

"You've got to. With three polio cases in the same grade, in the same school, we're dealing with an epidemic."

Lacey's heart tripped as that grisly word echoed in her ear. Epidemic sounded so oppressive.

"We need to isolate the healthy kids and make sure their parents know what symptoms to watch for," he said. "Education is imperative. Joe and Linda can assist with that."

"That'll be a big help." Lacey switched the phone to her right ear and rubbed the left. She'd pressed the receiver against it too firmly and it felt warm. "I just don't know what else to do to stop this."

Darrell sighed. "I wish I had an answer for you."

"Yeah, me, too."

"It's got me floored. I've never seen an outbreak like this. Not with polio."

"There's got to be something we're overlooking, Darrell. A common denominator that would link these cases together. A reason that would explain why well-vaccinated children are susceptible to a disease from the past."

"If this was a typical childhood disease, Holly's and Matthew's age and sharing the same classroom would be all we'd need."

"But this isn't the norm we're dealing with," she said. Lacey thumbed through the information. "I know tetanus isn't as unusual as polio, but two cases in two days in kids up to date with their shots is definitely not normal."

"Tetanus is sometimes seen in older adults who haven't had a booster since childhood, not children that are well-immunized."

"There's something really off about this."

"There's no logic in it, that's for sure."

"It's like we're in a time warp."

"Yep."

Lacey massaged her brow. "I'll get everything entered in the system and see to it the school is closed by noon today."

"Okay. Let me know if you need anything."

Lacey said goodbye and gathered her thoughts. She clicked the button for line two and called the school superintendent. He voiced his relief when she told him the school would be closed. Lacey guessed he'd been getting his share of flak from the community since this ordeal hit.

After she hung up, she opened Microsoft Word, took a slug of cold coffee, and got to work.

Five minutes later, she finished her combination letter to the parents/press release. The black-and-white print made it way too real.

There are three confirmed cases of polio in the first-grade class at Hoover Elementary School. Therefore, the health department will be closing the school effective immediately.

We recommend that your child receive an IPV (inactivated polio vaccine) booster as soon as possible. Also, parents and other family members living in the household are encouraged to get a booster, even if you have received one recently.

We ask that you keep your children away from congested places and keep them home as much as possible during the school closing to prevent any further spread of polio.

If your child develops any of the following symptoms, please contact your physician immediately: Fever, headache, nausea, vomiting, muscle pain, and stiffness of the neck and back.

Please know that your local and state health departments are working on this along with the CDC (Centers for Disease Control) in Atlanta, Georgia. Our hearts go out to the families who have been affected, and we sincerely hope to have this situation resolved soon.

The health department will be giving IPV (Inactivated Polio Vaccine) injections Monday through Friday, 8 a.m.-5 p.m.

For more information, call 555-2215.

She swallowed hard then set her feelings aside. She had to do this. *Okay, here goes.*

Lacey paused as her heart pulsed blood through the veins in her neck. Then she hit print. She was about to drop a bomb on Parkdale, but she had no choice. And she had a chill, radiating bone-deep, she couldn't shake.

CHAPTER SIX

"Joe. Linda." Lacey shot up from her desk and greeted the two epidemiology specialists—EPIs—from Springfield with a handshake. "Great to see you. I can't tell you how thankful I am you're here."

"Wish it could be under different circumstances," Joe said. He looked to be mid-forties in a light-blue pin-striped button-down shirt that was open at the collar and tucked into charcoal-gray slacks. He was average height and weight with the hint of a potbelly above his black belt.

"Your county has been hit hard." Linda shook her head. "Tetanus and polio, of all things. Who would've imagined?"

"Not us, that's for sure," Lacey said. "Especially the polio!"

"I understand you have three cases." Joe set his laptop and well-worn briefcase on the edge of her desk. "And two fatal tetanus cases?"

Lacey nodded.

"It looks like the polio cases are Type I, confirmed. No mutations. No variance. Your typical old-fashioned polio."

"That's right."

"It's been years since we've had a case of polio in the United States, and then it wasn't Type I. It was a vaccine-derived poliovirus from the oral vaccine used years ago." Joe's mouth was tight as a rubber band. Lacey wanted to tell him she'd had a hard time accepting it, too. But she kept quiet.

"The first thing I want to do is check the shot records." He lifted a brow over hazel eyes that were punctuated with deep crow's feet.

Oh boy. Here we go again. He probably thought he could breeze in like the hero on a white stallion, look at the shot records, and *voila!* The kids wouldn't be up-to-date, or the shots wouldn't have been spaced properly. Case solved. End of story.

Well, that wasn't going to happen no matter how hard Lacey wished for a miracle on four hooves.

"I've got copies of everything you'll need in the conference room." Lacey picked up the shot records and passed them to Joe. "Here's the originals."

Lacey watched Joe's face go pale as he scanned the records. He shook his head and shot her a deflated look. "It looks like we've got our work cut out for us."

"Big-time."

She hustled Joe and Linda across the building to the boardroom. It was stocked with two computers and two telephones and located away from the constant ringing phones and interruptions of the primary workspace. Perfect place for in-depth analysis.

"You guys can set up here." Lacey pointed to the long table where she'd set copies of the refrigerator temp logs, polio and tetanus case folders, and extra copies of the shot records. "You've got internet access and outside lines. Let me know if you need anything else."

"A wipe-off board, if you have one." Joe dragged his

hand across his head, leaving his dark, longish hair at a funny upward angle. Lacey had a sudden urge to smooth it down.

"Right here." Lacey walked to the south wall and opened the marker board cabinet. It unfolded into three sections, three feet each. "A dry-erase board and pens."

"That's great." Joe picked up a grease pencil and rotated it between his thumb and fingers. "I like to graph my work as I go." He divided the middle section into two halves. "Is the school closed?"

"It closed at noon." She squeezed her shoulder blades together and hitched them upward, trying to work out the tension in her neck.

"Tough call." Joe wrote *Polio* on one side of the board and *Tetanus* on the other. "You didn't have a choice. Had to be done."

Lacey shrugged. "Let's pray it helps."

Joe set the pen down and swiped his hands across his trousers.

"How many kids in the affected school?" Linda wiped her blue-rimmed glasses with a tissue and laid them on the table. She looked younger than Joe, early thirties maybe, and a little shorter although not by much, and rail thin. Her light-brown hair was cut fashionably short and fell in waves that just covered her earlobes.

"Hoover has three kindergarten classes and three first grades. A total of a hundred thirty-two students." Lacey handed her the school roster, which included addresses and phone numbers. "Twenty-four staff, including maintenance."

Linda scanned the list and passed it to Joe. "What about the bus drivers?"

"Already been taken care of. They had an IPV booster Monday along with the staff."

"So, we can concentrate on the students." Joe opened his briefcase and pulled out a couple of fact sheets on polio. "We've got to make sure the parents are aware of the outbreak and what to watch for in their children."

"And what to do if they do notice any symptoms," Linda said.

Lacey flinched. Did the big city EPIs actually think a small-town CD nurse would be that out of sync handling an investigation?

"A letter went out to the parents this morning." Lacey pointed to a pile of papers that included everything she'd sent out in chronological order. "It lists every sign and symptom of polio."

"Good." Joe raked fingers through his disheveled hair then tried to pat it into place. It still jutted out, especially around his ears, making him look more like one of the Branson Baldknobbers than an astute EPI specialist.

"Okay, I'll get back to work and let you guys do your job." Lacey went to the door then turned. "You know where the break room is. There's plenty of coffee and soda. Snacks, too. Make yourself at home."

"Thanks." Joe shuffled into a swivel chair and slid the CD reports toward him. "I'm good right now."

"Me, too," Linda said. She donned her glasses and took half the folders from Joe's stack.

Lacey stopped in the break room and filled her mug with the last of the coffee before making a fresh pot. After doctoring her drink to her liking, she opened the cabinet. She dug through the menagerie of snacks then palmed two mini candy bars and a bag of sour cream chips. Balancing them in her free hand, she headed to her office. Armed and ravenous.

Pulling in a long breath, she glanced at the two-inch stack of tasks needing her attention. She could work all afternoon and never make a dent. She opened the Mars bar and scarfed it down in one bite then tore into the second and let out a moan.

This was crazy. Lunch had been a salad because she'd noticed her waistband was definitely getting snug. As she popped open the bag of chips, she vowed to eat only twelve-hundred calories the next day.

Lacey spent the next hour or so at her desk returning calls, answering emails, and tackling the day's correspondence. She looked up at a knock on her open door.

"Amber!" Surprised to see her friend, Lacey scooted back in her chair, more than ready for a distraction. "Get in here."

"You looked so engrossed."

Amber, cute as ever, wore a pale-blue sweater over ochre slacks and two-inch heels.

"I don't want to bother you."

"You're never a bother. You know I'm always glad to see you."

"Ditto."

"Where's Suzie-Q?"

"Home. With Mom."

"Are you off today?"

Amber Lux worked at a local bank as a loan officer. She'd been with that branch for nearly three years, and Lacey could count on one hand the times she'd missed work.

"I took off when I heard the school was closing."

"I see."

"I'm scared, Lacey. All this talk about polio. And now the school closing?" Her eyes wide, she shook her head, making her short, dark curls wiggle across her cheeks. "Please tell me I don't have anything to worry about."

Lacey twisted her wedding band. She hated it when

she couldn't give her friends the reassurance they needed. Especially Amber.

"Here, sit." Lacey motioned to a seat beside her desk.

Amber lowered herself into a chair and Lacey sat across from her. Lacey studied her friend, wishing she could erase the tension from her face. But how could she? She touched Amber's arm and felt the soft cashmere.

"Did you get Suzy a polio booster?"

Amber nodded. "She had a wellness visit with Dr. Jenkins Monday afternoon and because of the polio scare, he gave her a booster just to be on the safe side."

"Good." Lacey offered her friend an encouraging smile. "Right now, the best thing you can do is keep Suzie home away from crowds. And especially away from anyone who's sick. And—"

"And what?" Amber snapped, her mouth a thin line. "That'll keep her from getting polio?"

Lacey hesitated. "It's the best preventative advice we have to offer right now."

"'Preventative advice we have to offer!'" Amber threw up her hands. "Quit talking to me like a nurse. I'm not your patient. I'm your best friend, for Pete's sake. Tell me what's going on. And I want the truth."

"Okay." Lacey rolled her chair closer. "Here's the truth. Friend to friend. We have a serious situation. We're doing the best we can, but to be honest, we are at a standstill. We've got two people from the state in our office looking into the outbreak, and the CDC is working nonstop, trying to get us some answers."

Her words tumbled over one another in frustration. How could she assure anyone, much less her best friend, who knew her better than she knew herself, that Suzie wouldn't get polio? She couldn't get a handle on this mess, much less a convincing one. She blew air out forcefully, lifting her bangs off her forehead.

"I promise you, we're doing everything humanly possible to control the outbreak," Lacey said.

Amber shook her head again. Her lips parted as she reached for a thought. But she just sat quietly meeting Lacey's gaze. Her eyes pleaded for answers. Answers that Lacey didn't have. Amber would never be fooled with false hopes. So, Lacey decided to try honesty.

"I know you're upset, and you have every right to be. But you're not the only one that's frustrated. I'm sick over this. I've got kids I worry about. So, I know what you're feeling because I feel it, too. And I'm doing everything I can to protect our children."

"Aww, I know that." Amber's voice softened, transitioning from agitated mother to lifelong friend. Her soft, chocolate-brown eyes brimmed. She blinked.

Lacey patted Amber's knee. Worry sprinkled over her like grains from a saltshaker. How she wished she could alleviate her friend's concerns.

"I know you guys are working on it, but I'm not handling this very well." Amber tucked an unruly strand of hair behind her ear and sighed. "Suzie is my life. I waited so long for her..."

"I know that, sweetie." Lacey leaned forward and touched her shoulder. "Believe me, I do understand what you're going through. And I'd give anything if I knew what to do to take this threat away."

She plucked a tissue from the box on her desk and handed it to her friend.

Amber wiped her eyes, blew her nose then wadded the tissue in her hand. Pain flicked across her features. "I need a hug."

"Now that's easy." Lacey gave her a big hug that lasted several beats.

"We'll get through this," Laccy whispered in her BFF's ear and tried hard to believe it herself.

CHAPTER SEVEN

Jake tucked the finished report under one arm and headed down the hall. He veered into the break room and poured the last of the coffee into a Starbucks mug. The brew smelled a lot like charred rubber. He wrinkled his nose as he tossed two sugar cubes into the thick liquid then took a sip. *Ugh.* It tasted as bad as it smelled. He dumped it in the sink and grabbed a soda from the refrigerator before hustling into Brad's office.

"The Benson account's finished." He laid the folder on his boss's desk.

"Great." Brad scanned the synopsis as he motioned to a seat.

Jake lowered himself into one of the plush chairs in front of Bradley Acuff's cluttered desk and took a fizzy swig of Diet Coke.

He liked his boss. Jake's senior by ten years, Brad looked even older with gray, wiry hair that framed a double-chinned face. He was aggressive in business but honest and up front with clients. No shortcuts just to land an account. Jake admired him for that.

"Everything seems to be in order," Brad said after a couple minutes.

Jake smiled and stood, anxious to call it a day.

Brad held up a finger. "Give me a second to look this over before you leave."

Jake slumped back in his chair and sighed. Yeah, right. The word *second* might have been in Brad's vocabulary, but he had yet to grasp its definition.

Sure enough, it was twenty minutes, and an empty soda can later before a satisfied Brad closed the folder and peppered Jake with questions. Jake was sharp with crunching numbers and knew his report was right on the mark.

"You did a good job." Brad pushed back in his chair and slid his hands across his abundant potbelly.

"Thanks."

"Get one of the girls to type it up. We'll meet with the vice president of Benson first thing in the morning and get it signed, sealed, and delivered." Brad laughed at his own cliché.

"Okay, boss. I'm out of here. See you in the morning."

Brad had already averted his attention to another folder on his desk. He'd probably work until eight or nine. Jake liked to get out at five but, thanks to an overzealous boss, that didn't always happen. Jake took the folder to the secretarial pool and gave the girls a hesitant look.

"Sorry. Brad wants this first thing in the morning."

The clerks' eyes rolled back in their heads. Jake smiled and walked away. They were used to Brad's last-minute assignments, and he felt confident the report would be finished before they headed home.

He swung into his office, shut down his computer, and picked up his briefcase. When he turned, Kimberly was in the doorway with a sly smile across her face. Looking good as always.

"Hi there." Jake stepped toward her. "Haven't seen

much of you today."

"Your own fault." She shook her head and tsked. "I'm always available. For you."

"I'll keep that in mind." He gave her a wink. "Hey, I talked to Brad this morning. He's agreed to let you handle Mrs. Jacobson on Friday. It's just a routine short form W2 but it's all yours."

"Oooh!" Kimberly squealed and her flushed face was animated with excitement. She bounced toward him and flung both arms around his neck. "Thank you, Jake. It's not like having a *real* client but it's a start. You are so sweet."

Jake sucked in a breath as her soft full curves pressed against his chest. He chastised himself for noticing. After all, she was just giving him a friendly hug.

She took a half step back and flicked a piece of lint from the front of his shirt.

"Wow." She slid her palm slowly over his chest. "Nice pecs. I can tell you work out."

You, too. His eyes moved to her tight tan sweater then, with deliberate effort, cut back to her eyes. "Yeah. I try to keep in shape."

"It's working." She ran her tongue over her lower lip and angled her head to the side. "How old are you, Jake?"

"Forty-two."

"Really? I would've never guessed."

"That must seem ancient to you."

"Huh-uh. I've always been attracted to older men. Guys my age are so immature. They don't know how to treat a woman. I bet you know all about taking care of a woman..." Her voice trailed off, but the meaning didn't.

Her finger moved to his mouth, and she traced the outline of his lips. "Nice. So soft."

Her face was only inches from his. For a second, he thought she was going to kiss him. And for a second, he wanted her to.

She let her hand drop back to his chest. His heart pounded against his ribs like a rapid-fire machine gun. He knew she could feel every beat banging against her palm. He was on fire. She had to know what she was doing to him.

She gave his chest a final pat and stepped back, sliding her hands down her hips. She shook her head. "We are definitely going to have to meet somewhere more private. You know, so you can help me with that ol' test."

Jake was an instant away from suggesting a place but knew his testosterone had kicked in, demanding action. He shook off the impulse. Tried to get a visual of Lacey. As hard as he tried, he couldn't. He wanted to kiss Kimberly so bad he could taste her.

His cell rang and he fished it from his pocket, dropped it.

"Well, see you, handsome," Kimberly whispered and gave him a once-over that made his gut churn. She turned and sashayed out slowly, giving him a full view of her firm tush.

Jake picked up his phone and looked at the ID. Lacey. He released a guilty breath and slapped the side of his face a couple times. With a calmness he didn't feel, he said, "Hi, Lace."

"Hey, Jake. Don't forget I'm going to be late tonight. Girls' night out, remember?"

"Yeah, sure." He hadn't remembered. Once a month, Lacey and her nurses went out to eat after work. A female thing. He smiled.

"The boys and I will batch it tonight. You guys have a good time, and I'll see you when you get home."

"I won't be late. Bye."

"Bye." Jake snapped shut his cell and rammed it into his pocket, his head still buzzing with Kimberly.

CHAPTER EIGHT

Lacey ended her call with Jake. She looked up and smiled at Ann, who leaned against the doorway.

"I wondered if you'd have second thoughts about our routine night out."

Apparently, Ann had overheard her conversation. No secrets around here.

"After the week we've had? Not a chance. We all need it." Lacey tucked her cell into her purse, grabbed the outgoing mail, and pulled her jacket from behind the door. "Pizza Hut, right?"

"Yep."

Both pushed through the back door, with Betty and Joan on their heels.

"I'll be there in a few minutes," Lacey said. "I'm going to run by the post office and mail the immunization reminders."

"See you in five," Ann said as she piled into the vehicle with the two nurses.

Lacey drove three blocks to the post office, slid her parcels into the drop box, and less than ten minutes later, pressed through Pizza Hut's door.

The aroma of tomato sauce and oregano hit her first thing, making her stomach growl. She saw her nurses had picked a rear booth by a window overlooking North Highway 5. Indirect light brightened the spot, and Lacey blinked away the brightness as she tucked her keys inside her purse.

The waiter ambled over. He smiled and aimed a pen at the pad in his hand. "The buffet, as usual?" he asked.

The four nodded and gave him their drink orders. They were early enough to beat the dinner crowd and breezed through the buffet in record time. Juggling plates piled high with pizza and salad, they settled into the booth.

"Any big plans for the weekend?" Joan slid a straw into her Diet Coke.

"Nothing big for me," Ann said. "Richard's out of town all week. Won't be home until late Friday night, and I'm sure he'll want a quiet time at home. Which is fine with me. I'm pooped."

"Me, too," Joan agreed. "But we've got company coming. My brother and sister-in-law had to pick this weekend, of all weekends, to come down."

Betty sighed. "We're going to Joplin. Tom's brother is having a huge farm sale and my gullible husband got snookered into helping. Believe me, I'm not looking forward to that."

Joan shook a heavy dose of parmesan on her pizza then reached for the red pepper flakes. "Eeew. That sounds like a lot of work."

"Yeah. And his brother thinks it'll be fun. He's so strange."

Lacey laughed and picked up a slice of steaming pepperoni pizza. She sank her teeth into the wedge and the first bite burst with flavor. Hot, salty, spicy. She chewed and swallowed. "We don't have any plans," she said. "Just hang out at home, I imagine."

The waiter stepped up to the table and eyed the

drinks. "Refill?"

"Yes, please," they answered in unison.

"Be back in a jiff." He scooped up four glasses in one swift movement, a feat Lacey knew she'd never be coordinated enough to manage.

"Mom's adopted a puppy." Lacey forked some salad and popped it into her mouth.

"From the shelter?" Ann asked.

Lacey shook her head. "Someone dumped him off. And you know Mom. She couldn't call the animal control."

"I don't blame her. Those places are wrong." Betty frowned and dabbed her mouth with a napkin. "He's lucky he was dumped on your mom's street."

"Yeah, I know. The little guy looks pretty healthy so hopefully he hasn't been mistreated."

"What kind is he?"

"Just a mutt. But he's adorable. Black with a white ring around one eye."

"Is she gonna keep him or find him another home?" Betty asked then bit into a slice of pineapple pizza.

Lacey shrugged. "She says find him another home, but we'll see."

"I'm betting your mom won't part with him," Joan said as the waiter set the drinks on the table.

"He sounds like a cutie." Ann tipped her head to the side and gave Lacey a sly smile. "Why don't you take him?"

Lacey pulled in a deep breath. Visions of Sophie flashed through her head and her heart thudded. She couldn't stand the thought of replacing the pet they'd lost six months ago. She took a drink of tea and abruptly changed the subject. "Did you see in the paper where the YMCA is taking over the Civic Center?"

The three nurses eyed her, but they let it go, didn't

push, and Lacey was relieved. They were well aware how uncomfortable she'd get when anyone talked about Sophie. Uncomfortable and sad. And she didn't want to focus on unhappy events. This was supposed to be a fun night out.

Light banter continued throughout the meal, but eventually the conversation drifted to things at the health department. It stifled their good moods and they fell silent. A nervousness Lacey couldn't explain settled over her. Suddenly she wanted to be home with Jake and her boys. Make sure her kids were okay.

"I'm ready to call it a night." Lacey pushed aside her plate and moaned. "I'm stuffed. I can't hold another bite."

"Me, either." Betty sighed. "I bet I've gained five pounds in less than two hours."

"Yeah, right! You know you never gain an ounce, no matter what you eat. I'm the one who's gonna pay." Ann frowned and pointed at her two empty plates. "Why do you guys let me eat so much?"

Lacey laughed and said, "As health professionals, you'd think we'd know better." She scooted back from the table, grabbed the bill, and stood. "My treat this time. See you guys in the morning."

CHAPTER NINE

At eleven thirty p.m., she pulled into her two-car garage and cut the engine. She walked through the utility room and turned left into the kitchen, poured a glass of merlot, and took a big gulp of the smooth wine.

Kicking off her shoes, she padded down the hall to the guest bedroom. After unloading and stashing the night's bounty, she praised herself for another successful trip.

After all this time, she thought she would have gotten used to the night raids. But she hadn't. Every heist was as nerve-wracking as the first.

It had been worth all the planning, pilfering, and waiting to see her plan kick in and start showing some results. She'd waited forever, or so it seemed, but finally things had started to pick up. There was no stopping her. Payback time was coming full force.

She headed back to the kitchen, scooted up to the table, and picked up a magazine. After pulling a long skinny cigarette from her pack of Capris, she lit it and took a long drag. The smoke hit the page of her newest *Cosmopolitan* and fogged back on itself like vapor from a steam iron.

As she watched the smoke curl upward, she smiled. Nobody suspected she smoked. Well, her husband knew, but he didn't care. He never cared what she did and would never reveal her nasty little secret.

Unable to concentrate as she flipped through the pages, she slammed the magazine shut. She took another long drink of wine and a drag of nicotine.

She stood and paced. Back and forth across her kitchen. Why was she so antsy? She opened the cabinet and pulled out a prescription bottle then swallowed a Xanax, chasing it down with the sweet wine. Maybe that would help her sleep.

The sexy blonde on the cover of the Cosmo looked a lot like Lacey. Little Miss Director of Nursing, who everyone thought was so perfect. Oh, how she despised Robert for giving Lacey the position that should have been hers. She'd never forgive him for choosing Lacey instead of her. She ground her teeth together and let visions of a defeated Lacey flood her mind.

She'd show Robert and Lacey. Before she was finished, both would be sorry.

CHAPTER TEN

Friday morning, Jake scooted up to his desk, blood still pumping from a vigorous hour at the gym. He opened his briefcase and slipped the report he'd worked on the night before into his desk organizer. He smiled as Kimberly walked in and set down a mug of steaming coffee.

"Two sugars." She winked. "Just how you like it, right?"

He nodded, wondering how she knew. "Thanks." He picked up the mug and took a sip. "Mmm. Perfect. What would I do around here without you?"

"You'd never make it." She leaned over and placed her hands flat on his desk. "But don't worry. You'll never have to find out. You're stuck with me."

"I've had worse burdens to bear." He caught a whiff of something fruity and tantalizing. Warmth flooded his veins as he remembered how her body had felt against his. He cleared his throat and set down the mug.

She looked classy and sexy all in one package, dressed in a form-fitting red top over black pants that hugged her hips like a second skin and red spike heels. Silver hoop earrings swayed whenever she moved her head. Her hair was loosely pulled back with a red clip, a few stray wisps teasing her cheek.

"You're looking good today," he said before realizing his thoughts turned vocal. Heat spread across his face.

"Back at you." She flashed him a half smile and held his gaze.

He looked down, picked up a pencil, and tapped the eraser end on his desk.

"You look so tense." Kimberly tugged at the bottom of her blouse, pulling it tight over her curves as she walked behind him. "Here, let me work out some of those knots."

She made slow, circular motions on his neck and shoulders. Her hands felt soft, warm. He closed his eyes and let his mind drift. To places he'd never admit out loud, not even to himself.

"Hey, what's going on?" Brad's gravelly voice brought him back to the present and his eyes flew open. "What do we have here, a massage parlor?"

"Not officially." Kimberly stepped around the desk and stood in front of Brad. "But I do give one heck of a back rub." She sent Jake a colluding look over her shoulder before turning back to the boss. "Poor Jake needed some kinks worked out. You know how hard he works? Well, gotta go. Work to do. See ya."

Feeling a little embarrassed, Jake leaned back and watched Kimberly sashay out. He could only imagine how things had looked to his boss.

Brad's brows lowered and vertical lines grew between his eyes. He situated his hefty frame in a chair and motioned to the door. "You need to be careful, buddy. Don't let this get out of hand."

"It's nothing."

Brad rubbed two knuckles beneath his double chin and kept focused on Jake.

"Really. Nothing is going on. You know Kimberly. She's a big tease."

Brad snorted, squared his shoulders, and pointed a meaty finger at him. "I'm warning you, Jake. You're playing with fire and you're gonna get burned."

"You worry too much."

"Somebody's gotta look out for you."

"It's just some innocent flirting. Nothing more," he said. But even as the words slipped across his tongue, he knew he'd crossed a line with Kimberly. A dangerous one at that.

"She flirts with me, too, Jake. But it's different with you. I see how she looks at you and I'm telling you, she's after more than a little fun."

Brad was right. Jake had seen the looks. "Okay, I'll watch myself."

"You better."

"You know I'd never cheat on Lacey."

"No." Brad dragged a hand across his forehead. "I don't think you'd deliberately plan to cheat on your wife. But things can get out of hand before you know what's hit you and escalate into something more than you intend. You've got to be careful."

"That'll never happen," Jake said. "You honestly think I'd let something—anything—come between Lacey and me?"

"I would hope not. You've got a lot invested in your marriage. Too much to risk throwing it away for some cheap romp."

"Well, I wouldn't. Not in this lifetime," he said. He was just having a few harmless fantasies about a gorgeous woman. All guys did that from time to time. It didn't mean anything.

"I didn't come in here to lecture you." Brad stood up and tugged at his belt. His pant waist was lost under his abundant belly.

"You didn't?" Jake threw up his hands. "You could've fooled me."

"You're not funny," Brad said, but he chuckled. "What I came in to tell you is you're going to have to rework the Henderson file."

"Why?" Jake pulled the folder from his organizer and held it up. "I finished it last night. Just have to get the girls to type it up."

Brad shook his head. "The office manager emailed me more information this morning and I forwarded it to you. Seems they didn't include two different accounts in the original report, so that's going to change everything."

"That's just great." Jake opened his email. He looked over the new information and felt his good mood plummet. "This will take me all morning."

"Sorry." Brad shrugged and headed to the door. "Let me know if I can help."

"Yeah, sure thing."

Jake took a swig of warm coffee, which reminded him of Kimberly's personal delivery. He didn't have time for that, so he got busy.

~ ~ ~ ~ ~

Jake spent the next three hours crunching numbers but finally finished. He stuffed the Henderson report into a folder and vowed to personally throttle that company if they handed him any more surprises.

Kimberly stuck her head through the door. "Jake, aren't you going to lunch?"

"Uh-huh. I wanted to get this report out of the way first."

"Mind if I tag along?"

Jake felt his jaw drop.

"My car's in the shop for an oil change." Kimberly

raised a brow. "I won't make you pay or anything."

"It's not that. It's just..."

Kimberly's lower lip turned down at the corners. Fluttering her eyelashes dramatically, she said in a bogus Southern drawl, "Don't tell me you're going to turn down a damsel in distress."

Jake had to laugh. She was definitely a charmer. Fresh out of excuses, he said, "Let's go. I'm starved."

"Lead the way."

"McDonald's okay with you?" He figured that would be safe. The place was always hopping, especially at noon. He wouldn't really be alone with her.

She slid a hand through the crook of his arm and smiled up at him. "Sounds great."

Jake's heartbeat increased a notch, and they hadn't even left the building. *This is not good.*

After holding the passenger door for her, he slid into the driver's seat. He cranked the engine and powered down his window. It was a warm October day with fall bursting out in bright shades of orange and brown. He glanced at Kimberly and reprimanded himself for feeling so uncomfortable. This wasn't like a date or anything, just a favor for a coworker. *I'll be okay,* he thought as his gut churned and definitely not from hunger. *This is not a date.*

Why did it feel like a date, then? His hands were clammy and his lips dry. Moisture beaded on his forehead.

Her cologne permeated the vehicle, making his senses stand at attention. Jake squirmed and rested a forearm on the steering wheel. Struggling for composure, he willed himself to act calm.

Thankful to see the big yellow M towering above the other fast-food signs, Jake turned into the lot. He found a spot toward the back. Kimberly hopped out of the car and found Jake's arm again. Reminding himself to be a gentleman, he held the door open and Kimberly breezed inside. She flung a smile over her shoulder and walked to the counter.

They ordered and settled into a booth by the window. Their usual light banter was punctuated with flirty innuendoes.

"You're kinda antsy today." Kimberly bit into her last chicken nugget.

"Me?"

"Uh-huh. Something bothering you?"

Yeah, you. "Nope." He took a bite of his Big Mac, followed by a swig of Diet Coke.

"I'm a good listener," she said. "If you need to talk to someone. I bet I could make you feel better."

Jake laughed. "I bet you could."

She eyed him over the rim of her Styrofoam cup. "I could get used to this. Looking at you makes the food taste better."

"Oh yeah? You'd get fat, then." Jake raked a fry through the catsup and popped it in his mouth.

"Would you still have the hots for me if I got fat?"

Jake nearly choked.

"You're cute when you get flustered."

Cute, right? He felt anything but cute. More like a junior high kid at his first dance with the most popular girl in school.

Kimberly giggled and leaned toward him. "You're so messy." Her hand snaked out. With an index finger, she dabbed at the corner of his mouth. Her touch sent a shock wave of warning through his brain, and he tried to muster a speck of composure.

"All clean now." She leaned back. Her foot lightly brushed his leg as she crossed hers.

Jake shifted in the seat, twisting his straw. "Are you ready to head back to the office?"

"If we have to." She sighed and gave him her pouty look. "But I wish I could kidnap you and have you all to myself this afternoon. Wouldn't that be fun?"

Would it ever. "You kid around too much." Jake popped up and waited for her to stand. "One of these days, someone is going to take you serious."

She jerked her head toward him and leveled him a look. "If you think I'm kidding, think again."

CHAPTER ELEVEN

Lacey's Friday got off to a bad start and didn't get any better as the day progressed. Six more children admitted to the hospital with probable polio. All the cases were linked to Holly. Same age. Same grade. The waiting room overflowed with anxious people demanding answers. The panicking public kept the phone lines tied up, and Lacey pulled a clerk from the WIC department to help man the front desk. Helplessness oozed through her, cold and bone deep. She hated feeling out of control. Her comfort zone revolved around the norm. Not a life-threatening illness popping up for no apparent reason. And more cases kept coming.

She gave a resigned sigh and grabbed one of the new cases from the growing pile of folders. As she looked over the data, a niggling in the back of her mind kept telling her something was really off about this. If only she could pull it to the front of her brain, make sense of it.

She skipped lunch break, eating snacks at her desk as she worked. By midafternoon, she was beat. She gathered her notes and stopped at the nursing station en route to the conference room. The staff looked as frustrated as she felt.

"I'll be with Joe and Linda if you need anything," she said. "I want to go over the latest reports with them."

"It just keeps getting worse, doesn't it?" Joan said. "Scary."

"Scary doesn't begin to describe it." Betty pushed her glasses up the bridge of her nose as she pulled a chart from the cubby outside the clerical window. "Good grief! I can't believe we have an epidemic."

Joan shook her head. "Scary," she said again, just above a whisper, and Lacey thought if she heard that word one more time, she'd scream.

"It's spreading so fast." Betty thumbed through the chart with her pale-pink manicured nails. "Just like it did in the olden days, before the Salk vaccine."

Worry clawed at Lacey's head. She thought about the work that lay before them. All the interviews still to be done, the frustration of trying to glean useful information from a community of stunned and angry parents. She needed to catch a break, be the in-control CD nurse she always strove to be.

"What do you want me to do with the new cases?" Ann narrowed her eyes. "I'm sure their contacts have already been in for a booster."

"Lot of good that'll do them," Joan mumbled under her breath.

The comment didn't get by Lacey, but she let it go.

"You know what to do without me telling you," Lacey said and aimed a look at Ann. "But just so there's no confusion, I'll spell it out. Check the immunization status of the family and close contacts. If they need a booster, get them in here ASAP."

Lacey didn't have the time or the energy to handle the nurses with kid gloves. They were upset. Well, so was she. As professionals, they would just have to deal with it.

Ann's mouth twitched and anger flickered across her features. "I'll get right on it." She crossed her arms over her chest.

"Hmph!" Betty said. "Like the boosters are doing any good. We're just wasting our time."

"Yeah," Joan said. "It's like we're running in circles and getting nowhere really fast."

"You guys have a better plan?" Lacey shot back, more sharply than she intended. "If you do, please share it with me. I'm always open to suggestions."

"Sorry, Lacey." Joan pushed back a stray strand of salt-and-pepper hair and tossed her a sheepish look. "We're just bombed. We don't mean to take it out on you."

"Forget it," Lacey said. "We're all under stress."

She walked down the hall, wishing she could make all this go away. Just blink her eyes and it would be over. She hated it when she was testy with her nurses. She knew what they were going through. They were at their wit's end, same as she.

"Wait up," Joan said. "Are you okay?"

Lacey stopped and turned. "I'm fine. Sorry I spouted off."

Joan dismissed her with a wave. "You've got a lot on your plate, and I want you to know if you need me to do anything, just ask. I'll be glad to step up and take some of the load off you."

"I know. And I appreciate you. More than you know. Besides, you more than carry your share of the work." Lacey was thankful she had Joan in her corner. Her oldest RN was an excellent nurse, and most important was a great team player. Lacey considered all three of her nurses good friends, but for some reason, she held Joan a little dearer to her heart. Working in a small clinic made it easy to bond, and her staff was easy to get close to.

"I worry about you. I don't want to see you let this affect your health." Joan chuckled. "You can't get sick on us. We need you."

"I won't get sick." Lacey raised her right hand. "I promise."

"I'm gonna hold you to that."

"Thank you for caring." She patted Joan's arm. "And thank you for being here for me. You always could read me like a book."

Joan smiled. "Okay, but let me know if I can do more to help."

Lacey nodded and headed to the conference room.

Joe and Linda looked up when Lacey pushed through the door. The marker board was full of neatly written names and symptoms. Beside the symptoms was a grid titled *Date of Onset*.

"How's it going?" Lacey pulled out a chair. The table was scattered with files and opened EPI books. The taut looks on their faces told Lacey how much this investigation was taking out of them.

Joe shook his head. "We've contacted all the parents of the first-grade class. They know what to watch for and what to do if their child shows any symptoms."

Lacey nodded.

Linda said, "We've told them to use face masks if they take their child to the doctor's office or ED."

"Yeah," she said. "We can't risk exposure in the waiting rooms."

"Most of the parents have been cooperative, but I've run across a few that were outright hostile." Linda frowned. "One mom even hung up on me."

Lacey's eyes settled on Linda, who had no children of her own. How could she possibly understand how frightening all of this was for a parent? Emotions ran wild when something threatened your child's safety.

"Every case is directly linked to Holly." Joe stood and tapped a rubber-tipped pointer at Holly's name. "We're almost certain she contracted polio in Lagos and brought it back to the States."

Lacey swallowed hard. She'd figured that out on day one.

Joe slid the pointer to the bottom of the board to the word *Delta*. "The airline faxed us a list of passengers on Holly's flight. Seventy-eight people from four cities were on that flight. We've faxed the information to the EPI specialists in those counties and they'll follow up on their end. So far, no cases of polio have been reported."

"No other county. Just Lester. Really weird." Linda shook her head. "I don't understand it."

"Me, either." Lacey was exasperated. "It seems to be confined to the first-grade class at Hoover Elementary."

Linda tapped her chin. "There is no logical reason why these kids should be getting polio. Every one of them was vaccinated right on schedule. They should have been protected."

Lacey blew out a breath. Yes, they *should* have been protected. So why in the world weren't they? If they could answer that question, they'd be well on the way to stopping the spread.

"And the two cases of tetanus really stump me. Those kids got a Td booster two years ago." Joe slid into a chair. "There has to be an explanation why the shot didn't work for them. Your first thought would be a bad batch of vaccine, but we've ruled that out."

"Yep," Lacey said. She had pored over the same information, time and time again, and still no breakthrough. She was beginning to doubt they would ever find an answer.

"Any news from the CDC?" she asked Joe.

"Not anything that would explain why the kids would have contracted either disease. They're still working on it. Maybe by Monday they'll have something for us."

"You guys are planning to come back next week, then?"

Joe nodded. "Until you run out of things for us to do, we'll be here."

"I appreciate all your help." Lacey studied the two. They had to be drained. The hour drive from Springfield in the morning then the evening drive back home must be wearing on them. "Why don't you knock off early today? Have a restful weekend and we'll start fresh Monday morning."

"Sounds good to me." Joe shoved stacks of papers into his briefcase and snapped it shut.

"What about all this?" Linda motioned to the paraphernalia strewn across the table. "Let me help you put it away."

"No. Just leave it." Lacey didn't want to put all the files and EPI books back in the library only to drag them back out on Monday. "We'll need all of it next week."

"Well," Joe said, "you know how to reach us if you need anything over the weekend." He gave her a crooked smile and slung the briefcase strap over his shoulder. "I hope you get some R and R the next couple of days. You look beat."

I'm way past beat. "I'm okay." Lacey pushed back her hair, thankful that the EPI team would return the following week.

CHAPTER TWELVE

Saturday afternoon, Lacey sat on the kitchen floor across from Amber. Lacey's back was propped against the wall and her legs were stretched in front of her on the large white and hunter green tiles. Her feet were bare, showing the chips in the toenail polish she'd been meaning to touch up. She felt cozy, if only because she was with the best friend she'd ever had.

On the floor between them was a shoebox of photos and an array of scrapbook material. On a nearby TV tray stood a platter piled high with fresh veggies and low-fat ranch dip. *Diet day today.* She was armed and salubrious.

"Any certain order you want these in?" Amber asked as she squinted into the box.

"Nope. I just want to get it finished."

"We'll need to crop some of the larger pictures. Unless you want to save the scenery in the background."

"You're the scrapbooking expert. I'll go with whatever you suggest."

"Expert, huh?"

"Well, better than me, that's for sure."

Amber dumped the box and shuffled through the

pictures. She picked one from the pile and wrinkled her nose. It had been taken at Branson when Amber was eight months pregnant. "I remember this one. I was big as a cow. Why is this one in here?"

"You're part of my family. I couldn't leave out that sexy picture."

"Yeah." Amber gave her a smack on the arm. "Real sexy."

Lacey felt a warm rush. She loved hanging out with her longtime pal. They'd been friends since the sixth grade when the Lux family had moved from Kansas and bought the house across the street from Lacey's. The two girls had bonded right from the first day and remained best friends since. Amber was creative and naturally gifted in so many ways. Lacey would always be a little ho-hum in comparison. Like scrapbooking. Amber had a knack Lacey couldn't quite muster.

After making neat piles, Amber separated the pictures according to date. "So, how's Jake? Have you talked him into going to the picnic tomorrow?"

"Nope. He's just so stubborn. I swear, I don't know what to do anymore."

"What?" Amber's eyes narrowed. "Is something else going on?"

"Not really."

"Something's bothering you. You can't fool me."

Lacey laughed. "So why do I even bother to try?"

"Because you think you can solve your problems all by yourself. You know, kiddo, we all need help from time to time."

Lacey wrinkled her nose and smiled at her BFF. "You know me too well."

"And don't you forget it. Now, out with it. What's going on?"

"Oh, I'm probably just worrying over nothing. But Jake has been acting different lately."

"How?"

"I don't know. Like he's preoccupied. He seems so distant." Lacey's voice went thick, and she thumbed through a pile of pictures. "Sometimes I think he doesn't love me anymore. Like he used to, you know what I mean?"

Amber nodded. "Maybe you two need to get away. Take a weekend and go off by yourselves."

"Maybe."

"You guys talked about this, right?"

Lacey shrugged. "A little. I've asked him if something is bothering him, and he tells me no."

"Well, there you go." Amber raked a carrot stick through the dip. "Jake adores you. Always has."

Lacey mulled it over, but something nagged at her. "I can't put my finger on it, but it's like he's pulling away from me emotionally."

"If he's acting different, I'm sure it's not because he doesn't love you. Come on, you guys have the best marriage around." Amber gobbled down the carrot like a hungry bunny and reached for a cucumber slice. Unlike Lacey, she didn't have a fetish for sweets and fats.

"Maybe I'm just being paranoid." Lacey sighed and picked up a stack of pictures. "This thing at work has got me so rattled I can't think straight."

"You and me both." Amber frowned. "And Suzie's really bored hanging around the house. The only place I take her is Mom's."

"You could have brought her with you today."

"And have her right in the middle of this?" She laughed and motioned at the clutter. "No, thanks. But I will be glad when things in this town get back to normal and I don't have to keep her corralled."

"I know what you mean. Everyone's mad and confused. They don't understand why polio and tetanus are attacking our kids. I don't, either." Lacey met Amber's gaze and shook her head. "I wish I knew what to do to stop it."

"Give yourself a break, Lacey. You can't be in control of everything."

"But I should be in control of this. It's my job to protect our community from communicable disease and I'm failing miserably."

"You are not! You're working your butt off. And you're exhausted trying to keep everyone calm. Then I had to go off on you Wednesday." Amber's eyes filled with tears. She blinked. "I'm sorry. When it comes to Suzie, I just get so..."

Lacey held up a hand. "I understand. I told you, I feel the same way. I'm scared, too. Really scared. I have this terrible gut feeling something sinister is attacking our town."

"I hate when you get your gut feelings. They usually pan out."

Lacey gave her friend a hug that lasted longer than usual. Then she focused her attention to scrapbooking and put frightening thoughts behind her.

~ ~ ~ ~ ~

An hour later, Jake stepped through the back door. He was sweaty and smelled of newly mown grass. He eyed the half-finished scrapbook and pulled a pitcher of lemonade out of the refrigerator.

"Hey, Amber. How's it going?" he asked.

"Hi, Jake. If you're done with your yard, you can head over to my house. Daniel would love the help."

"And deprive him of the pleasure and satisfaction of doing it himself?" Jake filled a large glass and swallowed half the liquid in two gulps. "No way. You tell Dan I'd never move in on his territory."

"You're just too thoughtful," Amber said.

Jake gave a two fingered salute then polished off his drink and wiped his mouth with the back of his hand. "I'm gonna hit the shower. I can't stand my own self."

Lacey eyed her husband. Even dirty and reeking of man scent, Jake was adorable. "Hey, you want to go to Bennett Springs later? We could eat at the Lodge."

"Sure." Jake gave her a smile that melted her heart. Maybe she was just inventing problems that weren't there. She watched him walk away and chided herself for having doubted his love.

Todd ambled in, as grungy as Jake, and made a beeline for the lemonade. So much like his father with dark, wavy hair and slate-blue eyes. He reminded her of Jake when she'd first met him in high school. Todd threw up a hand in greeting as he belted down sixteen ounces without coming up for air. Lacey noticed a dark circle of blood on his sock.

"What happened?" She pointed at his foot.

"The lawnmower threw a twig or something. No biggie." He refilled his glass and walked to the table.

"Okay, if you say so. But let me check it out." Always the nurse, Lacey wanted to see firsthand how bad the injury looked. She hoisted herself up and wet a paper towel at the sink.

Todd tugged off his shoe and sock. Lacey propped his foot on the chair across from him and wiped away the blood. "You're right, kiddo, nothing serious."

Todd rolled his eyes and looked at Amber. "I told her."

Amber laughed.

Lacey swatted his leg. "After your shower, put antibiotic ointment and a Band-Aid on it."

"Yes, Mom. Sheesh, it's just a scratch." He grabbed his shoe and sock then meandered through the doorway.

Lacey knew Todd was up to date on his immunizations, but just to make sure, she pulled his record out of the kitchen catch-all drawer. He'd had a Td booster two years ago, so he was fine with his tetanus.

As she put the record away, a cold clammy sensation chewed on her spine. *Those two boys who died from tetanus were up to date on their shots, too.*

"You okay?" Amber asked.

"Yeah. Just having an attack of motherhood."

"I hear you."

Lacey gave Amber a half grin, thankful to have a friend who understood. She squirmed back into her spot among the pictures and other paraphernalia, feeling like her life was spinning out of control. Would she ever be in charge again?

CHAPTER THIRTEEN

She turned over in bed and felt her husband's warm breath on her shoulder. His even breathing told her he was out for the night. Unlike her, he had no problem falling asleep.

The clock read almost midnight. She threw back the sheet, rolled out of bed, and padded silently to the window. Cars parked at the curb up and down the neighborhood were shrouded in shadows under the streetlamps. All was quiet. No breeze, the leaves perfectly still, the night dismal and dark. Just like she felt.

I am so tired of not sleeping, she thought as she walked to the kitchen and retrieved a bottle of wine from the cabinet and poured half a glass before plopping down at the table. She lit a cigarette and inhaled deeply, the nicotine burned her throat and esophagus. She coughed and cursed. One of these days she'd quit.

She guzzled the dregs from her glass and poured another. She was determined to get some rest one way or the other. She hated her insomnia and envied people who could drift into a sound slumber so easily. She couldn't remember the last time she'd had a good night's sleep. The last few weeks, it had become impossible to get enough rest to function at top speed. It took her forever to doze off at night and then she didn't want to get out of bed the next morning.

I need to see Doc John and see if he'll write me a script for a sleeping pill.

She needed more Xanax anyway. She'd call him first thing in the morning.

She'd bet money Lacey was sleeping soundly. Who wouldn't with a hunk like Jacob Bookman beside her? Ripples of rage gyrated through her veins as she pictured Lacey lying next to that gorgeous man. Lacey, who had always been a pain in the butt, taking what she wanted no matter who got hurt along the way, would pay dearly. She'd make sure of that.

She stubbed out the cigarette, grabbed her glass, and went to the living room and turned on the TV. But when QVC assured her that she'd sleep better if she had a Posture-Perfect mattress, she muttered an expletive and switched the channel to find the Golden Girls arguing over a man. *Eeew.* She hit the off button and tossed the control onto the end table. As she snared a novel from the bookends by the phone, an idea formed.

If I can't sleep, neither will Lacey. She dug her burner phone from the drawer—couldn't let caller ID show her number—and punched in the Bookman's home number.

"Hello?" A sleepy, yet sexy, Jake asked on the third ring.

After all these years, the sound of his voice still shot shivers through her body. She breathed into the phone, waiting.

"Hello. Is anybody there?"

She almost laughed then stifled herself. All the while, she made deliberate breath sounds.

"Who is it?" She heard Lacey's voice in the background. The image of her snuggled next to Jake made her want to hurl. Her jaw clenched tight, and she resisted the urge to tell Jake what kind of person he'd married.

And he could have had me.

"Someone who thinks they're funny," Jake said then he cut the connection.

She waited thirty minutes to give them time to doze off. Jake didn't sound sleepy when he answered this time. He said hello only once before he hung up.

The next several calls were fifteen minutes apart. Jake's voice grew angrier each time he answered. On her final call, Jake bellowed into the phone, and she had to hold the receiver away from her ear. "Who is this and what the crap do you want? It's three in the morning, you slime bag!"

She clicked off the phone and slipped it back in its little hiding place. Satisfied she'd successfully disturbed that serene little household, she headed back to bed.

If I am going to feel rotten tomorrow, so are you, Lacey.

CHAPTER FOURTEEN

Monday morning, Lacey watched Todd pour a white stream of milk into a tumbler. Then he limped to the table.

"What's wrong with your leg?" Lacey asked.

"It's not my leg." Todd rolled his eyes theatrically and Lacey wondered if he had a patent for that eye thing. "It's my ankle."

Lacey frowned and squatted down. "Good grief." She placed the back of her hand against his ankle. The entire area was hot, red, and swollen. The Band-Aid was saturated with yellowish-brown drainage. The wound looked infected.

"How long has your ankle been like this?"

"Since last night."

"Why didn't you tell me?"

Todd shrugged and took a drink of milk. "I didn't think it was a big deal."

"Don't give me that." Lacey's nerves pricked and she couldn't keep the irritation from her voice. "You knew."

"Well, I thought it'd be better by today."

"Well, you thought wrong, young man." What was wrong with him? His foot looked terrible, and he should have told her. Or maybe if she'd paid closer attention...

Jake and Brian walked in the kitchen with their heads together, discussing the upcoming football game at school. They stopped short and looked from Lacey to Todd's angry-looking foot. Brian grabbed a banana, pulled back the peel, and took a bite as he poured a glass of milk.

"What's up, buddy?" Jake peered at Todd's wound. He let out a low whistle. "That looks bad. What happened?"

"That stupid cut where the twig attacked me."

"And he never told me how bad it was getting," Lacey said and narrowed her eyes at her oldest son.

"Infected?" Jake asked.

"Definitely. I'm going to get him in to see the doctor this morning. He's going to need an antibiotic."

Brian eyed the foot. "Yuck. Nasty." He polished off his milk, set the glass in the sink, and bolted through the door.

"No school for you this morning." Jake squeezed Todd's shoulder. "Do you want something to eat? Cereal? Toast?"

"Naw. I'm going back to bed." He shuffled toward the door.

"I'll call you when I get an appointment," Lacey said. "Give you enough time to shower and get ready."

"Okay," he mumbled.

"That ankle is hurting him." Lacey was still peeved he'd let it go so long. And ashamed that she hadn't checked it herself last night.

"It looks pretty bad," Jake said. "What do you think?"

"Maybe staph."

"Will you be able to get away from work to take him to the doctor?"

"Yeah."

"Are you sure? I know you're swamped. I'll take him if you want."

"I can do it. I want to hear firsthand what the doctor says." Her hand settled on his arm. "But can you drop Brian off at school on your way to the office?"

"Will do." Jake pulled out a chair and plopped down.

"And he'll just have to ride the bus home tonight." Lacey picked up the carafe and poured him a mug of coffee. He'd need the caffeine if he was as pooped as she was.

"What do you make of the prank calls last night?" she asked.

"Probably some bored kid with nothing better to do." Jake frowned as he dropped two sugar cubes in his cup and stirred.

"I don't know. Three in the morning is awfully late for some kid to be up."

"I hope whoever it was has to get up early this morning." Jake tipped up his mug and took a long drink. "Were you able to get any sleep?"

"Some. But it took a while. How about you?"

"No. I tried but it was useless, so I just got up and read. I'm paying for it this morning."

"I wondered why you were up so early." Lacey squeezed his shoulder. "Poor baby, you look terrible."

"Ooh. You wound me."

She gave him a swat. "You know what I mean. You look good even when you're looking bad." She leaned over and planted a kiss on his forehead.

"Don't try to make up now."

Lacey laughed and grabbed her purse. "Gotta go. See you tonight."

~ ~ ~ ~ ~

Lacey walked through the back door of the health department and checked the fax machine thankful it was empty. She headed to the break room and made coffee. The Bunn was fast and in no time, she had her fingers wrapped around a full mug. She hustled down the hall and settled into her chair.

Lacey watched the clock as she typed the morning report for the media. It was simple. When nothing new was known about the cases, there was not a whole lot that could be reported. *We will keep you informed as we become aware...*seemed to be repeated every morning. She was grateful Robert was handling the press. All Lacey had to do was type the release and send it to the three local radio stations and the newspaper.

At eight thirty, she phoned the doctor's office. They could see Todd in an hour. She'd have to hurry. She phoned home then grabbed her purse and sprinted to the nursing station.

Ann looked up as Lacey stepped to her cubicle. "Hey, Lacey. Did you have a good weekend?"

"Yeah, I did. It was nice to get away for a couple days." Lacey repressed a yawn. "How about you? Are you revived and ready to face another week?"

"Uh-huh. I hope this week's better than last."

"You and me both." Lacey hoisted her purse over her shoulder. "I'm going to be out of the office for a while. I'm taking Todd to the doctor."

Ann lifted an eyebrow. "Is he sick?"

"No. He hurt his ankle Saturday mowing the lawn. I think it's infected."

"Sorry to hear that. Hope it isn't anything serious."

"Probably not. But he's gonna need some antibiotics."

"Why not have the doc call in a script?"

Lacey lifted a shoulder. "You know me. I want to be on the safe side and have it looked at."

"I don't blame you."

"If Joe or Linda need anything, I told them to check with you. The girls up front know I'm leaving. They'll refer everything to you while I'm out. I shouldn't be gone long, but you know how that goes. With them working Todd in, we may have to wait a while before he even sees the doctor."

"Don't worry about things here. We'll be fine." Ann smiled and patted her hand. "Just take care of your son."

Lacey hustled out of the building and ten minutes later parked in her driveway. As she walked through the front door, she gasped. Todd was hobbling toward her with one shoe on and one shoe off; he was practically dragging his injured foot.

"I couldn't get my shoe on. Sock, either. Too swollen."

"Oh Lord, help him," Lacey cried out to God.

She helped her son sit on a nearby chair. When she looked at his foot, concern tugged at her heart, and she shivered. It was redder than earlier and very warm to the touch. Purulent drainage oozed from the point of entry. "That foot is getting worse. Hold on, I'll be right back."

She sprinted up the stairs two at a time, flew into the bedroom, and grabbed one of Jake's old, stretched-out house shoes. She quickly retraced her steps.

Todd offered his hand, but Lacey shook her head and said, "Here let me."

She slid the cloth-like shoe gently over his edematous foot.

Todd stood and leaned against her as they headed

outside. She helped him into the car then rushed to her side. She was worried. Really worried. She did not like the look of that foot. She sped down the street and a few minutes later, pulled into the crowded parking lot at Dr. James's white brick office.

The waiting room was almost full. She guided Todd to a seat, signed him in then lowered herself into a seat beside him. An elderly man to her right was coughing into a tissue. His cough rattled, making Lacey suspect an upper respiratory infection. She hoped it wasn't contagious.

A young woman with two small children sat across from her. The kids were fussy and wanted to go home. The young woman patiently explained why they couldn't leave just yet.

Lacey didn't want to stare at the clients, but there was nowhere to look except at the people. She crossed to the magazine rack and randomly grabbed something and sat back down.

Sports Illustrated. Smiling at her poor choice, she held it out for Todd. He thumbed through the pages then laid it down.

It seemed like hours had passed before the nurse finally called Todd's name. Lacey looked at her watch. Ten thirty. They'd been there for over an hour. She inhaled deeply and tried not to show her irritation as she fell into step behind the nurse that guided Todd to an exam room. Another fifteen minutes slid by before Dr. James came through the door.

"Hello, Todd," he said. "Foot problems." It was more of a statement than a question as he looked down at the iPad for a beat then laid the apparatus on the counter and lowered himself onto a stool with wheels.

"What did you do to your ankle?"

"I was mowing the yard Saturday and the mower

threw a twig. Caught me right here." Todd pointed at the angry ankle.

"It just looked like a minor scratch." Lacey felt a fresh ping of shame shoot through her. She should never have let it go this long.

"Well, let's take a look." The doctor snapped on latex gloves and rolled his stool to the exam table. He slipped off the shoe and examined Todd's ankle. He turned toward Lacey. "I think there's something in the wound. I'm going to move him to the minor surgery room so I can take a better look. If there's something in there, it'll have to be removed."

Todd groaned. So did Lacey.

The doctor patted Todd's arm. "It'll only take a few minutes, and I'll give you something for pain. You won't feel a thing."

"Yeah, I bet." Todd chuckled, but Lacey heard dread in his voice as Doc helped him through the door.

All kinds of thoughts raced through Lacey's mind while she waited. She should have checked the ankle the next day. *Should have but didn't.* She berated herself for not having paid closer attention to things at home. It seemed she was always more wrapped up in work than her own family.

Guilt wracked her and she was on the verge of tears by the time the door opened. Dr. James and Todd stepped inside. Both were smiling. That had to be a good sign. Todd fell into a chair.

"Well?" Lacey hesitated.

"Two tiny pieces of bark were embedded in the tissue," Dr. James said. "I removed them and deep-cleaned the area. Getting that junk out of his wound will decrease the edema, and I'd say by morning, you'll see a big difference in the size of his foot. Keep him home from school for the rest of the day with his leg elevated. That will help to decrease the swelling. Antibiotics for a week, and he'll be as good as new."

"Can I go back to school tomorrow?" Todd asked.

"Not tomorrow." The doctor scribbled on a prescription pad. "Maybe Wednesday if the swelling is down."

Todd knit his brows in a disapproving scowl but didn't protest.

"You're sure it's nothing serious?" Lacey pushed her hair back from her face. "You know we've had some crazy things going on in our county. For instance, tetanus."

Dr. James nodded and a frown crimped his forehead. "Yeah, I've heard. But Todd's symptoms are entirely different than tetanus. Lacey, you know that. The first symptom of tetanus is a stiff jaw, drooling. That's why it's called lockjaw."

"I know. But when it's your child, it's hard to be objective." Lacey heard her voice tremble.

Don't start blubbering and embarrass Todd.

"I know without asking, Todd's shots are up to date," the doctor said.

"Yes. They are. But just to be on the safe side, can you give him a tetanus booster while we're here?"

"Mom!"

Lacey held up a hand to shush Todd. She wasn't taking any chances where her son was concerned.

Dr. James laughed. "I'll send the nurse in with a tetanus shot before you leave. An extra one won't hurt. And I can see it will ease Mama's mind."

"Thank you." Lacey gathered a breath and looked at the doctor. "The kids who contracted tetanus were up to date on their shots."

The doctor tented his fingers and met her gaze. "Trust me, Lacey. This isn't tetanus."

"But where does tetanus come from?" Before he

could answer, she continued, "Dirt, that's where. Todd had a dirty wound, so dirty in fact, he has a rip-roaring infection..."

"Look at me, Lacey." Dr. James took both of her hands in his. "This is not tetanus. Todd has an infection caused by the dirty debris embedded in the tissue. That's all. I'm starting him on antibiotics and he's gonna be okay, believe me."

Lacey nodded, willing herself to let go of the irrational fear that gripped her heart. She trusted Dr. James completely. He'd been their family physician for years. He would be straight and honest with her. He wouldn't let anything happen to Todd.

She was still glad Todd would be getting an extra booster.

CHAPTER FIFTEEN

Jake opened his phone calendar and scanned Monday afternoon's schedule. Four o'clock meeting with the CEO of Sunblazer Boats. Why did Brad always schedule meetings so late in the day? He pulled out the file on the boat factory and set it aside. He'd go over it one more time before the meeting.

He checked his watch and wondered if Lacey had taken Todd to the doctor yet. She was a tiger when it came to her kids.

Sometimes he wished she'd be a little more that way with him. She was always so busy with her job and church, she didn't do the little things for him that she used to. He flashed on the times early in their marriage when she'd meet him at the door dressed in a slinky gown that barely covered anything. He'd forget about dinner until much later in the night. That hadn't happened since the kids passed the toddler stage.

His cell rang, jarring him back to the moment. *Lacey.*

"Hi, hon. How's Todd?"

"He's okay. Thank goodness."

"Good deal."

"He had a couple splinters embedded in his ankle. Doc took them out and ordered antibiotics. Says Todd will be good as new in a couple of days."

"Great. I know you're relieved."

"Yeah. I was kinda freaked out this morning when I saw how bad that ankle looked."

"I could tell." He chuckled. He had to admit, he worried about the kids as much as his wife did. "It did look pretty yucky. Has he started the antibiotics yet?"

"Yes, Dad." She laughed. "We stopped by the pharmacy and filled his script then swung by McDonalds and got lunch to go. He's at home with his leg propped up and I gave him strict orders to keep it that way."

"Are you at work?"

"On my way. I figure I can get a good half day in."

"Don't worry about dinner tonight. I'll bring pizza home, okay?" Jake knew Lacey was as bad about pizza as Brian was with spaghetti.

"Sounds perfect."

"Okay. I have a meeting at four, so if I'm late getting home, you'll know why."

Lacey chuckled. "If the meeting's at four, you'll definitely be late. I'll swing home and check on Todd then change and go to the park. I missed my run this morning."

"Okay. See you later, babe."

Jake slipped the phone back in the holder on his belt. He knew Lacey felt relieved. She was a good mother. And, he had to admit, a great wife. He needed to get back on track with her. Open up to her more like he used to. Be more involved.

Their Saturday evening at Bennett Spring State Park had been nice. Just him and Lacey feeding the fish in the hatchery, strolling around the grounds, browsing at various shops then ending their day with a late dinner at the Lodge. He'd ordered a whole catfish, complete with eyes, and laughed when Lacey swore the eyes were staring at her. On the way home, she asked if he was planning on going to the picnic Sunday. When he'd begged off, she'd let it slide.

"Here's the preliminary on Sunblazer." Kimberly pushed through the door, bringing him out of his reverie. Ended thoughts about his wife instantly when he inhaled her aroma.

"Thanks. Are you sitting in on the meeting this afternoon?"

"Yeah. Brad thinks I need the 'experience.'" She made air quotes.

"And you don't think so?"

"What kind of experience is that going to give me? I want to do hands-on. I wish he'd let me have a client of my own. A *real* client."

"He will. As soon as you pass that test."

Her eyebrows shot up. "You really think I'll pass it?"

"It's not that hard if you've studied. Everything you need to know is in the manual Brad gave you."

She shrugged. "I've studied. Hard. Every night."

"Then you'll do fine. Trust me."

"I do trust you, Jake." She shut the door and clicked the lock.

Uneasiness crept up his spine. But what could happen? Good grief, this was an office complex, not a motel room.

She eased into the chair across from him. She crossed her legs, showing tanned, muscular calves and six inches of thigh. Jake sucked in a gulp of air.

The locked door nagged at him. He had the urge to march across the office and unlatch it. But he just sat there, sculptured to his chair, like a clump of clay.

She swung her leg then extended it. "Like my legs?"

"What's not to like?" He surprised himself with such a quick answer.

She laughed, uncrossed her legs, and sat up straight. "Anything else interest you?"

Her movement outlined her perfect physique, leaving little to his imagination. Jake picked up his cup, but it was empty. His tongue felt glued to the roof of his mouth. Warmth flooded his cheeks and he had to force his gaze above her neck.

"There's nothing to be embarrassed about. I like it that you like my body." She adjusted herself in the chair, causing her skirt to hike up even more. "I like your body, too, Jake. You are one gorgeous man, and you turn me on big-time."

Jake moistened his lips, wondering if her legs felt as smooth as they looked.

"And what's so cute about you is you don't have a clue how you affect women." Raw passion flicked across her eyes. "Do you know how hard it is for me to keep my hands off you?"

Her voice was low and husky with not a hint of jesting. She was dead serious, and Jake had to make a quick decision. He had to admit he was attracted to her. But was he willing to toss everything aside for her? Lacey, his kids, his self-respect? His indecision made him crazy. He'd never thought he'd ever want another woman besides Lacey. And though Kimberly was a temptation, Lacey was his life. Had been since high school.

"Jake?"

Tell her to get out of here. Go. Now. He looked at her, couldn't speak. He couldn't even think.

She held his gaze like a lion about to pounce on her prey. Part of him wished she'd leap on him with all fours. He couldn't control his throbbing pulse or the sweat that popped on his forehead. He gripped the arms of his chair.

"I know you like me." She purred like a kitten.

He raked fingers through his hair.

"Don't fight it." She unbuttoned the top of her blouse.

He swallowed hard and his mouth was so dry he thought he was going to choke. He needed a drink of water, bad.

She twiddled with the second button as she looked up through her thick lashes. Her invitation hung heavy between them.

Jake pushed back from his desk and stepped toward her. *I've got to get her out of here.*

The doorknob rattled and Jake jumped.

"Jake?" Brad called out. "Open up."

Kimberly buttoned her blouse as she walked to the door. She stepped across the threshold without a word.

Brad pushed in and looked from him to Kimberly and back. Unsmiling lips pressed tight like a rubber band about to snap. Jake felt blood pulsing through his veins. The look in Brad's eyes told him that his boss knew what he'd almost done.

~ ~ ~ ~ ~

Jake went back to his office after he'd splashed cool water on his face in the restroom. His shirt had not escaped the splatter.

"What is the matter with you? Are you crazy?" Brad asked.

"I don't know." Maybe he had gone crazy. He sure hadn't acted sane.

Brad paced around the office then plopped a hefty hip on Jake's desk. "Let me ask you this. Are you ready to ask Lacey for a divorce?"

"No, of course not. No matter what you think, I do love her."

"But you're drawn to Kimberly."

Jake didn't answer.

Brad blew out a frustrated breath. "Jake, what you're feeling for Kimberly is more than attraction. It's lust. Nothing but your testosterone working overtime. And you're going to lose Lacey if you keep this up."

"I haven't done anything—"

"Not yet. But don't kid yourself, you're headed that way." Brad hit his head with the heel of his hand. "Use your brain, man. Not your—"

"I *am* using my brain." Anger sliced his words. "If I hadn't been using my brain, I would have already slept with her."

There, he'd said it. What had been in the back of his mind for weeks. He dropped his head and looked at his feet, hating himself for allowing such lewd feelings.

"Jake, look at me."

Jake shifted and met his boss's gaze.

"You've got to stop this."

"I know."

"I mean it. You've got to get a grip. Now!"

Jake snorted. "I know. I said, I know." He plopped down in his chair and adjusted his tie. His collar was damp. "I don't want to hurt Lacey."

"You will, you know. If you don't stop this crap." Brad shook his head. "A moment of pleasure can cause you a lifetime of regret."

"This is so crazy." Guilt choked Jake's voice. His skin crawled with self-disgust. If Brad hadn't interrupted, would he have asked Kimberly to leave? "It's like I'm addicted to her."

"I know what you're going through. It happened to

me once. Almost cost me my marriage."

"You?"

"Yeah, me." Brad got a faraway look in his eyes. He walked to the window and stood looking out while Jake stared at the back of his head.

Brad finally turned. "She was a knockout, man. Young. Very sexy. She made me feel like a real stud. She was everything I thought I wanted." He shook his head, laughing without mirth. "Notice I said, what I *thought* I wanted? Sometimes we think we want something and when we get it, it blows up in our face."

"Did you..."

"Yes. The affair lasted three months."

"Did Harriett find out?"

"Oh yeah. Broke her heart. She kicked me out."

"But you and Harriett are still together."

Brad harrumphed. "After a one-year separation, almost divorce. I went to counseling and finally got my head on straight and realized what I'd done was the worst thing I could've done to my innocent wife. Harriett forgave me and took me back, but it was a long time before she could completely trust me again. I was lucky. Some wives wouldn't have been as forgiving."

Jake let Brad's words sink in. He shuddered as he pictured how hurt Lacey would be if he betrayed her. He had to stop panting after Kimberly. No matter what was going on between him and Lacey, he loved her and didn't want to live his life without her. Not with Kimberly or any other woman.

"So, what happened to that woman? Where is she now?"

"Don't know. Don't care. Last I heard, she'd moved to Kansas City, but that's been quite some time ago."

Jake stood and laid his hand on Brad's shoulder.

"Thanks for sharing, man. I came this close"—he held his thumb and forefinger a fraction of an inch apart— "to messing up. Big-time!"

"But you didn't, thank God." Brad slapped him on the back. "Just tell her you're not interested then keep your distance. If you slip up, you get your butt in my office pronto. Hear me?"

"I hear you."

And he did, loud and clear. He'd been stupid to let this thing with Kimberly go this far and he was done. He vowed he'd concentrate on his marriage. Focus on his wife.

He had no intention of jeopardizing his life with Lacey.

CHAPTER SIXTEEN

After work, Lacey found Todd sitting in Jake's overstuffed recliner with the footrest up and his legs stretched out. *Good boy.* He was playing some game on X-Box. Lacey shook her head. She'd never understand her guys. Jake included.

Todd smiled as he hit the pause button. "Hi, Mom."

"Hey, you." Lacey squatted down. The ankle still looked angry. "How's the foot feeling?"

Todd shrugged. "The same."

"It's going to take the antibiotic a while to get in your system, so don't worry."

"I'm not worried." He did his annoying eye-rolling thing. "It's you."

"So, sue me. I can't help it. I love you."

"Whatever." He resumed his game.

"Dad's bringing home pizza for dinner, but it'll be a while. I'm gonna change and get in a quick run. You need anything before I go?"

"More soda." He glanced toward his empty glass. "Lots of ice."

After Lacey delivered the drink, she dashed upstairs, changed into sweats and running shoes, and drove to the park.

She tossed her tote on a bench. It was another splendid fall day in the Ozarks, and she liked to take advantage of pleasant weather. When winter arrived, she'd have to use the treadmill at the gym, which was boring. Staring at a monitor did nothing for her. While the mild weather lasted, she would enjoy the beautiful scenery.

She slipped her phone from her bag and inserted the earbuds. She flipped it on and listened to "That Old Time Rock and Roll" while she did her stretches. By the time she hit the trail, "Rockin' Robin" was blasting away, making her shoes pound the track in rhythmic strides. The farther she ran, pumping her arms and breathing harder, the better she felt.

Forty-five minutes later, she sprinted to the bench, her lungs feeling like they could ignite. She bent over with hands on her thighs, gulping in fresh air.

Saturated with perspiration, she grabbed a towel from her bag. She tipped up the bottle of water and took a long drink then draped the towel around her neck. She clicked off her music—sorry, Chubby Checker, but she'd heard enough of "The Twist" for one day—and plopped down on the bench under an ancient oak. Acorns attracted a pert bushy-tailed gray squirrel that seemed indifferent to her presence. He sat on his hind feet with a nut cradled in his cute little paws, nibbling away.

A white, neatly trimmed miniature poodle, nose to the ground like a blood hound, trotted across the grass. The squirrel scampered up the gnarled tree in a blur. The pooch looked at Lacey with warm, brown eyes, gave his head a hearty shake then pranced over and sniffed her legs. She scratched the wooly fur behind his ears.

"Are you lost, little guy?" she asked in her dog-savvy lingo.

The poodle gave her a wet doggy smile, wagged his tail, and whimpered as if he were trying to answer. She was just checking his collar for identification when she heard someone call.

"Fritz! Here, Fritz, over here..."

Fritz. That's cute. You look like a Fritz.

The dog's ears stood up and his head cocked to one side. After he gave himself a good shake, he ran toward his owner's voice. Lacey watched him reunite with a middle-aged lady dressed in lavender sweats. Her nutmeg hair was pulled back in a tight ponytail. The woman bent forward, and immediately the dog jumped up to lap her face. By the way she was shaking her finger, Lacey knew the pet was getting a royal chewing out. Fritz sat back on his haunches. The tail never stopped wagging. He was not one bit afraid of the reprimand. Lacey smiled.

"You really do like dogs, don't you?" a voice said.

Startled, Lacey turned. Ann stood beside her, clutching a diet soda.

"Yeah, I love dogs." Lacey scooted over and Ann lowered herself onto the bench. "What are you doing here?"

Ann shrugged. "Just trying to wind down."

"I hear you." Lacey took another drink from her bottle. "I didn't get my run in this morning, so I did it after work. Then I had a small canine visitor." Lacey looked toward Fritz and the woman who were heading out of the park.

"I saw. It looked like both you and the mutt were enjoying each other's company." Ann tilted her head and smiled. "You know, you really need to consider getting another dog. It would be good for you."

Memories of Sophie opened old wounds. They'd gotten her as a puppy and had her until they said goodbye six months ago. She'd been part of the family for fifteen years and they still missed her like crazy. They hadn't even talked about getting another pet. It was way too soon to even think about it.

"You should take that stray off your mother's hands," Ann said.

"Are you kidding? Mom would never give him up. Despite her protests, she's bonded with him."

"Then go to the animal shelter. There's plenty of wanna-be pets there."

Always the one ready to dole out advice, Ann had an answer for everything. Or thought she did. But she couldn't possibly understand how hard it had been to give up Sophie.

"I'm serious. You guys need to get a dog."

"We probably will eventually..." Lacey hesitated. Her heart rose into her throat at the thought of replacing Sophie.

Sophie, a big blond dog, was part lab and a mixture of a couple of other unknown breeds. It hadn't mattered to them when they had picked her out at the animal shelter. Todd had only been a year old, and Brian hadn't even been born when Sophie had joined the family, so the boys had grown up with her. She had been such a loving animal and oh-so smart. She'd captured their hearts from day one despite her habit of chewing their socks to pieces every chance she got.

The year before she'd died, it had been obvious she was failing fast. They had taken her to the vet several times and he'd said Sophie was just getting old.

"I know how easy it is to get attached to a pet." Ann sighed. "We have a dog and a cat. It sure doesn't take very long for them to wedge their way into your heart and become a big part of your life."

Lacey changed the subject. She liked Ann in spite of her know-it-all attitude. Ann meant well, but Lacey wasn't in the mood to sit through one of her advice sessions. Especially when it concerned replacing Sophie with a new, improved model.

Things at the office had been so hectic lately, there hadn't been much of a chance to visit about trivial things not work-related. So, sitting in the park away from the hustle and bustle of the office, Lacey and Ann slipped into easy conversation. Occasionally the subject turned to issues at work, but overall, the banter was light and relaxing.

When Lacey glanced at her watch, she was shocked to find it was after seven. She jumped up. "Geez. My family will be wondering what's taking me so long. I've gotta go."

"I'm going to stay a little while longer." Ann stood. "No reason to rush home. Richard's putting in a lot of overtime lately."

Ann's six-foot frame towered over Lacey. She was a large woman. Not fat, just muscular and big-boned. She carried herself gracefully and came across as attractive, if not outright beautiful.

"See you in the morning." Lacey stuffed her things into her tote and raced to the car.

She snapped to attention when she noticed something stuck under her windshield wiper. Probably a political flyer. It was getting close to election time and the candidates were busy making their last-minute pitches. She yanked it free and unfolded the paper. Her eyes rolled over the note.

The gasp was out of her throat before she could suppress it. Her skin turned clammy.

She scanned the park expecting to see the perpetrator lurking behind a bush. Nothing. The area was deserted. She looked carefully at each parked car to see if anyone was sitting inside, watching her, laughing at her shock. No one.

She jerked open the door, jumped in the Nissan,

and quickly clicked the lock. She cranked the engine and shivered as she rammed the gear into reverse and trounced the gas.

CHAPTER SEVENTEEN

Lacey gunned the engine and shot out of the park, tires squealing as she turned right. Her eyes flicked to the rearview mirror. No one behind her. She shoved her hair back and wiped the dampness from her forehead. Why would someone leave a note like that? Maybe they picked her car by mistake. But that didn't make sense; she wasn't thinking rationally. The note was obviously meant for her.

She drew in a breath, relieved to see her driveway and thankful she'd made it home without wrecking. She pulled into the garage, jumped out of her car, and banged through the kitchen door.

"What's up?" A frown creased Jake's brow.

Two open pizzas boxes sat on the counter with several pieces missing. Glasses and half a two-liter soda bottle dripping condensation stood beside the boxes.

"This." Lacey thrust the note at him with trembling hands. "It was on my windshield."

Jake opened the note while Lacey paced back and forth.

What kind of person would write something like that? Someone she didn't want to meet, that was for sure.

Jake handed the note back. He pressed his lips together.

"Why would someone want to threaten you? Us?" he asked.

Lacey shrugged and grabbed a piece of cheese and pepperoni pizza, and bit into it. She swallowed and took a swig of soda directly from the bottle.

"Do you think we need to call the police?" she asked.

"No, not call." Jake scratched his head. "I'll take it down to the station and let them look at it. It's hard to believe this isn't just a stupid prank, but I'm not taking any chances."

He reached for the note. Lacey hesitated and looked down at the paper. The words jumped out at her in bold, large font.

Thanks to you, things are in a mess at the health department. It's time for you to get out. Now. Before you regret it. You have a family to consider and you wouldn't want anything to happen to them, would you? I'm watching you. I know your every move. I know every step your husband and those two boys take. Get out now or you will be sorry.

Lacey's hands trembled as she handed the note to Jake. "I don't like this. First the calls, now a threat. I'm scared."

Jake slid the note into his pocket then laid a hand on her shoulder. "Someone is just upset about the polio cases. They can't possibly think it's your fault. Don't worry, nothing is going to happen to us."

He gave her shoulder a squeeze. His firm grip was reassuring, making her feel, for just a moment, that she'd be okay.

"It was just so eerie, getting it on the windshield

and all. Like someone knew where I'd be and when. But how would they know? I usually run in the morning."

Jake looked thoughtful and shook his head.

"I feel like my privacy has been invaded."

"I know." Jake wrapped his arms around her and gave her a hug. "I'll take care of it, Lace. Todd and Brian are upstairs—they've already eaten. You go ahead and eat before the food gets cold. I'll be back in a few minutes."

A sudden chill crawled over Lacey. She didn't want him to leave her.

"Better yet, you come with me." It was like Jake had read her thoughts.

"Okay. Let the boys know and I'll put the food away."

Jake went upstairs then returned in a flash. "I told the boys we're going out."

"Did you tell them about the note?"

"No. We can tell them after we get back. I'm sure we'll both be feeling better by then."

"Todd's foot..."

"Don't worry, Mom, he's keeping it elevated." Jake smiled and opened the door to the garage.

~ ~ ~ ~ ~

Less than an hour later they were back. Jake had been wrong. The trip to the police station hadn't made them feel any better. Not her anyway.

They'd been ushered to the cubicle of Detective Douglas Prater. Detective Prater looked mid-fortyish with a muscular build, a pleasant face, and a no-nonsense yet friendly demeanor. He'd read the note then asked questions as he scribbled on a yellow legal pad.

He was sorry, he'd said, but things like that happened, and there wasn't much they could do since no one had seen who had put the note on the car. And he wasn't convinced the note and the phone calls were related. He instructed them to contact him if anything else unusual occurred.

"You know," Jake said as he held the kitchen door open, "this is probably just a prank. But we ought to be careful until this polio stuff blows over."

Lacey sighed. "That could be awhile."

CHAPTER EIGHTEEN

After poring over the files of the nine children under investigation, Lacey stacked the folders in order of date of onset and put them in her desk organizer. She leaned back and took a sip of coffee. There still was not one single thing to indicate why these children would have contracted polio. She stood and paced in her small office. Something she'd been doing a lot lately.

She strode to the window, peered through the blinds, and rubbed her forehead. *What am I missing?* She trekked to her desk then returned to the window. *And I know I'm missing something. Something important. I can feel it.* Back and forth she went, asking herself the same questions, getting the same answers. Finally, she rubbed her eyes and plopped her weary body back into her chair.

She hadn't slept well last night. Too much on her mind. Jake had told Todd and Brian about the threatening note found on her windshield. The boys had laughed it off and agreed with Jake—it was just a stupid prank that didn't mean anything. The pair had almost convinced her. Almost. But not quite.

Even at work this morning, she couldn't shake the

uneasy feeling that gnawed at her. If someone was vicious enough to threaten her and her family, it couldn't be taken lightly.

Jake had warned her to be careful. She'd reminded him she was careful. He knew that. Safety was the option she always chose. She never took risks. Didn't jog in out-of-the-way places, and never ran after dark unless she went to Cowen Park. She didn't open her door to anyone until she looked through the peephole. What more could she do to be on guard?

She shook off her doldrums and riveted her attention on the paperwork that dominated her desk. Even with the polio and tetanus cases consuming so much of her time, business at the health department continued. Other communicable disease cases drifted in and demanded attention.

Starting at the top of her pile, she pulled out two food-borne illness reports. Salmonella and campylobacter. Joan had finished them with a follow-up investigation yesterday, so they were ready to file in the "closed" drawer. A case of giardia was still pending; lab results hadn't been conclusive, and another specimen was obtained and sent to the state lab in Jefferson City. That case couldn't be closed yet.

Betty was working on a couple STI cases that needed a follow-up. Lacey laid them to one side and jotted a reminder on a Post-it note to check them later.

Thumbing deeper into the pile, she found Betty's completed follow-up report on the E.coli case that was reported two days ago. The origin had been traced to a bucket-calf on a dairy farm. Betty's notation indicated she'd spent a great deal of time educating the family on the importance of handwashing to prevent further spread of the disease.

Lacey silently praised her nurses. Even with the

polio outbreak, they were right on the mark.

She arranged the enteric disease case reports in order of priority and drained her cup. Satisfied that she and her nurses were still on top of everything in the community, she looked at her watch. A little after eight.

She pressed the intercom button and announced overhead, "Will the nurses and EPIs please report to the break room for a brief meeting?"

Lacey had nothing new to report on the polio and tetanus cases. But looking at the data as a group might stimulate some insight. She was all for brainstorming.

Joe and Linda were filling mugs with freshly brewed coffee as she stepped into the break room. Her nurses slipped in and headed to the cabinet for cups.

"This won't take long," Lacey said. "I know everyone is busy."

She passed out copies of the disease case reports. She'd been over the files more times than she could remember. But she summarized them to the staff yet again, keeping it short and to the point. No speculations. Everyone listened in silence, nodding from time to time as they shuffled through the data.

"I keep thinking if we look long enough, something will jump out at us," Lacey said as she tucked the reports into a folder. "So far it hasn't. Not for me anyway."

"I even look at them in my sleep," Joe said.

By the looks of the dark circles under his eyes, he hadn't been getting much of that lately.

"It's frustrating." Lacey tapped her pen on the table.

"No new cases reported today," Joan said. "Maybe that's a good sign."

"The day isn't over yet," Betty said.

"Don't be such a downer." Ann took a bite from a

caramel sweet roll and dabbed at her mouth.

Lacey's gut growled, begging for a taste of the gooey pastry. She hadn't had anything sweet in two days and she was overdue for a sugar fix.

She aimed a look at Joe. He'd be the first to hear if the CDC came up with something. "Any news on the autopsies?" she asked.

Joe shook his head. "I talked to the disease prevention department at the CDC last night. There could be a preliminary report by Friday."

"What's the hold up?" Betty looked at Joe with narrow eyes.

"It just takes time."

"What about the labs on the polios?" Lacey asked.

Joe shifted positions. "The CDC lab has ruled out any immunosuppressive diseases. The kids' immune systems are fine."

"So, it's back to square one," Linda said.

"I'm afraid so." Joe walked to the counter and poured coffee for himself before carrying the pot to the table.

"I guess that's it for today," Lacey said as Joe topped off her mug. "I'll let you guys get back to work."

Linda placed a palm over the top of her mug when Joe held the pot toward her.

"Are you feeling okay?" Lacey asked. Linda had been quiet throughout the meeting.

Linda shrugged. "Just a little tired. I was up until two this morning doing some research on the CDC site. It would've been worth it if I could have found something that would give us some answers. But I didn't."

Joe put the carafe back on its stand. "We'll find something—"

"You think?" Linda snapped. "We've been at this

almost a week and haven't turned up one single bit of information that would explain why these kids are sick."

Joe headed to the door and paused. He caught his lower lip between his teeth and gave Lacey a disgruntled look then shook his head.

Lacey could identify with them both. Joe and Linda had been stretched to their limit and had to be frustrated with this entire ordeal. She felt a knot tighten in her chest.

What would happen if no one ever came up with an answer?

CHAPTER NINETEEN

Lacey absently scooped coffee grounds into the paper filter. Her thoughts centered on Jake. Although he did seem more like himself lately, his antichurch stand remained steadfast. She wondered what could have changed him so much. She wished he would talk to Pastor David but had veered away from that subject, not wanting to push. She'd let him work out whatever was troubling him in his own way. When he was ready to confide in her, she would be there for him.

He knows that, doesn't he?

Lacey shrugged off her misgivings. She put the container of Folgers back in the cabinet then filled the glass pot with tap water.

"Coffee ready yet?"

Lacey glanced over her shoulder as Ann stepped into the break room.

"It will be in a minute." Lacey poured the water into the top of the Bunn, put the empty pot in the machine, and closed the top flap. She opened the cabinet above the coffeemaker and pulled out two mugs.

"How's Todd's foot?" Ann opened the cupboard next to the sink and set the Coffee Mate and box of pink sweetener on the counter.

"Better. He went to school today. Thank goodness."

"Getting a little stir crazy on you, huh?"

"More than a little." Lacey rolled her eyes. "I think I was getting on his nerves as bad as he was mine. He hates it when I fuss over him."

"He's lucky he's got a mom that cares so much."

"Yeah? Well, try telling him that."

"I will." Ann laughed. "The very next time I see him."

"How come you're so early this morning?" Ann was never late for work, but she was never this early, either. Usually, she walked in the back door at five 'til eight.

"My coffeepot went out this morning." Ann frowned and shook her head. "And I just got the freakin' thing a couple months ago."

"So, you're not really that dedicated! You're just after a caffeine fix, right?"

"Yeah. I knew you'd be here making the brew and I didn't want to mess with stopping at Casey's."

"See how you are?" Lacey poured coffee in two mugs and handed one to Ann. "Here's your fix."

"Thanks." Ann chuckled. She took a gulp and held up her cup. "It's terrible to be this dependent on something."

Lacey added fake cream and sweetener to her brew and grinned. "You know I really enjoy working with you and the other nurses. I couldn't do half of what I do without you guys. Especially you, Ann."

Ann shrugged and her face reddened. "I enjoy working with you, too. You're not just a friend, you're a great boss."

Lacey hadn't meant to embarrass her coworker; she just wanted her to know how valuable she was. Lacey appreciated all her nurses, but Ann was the one she leaned on. Ann could take care of things even in

Lacey's absence. She was a decision-maker and could function independently. She didn't have to be told every step to take during a situation and that was critical. Especially in a crisis like the one they were going through.

"I just want you to know I appreciate all you do around here," Lacey said. She squeezed Ann's arm. "I know I can depend on you."

"Thanks." Ann glanced at Lacey's hand then met her gaze. "I'm glad you feel you can count on me."

"And you're more to me than an employee. I hope you know that. You're like family. Always have been." She released her grip. "Now let's get to work."

Ann arched an eyebrow and tossed her a fleeting look that made Lacey wonder if she'd been too maudlin. She didn't make a habit of getting gushy with compliments, but with all that had been going on lately, she couldn't depend on a predictable future. If you had something to say, better to say it right away than later regret having held back.

The two nurses made their way down the hall and the escalating sound level signaled to Lacey the front doors had been opened. It was time to get the press release ready. Chagrin crept up her spine as she considered how little she could report. The community craved good news for a change and all she had was no news. Wishing she had something positive to tell the media, she plodded into her office and dropped into her chair. Her phone beeped just as she flipped on her computer. She answered before it beeped again.

"It's me," the infection prevention nurse said.

Oh God, not another case of polio. Or worse, a fatal tetanus.

"Susan? What's going on?"

"The first little girl with polio. Holly. She died an

hour ago. Columbia just notified us."

Lacey sucked in a lung full of air and clutched her throat. "Oh, Susan, this can't be happening."

"I know. I can't believe it, either. Two of the other polio cases are out of danger now but..."

"But what?"

"They're showing signs of permanent paralysis." Susan's voice cracked and she blew her nose. "Lacey, those two kids are going to be physically disabled for the rest of their lives."

Lacey felt like she'd been run over by a semi. Her gut churned, and for a moment she thought she was going to be sick. She swallowed, choking back waves of nausea.

It looked like there would be news in the press release after all.

After Lacey ended the call, she gathered the team together to relay the dismal news. Her nurses cried openly. Everyone was speechless. They'd all worked so hard to prevent this kind of situation.

Broken spirits. Sad faces. Heavy hearts. No doubt they were feeling the same thing as her. Failure.

"We can't give up." Lacey cleared her throat, but a lump the size of a golf ball refused to budge.

Betty wiped a hand across her eyes. "What more can we do? Kids are dead. Kids are physically disabled. Everyone is looking to us for answers and we don't have any."

"Lacey is right," Joe said. He stepped beside Lacey and laid a large, supportive hand on her shoulder. "It's not hopeless."

~ ~ ~ ~ ~

Later that afternoon, Lacey called Jake to tell him she'd be working overtime.

"I figured," Jake said. "I heard the bad news on KTEL at noon. I'm so sorry. Are you okay?"

"Hanging in there." Lacey gave a long low sigh and tried to maintain her composure. "I shouldn't be too late. I have a conference call at four and then I need to finish a report."

"You're not going to be there by yourself, are you?"

"No. Joe and Linda will be here until I leave."

"Okay. I'll see you later, babe. Love you."

"Ditto."

Lacey pulled the aspirin bottle out of a drawer and swallowed two pills with cold coffee then headed to the board room to join the two EPIs. Joe linked Darrell Parker and the CDC onto the line then hit the speaker button. The conference call lasted forty-five minutes, and Lacey's head continued to throb as she returned to her office. Neither the CDC nor the State had any more answers than she did. And that equaled zero.

She finished her report quickly without the usual interruptions she dealt with during working hours. She shut down her computer and looked up when Joe tapped on her doorframe.

"Are you about finished?" He walked across the threshold, holding his briefcase. Linda followed, looking worse than she had this morning.

"I just finished. You guys are welcome to stay at my house tonight. I'm sure you're not looking forward to the long drive." Lacey scooted back from her desk.

"Thanks for the offer," Joe said. "But I've got to get home."

"And I can't wear these same clothes tomorrow." Linda looked at her wrinkled pantsuit. "Don't worry. We'll be fine."

Lacey walked with the EPI specialists to the parking lot where they said their goodbyes. She waved at the pair as she turned left and they made a right.

Less than five minutes later, she pulled into her garage and blew out a relieved breath. Good to be home. She understood why Joe wanted to head home, even if it was just for a few hours. There was definitely no place like your own surroundings when things looked dismal.

It was going on six o'clock when Lacey stepped into the kitchen. Jake greeted her at the door with a smile and a kiss on the cheek. A wonderful aroma tantalized her senses and made her mouth water. She gave Jake a puzzled look.

"I started dinner," he said. "It's almost ready. I figured you could use a break."

"Thanks. You don't know how good that sounds. Where are the boys?"

"Youth group meeting tonight. Remember?"

"I guess I forgot."

"Bad day, huh?"

"Yes." She set her purse on the counter.

"Want to talk about it?"

"We've got nine cases of polio now. One of them died, two are physically disabled."

Her voice broke and tears welled up in her eyes. She wiped at them with the back of her hand. Jake stepped closer and put both of his arms around her.

"I'm so sorry, Lace. I know how hard you've been working."

She leaned her head on his shoulder and gave in to the tears, letting out all the pent-up frustration. She cried for the children. She cried for their parents. And she cried because she knew more children and parents would suffer unless she could find an answer.

Jake held her and gently rubbed her back until no more tears would come. When she pulled back, he handed her a tissue.

"You okay?"

She nodded and tried to regain her equilibrium. She knew he was worried; her tearful outburst had been uncharacteristic. "Really, Jake. I'm going to be okay."

He guided her to the snack bar where he had framed two plates with napkins and forks. While she spritzed hand sanitizer on her palms, he dished up a large bowl of barbeque beef and set it on the counter.

"How was Todd's foot after being on it all day at school?" She kicked off her Danskos and wiggled her toes, trying to work out the ache in her arches.

"Looked great. He said it's feeling a lot better, too." Jake pulled a huge potato from the oven, sliced it down the middle, and placed half on each plate. He completed the arrangement with salad and ranch dressing. "All set. Hope you're hungry."

"When have you ever seen me not hungry?"

"Exactly, never." He hopped on the stool beside her, gave her a sideways glance, and laughed. "No matter how upset you are, the only time I've ever seen you refuse food is when you're hurling. And then it's only because you know you couldn't hold anything down."

"People with food addictions are like that." She pretended to be joking but was only half kidding. She must have an addiction. Why else would she eat the way she did?

After dinner, Jake shooed her out of the kitchen and insisted on cleaning up alone. "Call your mother and see how she's doing with Bandit."

She smiled. Her mom had already named the puppy. She punched in the number as she collapsed on the couch in the family room.

She laughed as her mom described the puppy's antics. Bandit wasn't any closer to being housebroken, but Mom wouldn't give up until she'd conquered the pup's stubbornness. That puppy would find out who was boss. Until then, he'd just have to stay in the yard while she was at work. She would have him trained for inside before bad weather set in.

Jake walked over as she ended the call. He took her hand and said, "Come with me."

She twined her fingers through his. He led her to the master bathroom where the tub had been filled with water and topped off with bubbles. She gave him a slow grin. The scent of lavender wafted over her, and a candle glowed beside the sink. A CD player had been set up with soft classical music.

"Enjoy." Jake left her to the spa-like surroundings.

She peeled off her clothes and sank into the welcoming warmth. The water was soothing. Warm but not too hot. The bubbles tickled her nose as she eased her head back on a tub pillow.

How could she have thought Jake didn't care about her anymore? She chided herself for entertaining such a foolish notion as she sank deeper into the velvet oasis. This was wonderful. Just what she needed. Her mind drifted over the day's events, growing jumbled and fuzzy.

Sometime later, she jerked to attention. She must have dozed off because the water was cool against her skin. She pulled herself up and slipped into her white terrycloth bathrobe. She blew out the candle and clicked off the CD player. Wrapping a towel around her wet head, she stepped through the doorway. Jake, propped up in the king-sized bed, was watching the ten o'clock news.

He gave her a wide smile. "I wondered how long you were going to soak."

"I think I went sound asleep."

"Good for you. You need the rest."

"Are the boys home?"

Jake nodded. "Safe and sound in their rooms."

"I can't believe I didn't hear them come in."

"I told them to keep it down and let you enjoy your bath time."

"What did you do tonight?" She dried her hair and tossed the towel over the back of a chair.

"Looked over a report for tomorrow. Then watched a little TV."

Lacey slipped out of the bathrobe and wiggled her arms into a silky Cardinals jersey and slid into bed. The sheets were cool and inviting as she nestled into the cocoon of Jake's arms.

"I feel like I could sleep for a week." She traced her finger down Jake's cheek and inhaled the familiar scent of lime and Dial soap. "Thank you for the night off. Fixing dinner, doing the dishes, and the bath. I love you, honey. You're the most important thing in my life."

"I love you, too, Lacey."

She felt her hand slide down Jake's face as the fingers of sleep pulled her under.

CHAPTER TWENTY

The first thing Jake noticed when he walked into the CPA firm Friday morning was Kimberly. She stood by the water fountain talking with the boss. Brad, wearing a cream-colored button-down shirt with a bright blue and burgundy tie, had a smile plastered across his face. His head bounced like a jack-in-the-box and his mouth spewed words Jake couldn't hear. Apparently, his story was funny because when his mouth stopped flapping, Kimberly threw her head back and laughed.

A twinge of jealousy shot through him. Heat grew at the base of his neck then moved up until his face was on fire. Maybe Brad's little talk had been meant to get Jake to back off so he could move in on the soon-to-be accountant himself. He knew what to do after all. He'd done it before.

Good grief, get it together. What's wrong with me?

Jake had to pass the pair to reach his office. He straightened his tie and headed down the hall, nodded, and mumbled good morning. The scent of aftershave and cologne blended together and wafted over him as he breezed by.

He shuffled out of his jacket and hung it on the

coat-tree in the corner. From his desk, he could hear Brad and Kimberly's muted voices. Stray words occasionally filtered in and Kimberly's tone, punctuated with sexy laughter, told him the conversation wasn't strictly business.

Jake was rattled. Why did another woman have such a strong effect on him? Chiding himself for his ambivalence, he told himself he didn't care. This whole mess was his fault. He'd been so sure he could control the situation. Had convinced himself he wasn't doing anything wrong. He should never have toyed with the sexy Ms. Ames. He'd led her on, encouraged her advances from day one. He'd fed on the attraction, enjoying the high he felt around her. *Now he couldn't even do his work without wondering where she was or what she was doing.*

The phone interrupted his thoughts. He snatched it up, glad to have a distraction.

"Hey, Jacob. It's Warren Boston."

"Yes, Warren, thanks for returning my call." Jake scanned the J&B Construction file. "I need last quarter's financial statement."

"I thought I sent it to you."

"Nope. Don't have it."

"I'll shoot it to you in an email, then. Did I tell you about the real estate deal I'm looking at?"

"Uh, no."

Jake had to catch up with the abrupt change of subject. And he didn't really want to hear about any deal Mr. Boston had in the works. Warren chattered on about some property south of town he planned to purchase so he could build another mall. Jake zoned out while Warren explained everything in detail.

When the call finally ended, the hall was quiet. Jake walked to the window and gazed out. Maple and oak trees dotted the street and orange, brown, and rust leaves caught the light. As they swayed, they sparkled like a kaleidoscope.

The sun filtering through the window was warm on Jake's face. He leaned his forehead against the pane, confused. Not about Lacey. He loved her, no doubt about that. What confused him were his strong feelings for Kimberly. Until a few weeks ago, Lacey had been the only female on his mind. He hated that he'd allowed himself to become so consumed with that young woman.

A blue jay perched on the windowsill. Its head bobbed as it pecked at something Jake couldn't quite make out. Growing tired of its labor, the bird flew away. Like Jake wanted to do.

If he didn't have to see Kimberly every day, he'd be okay. He could shake her out of his system, quit fantasizing about her. Being around her was a bad thing for him, stirred up too many unwanted feelings. How could he concentrate on his marriage with his mind consumed with constant thoughts of Kimberly?

His heart lurched at the thought of his unsuspecting wife and how he'd shut her out lately. All because he wanted to feel young again. He vowed to change. He was not going to hurt her.

"Thought you might need this." Kimberly's voiced startled him.

She set a cup of coffee beside his computer.

"Thanks. But you shouldn't have bothered."

"No bother. I like taking care of you."

Yeah, right. Jake bit back his usual flirty response and lowered himself into his chair. *No better time to cut this off—whatever this was—than now.*

However, that all too familiar ill-at-ease feeling which always materialized when he was around her consumed him. Her perfume, smelling like fresh-picked apricots, made him dizzy.

He shook his head to clear it and cradled the warm mug in his hands. Kimberly just stood there with her head slightly cocked. Confusion clouded her eyes.

"Thanks again, Kimberly. I better get back to work." He picked up a report and faked reading it. He wanted her to go. He wanted her to stay.

"What is this, a brush off?" Kimberly frowned and plopped a hand on her hip. "I'm crushed."

"I'm really busy this morning."

"Yeah, I could see how busy you were when I came in." She met his gaze. "What's going on, Jake? Talk to me."

Jake released a heavy sigh. "I've been thinking, Kimberly, and well, I think we need to keep things a little more professional between us. I've been way out of line with you and I apologize. I won't let it happen again."

"Nice speech but I'm not buying it. Not for one minute. Now out with it. What's wrong?"

"You know, I'm married—"

"So? A piece of paper doesn't make you happy."

"But that's the thing, don't you see? I *am* a happily married man and it's time I started acting like one."

"Shame on you." She tsked and shot him a toothy grin. "If you were that happy, you wouldn't have to act."

"Come on. You know what I'm saying."

Kimberly fanned her face with a dainty hand and segued into her ersatz Southern drawl. "My, my, sir. I think the furnace has been kicked up a notch and you can't take the heat."

"Whatever."

He resisted the urge to laugh. She was so smooth, and he did like her. He just couldn't like her in that way. He owed it to Lacey to cut it out before something happened that he couldn't take back.

She headed to the door then turned.

"You're cute when you play hard to get," she said then traipsed across the threshold.

Jake felt good that he'd set things straight. That was a start. So why didn't he feel any less attracted to her? He could still remember how soft she'd felt against his body.

He curbed his mental gymnastics and rebuked his all-too-vivid imagination. He couldn't have an affair of the mind with her and ever get her out of his system. He turned to his computer and tried to concentrate. Usually, he could switch into business mode at will. *Not today. Today, my mind is crowded with other thoughts.*

Maybe he did need to talk to Pastor David.

CHAPTER TWENTY-ONE

At the back door of the health department, Lacey jiggled the key in the lock. Suddenly she felt strung out. It had been a long week. She was losing her grip on her purse along with a bag of glazed doughnuts from Winston's bakery. The aroma of fresh pastry wafted from the top and teased her stomach as she twisted the key harder.

The lock finally opened with an irritating grind. She pushed through the door and flipped on the light, looking forward to the coming weekend. Two days away from the office would be sovereign. Not that she'd escape thinking about polio and tetanus the entire time, but she'd have a glorious forty-eight-hour reprieve from the hassle and clamor of a crazy workplace. At least that's what she hoped for.

The polio and tetanus cases had made the national news and though Robert handled the media, the effects spilled over to the entire staff. Every day, the parking lot and waiting room were filled with agitated citizens seeking answers. Most days felt like a circus.

Stopping in her office, she shrugged out of her jacket and set her purse on the desk. She trekked to the break room where she made a pot of coffee and gobbled down one of the goodies while she waited on the Bunn. With a steaming cup in hand, she fished out another doughnut and detoured through the clerical area to the fax machine.

Her chest tightened as she looked at the dozen sheets of paper. *Oh great.* After securing the doughnut between her teeth, she snatched the papers from the tray and hurried into her office. Dread squeezed her stomach as she sorted through the faxes. The all-too-familiar communicable disease forms stared her in the face.

One, two, three, four, five new probable polio cases. Same age group.

She stared at the case reports. This was unbelievable; the rate was picking up speed.

Well, why not? We have found absolutely nothing to explain this, much less stop it.

She booted up her computer then entered the basics on each report. This would let the state know she was aware of the new cases and was actively working on them. Lacey looked up when Ann paused in her doorway.

"Good morning." She pointed at Lacey's half-eaten doughnut. "Hope there's more."

"There is. In the break room, help yourself. You're gonna need fortifying."

"What's wrong?" Ann slipped off her sweater and folded it over her arm.

"Five more polio cases."

"No way!"

"Not confirmed yet. But they will be. Symptoms are textbook, just like all the others."

"From Hoover?"

"Yep. All six-year-olds. Two girls and three boys."

"Oh wow." Ann took the investigation forms and scanned the reports. Her head tilted so that her dark-blonde hair fell into her face. She looked chipper with a ribbed white pullover under her Scooby Doo scrubs top, baggy scrubs pants, and tan Dansko box leather nursing clogs with an open heel. "I'll get right on these."

"Have the clerks pull the immunization cards for me," Lacey said. "I need to make sure these kids were up to date."

"They were. You know it as well as I do."

Lacey nodded. She knew. All too well.

As Ann headed to her cubicle, Lacey called, "Don't forget the doughnuts!"

"Are you kidding? I'm on my way!" Ann laid the reports in her small cubicle, draped her sweater over the back of her chair, and disappeared down the hall.

Twenty minutes later, one of the clerks handed Lacey the immunization cards. It didn't take long to find the information she was after. All five children were up to date and had received their shots at the health department.

Lacey made copies of the shot cards then hustled across the building. Joe shut his cell phone and pointed it at Lacey as she stepped into the conference room.

"Just hung up with the CDC," he said.

"Any news?"

"The preliminary report on the autopsy of the first tetanus case is complete. And to make a long story short, the autopsy didn't reveal anything unusual."

"Nothing?" Lacey's spirits soared downward if that was possible.

"Nothing out of the ordinary. Nothing that would explain why the child would have contracted tetanus."

"No immune deficiencies?"

"None. Nada. Zip."

Lacey shook her head. "I just got five more polio

cases." She set the copies of the shot records on the table.

Joe studied the records. He leaned back, and she could read the bewilderment in his face. He shook his head.

"Not only did they get an IPV booster before they started kindergarten," Lacey said, "they had another booster right here last Friday."

Linda's eyes narrowed. "The polio antibodies should have kicked in."

"They should have been more than covered." Joe raised an eyebrow and gave her an intent look. "I just don't get it."

"Something's wrong with the vaccine." Lacey tucked her hair behind her ear. "That has to be it. For some reason, it isn't working. It's not protecting our kids."

"I don't see how that's possible," Linda said. "We aren't dealing with one lot number. A bad batch is one thing, but how can you think there would be several bad batches?"

Joe nodded in agreement.

"Well, something's going on." Lacey shifted positions. "And I still say it's the vaccine."

"I don't know." Joe rubbed his chin, taking care to miss the scabbed-over nick at the center. "But I think it's time we trace the vaccine, find out exactly where and when it's been used."

Lacey nodded.

"We'll need the lot numbers."

"No problem. The lot numbers are documented on the shot records."

"Start with the first dose each child received. You'll have to go back six years."

"I can do that," Lacey said.

"How many different lot numbers are we talking

about?"

"Several, I'm sure. Forty to fifty, I'd say."

"And the manufacturers?"

"Two. Sanofi and GSK."

"If you'll get that information to me, Linda and I can start tracing the vaccines. I want to go over everything with a fine-toothed comb." He raked his fingers through his hair. "Who knows? Maybe we missed something the first time."

Lacey felt the tiniest spark of hope fire through her, and she willed it to ignite. If they could confirm her faulty vaccine theory, then they would be well on their way to turning this around. And even though Joe didn't share her hunch, her gut told her it had to be the vaccines.

"I want to find out where each vial of the identified vaccine went," Joe said, "who received a dose, and the status of the persons who received it. I know this will entail some extensive crosschecking and take a great deal of time, but we plan to work through the weekend."

"The weekend?" Lacey was surprised.

"Yeah. We've got to get a handle on this. It's gone on way too long."

"The drug companies will be able to help," Linda said. "They can trace where each shipment went, who got them, and when."

Joe nodded. "After we get that information, we'll call the facilities that used those particular lot numbers and do some checking."

"The hospitals, clinics, and urgent cares can follow up with clients who received a dose, find out if they've had any type of illness." Linda looked less frazzled this morning. She wouldn't after this was over.

"What can I do to help?" Lacey asked. "I can work through the weekend if you need me."

Joe shook his head. "No need. All we'll do is track lot numbers and make phone calls. If we have any questions, we'll call you."

"Joe's right," Linda said. "By Monday morning, we should have a list of every health care facility that used the vaccines. That's when we'll need your help. You guys can contact the offices that are closed on weekends. Get specific information, times and dates the vaccines were used, and the status of the clients who received them."

"I still don't think there's a problem with the vaccines." Joe picked up the shot records.

"That's how we differ," Lacey said. She was convinced it was compromised vaccine. There was absolutely no other feasible explanation.

"If there was a problem, we'd be seeing cases of polio in other counties by now, don't you think?"

Lacey shrugged.

"But we've got to check it out," Joe said.

"I'll start calling the drug companies." Linda slid her reading glasses over her pretty blue-gray eyes. "We already have some lot numbers to work with. Might as well get the drug companies alerted, get them going on this."

"My nurses are working on the new cases," Lacey said. "They should have something for you before long. And I'll get the rest of the lot numbers."

Lacey felt excited as she headed to the administrator's office. She wanted to speak with Robert before she got down to business.

As she updated him, he nodded from time to time in his composed way, letting her know he was absorbing everything she said.

Robert opened his top drawer and pulled out a key ring. "Give this to Joe and Linda so they can come and go as they need to this weekend."

Lacey slipped the key into her pocket. "Thanks."

"Sounds like a busy weekend for the EPIs." He leaned back and laced his hands together in his lap. "I appreciate all their hard work."

"I don't seem to be getting very far—"

Robert threw up an arm like a crosswalk attendant and she fell silent.

"Lacey, two years ago when I put you in as Director of Nursing, I did it because I knew you were a leader. Not only were you more qualified than other applicants, you were the smartest and brightest. You've proved yourself a hundred times over and I've never regretted my decision. You're doing great with these investigations, so I don't want to hear any more about you not getting very far."

Lacey's face grew warm. "Thanks."

Robert waved a large hand in the air and the wide gold band of his Timex slid back toward his elbow. "I know I give you a hard time sometimes. Well, a lot of the time. But I have every confidence in you. Now get out there and do your job."

Lacey left Robert's office and gathered the immunization cards. She jotted down the lot numbers of the vaccines given to each of the polio cases, as well as the two tetanus cases, and sent the information to Joe. She worked through lunch, grabbed a bite from the refrigerator in the break room, and consumed more fats and carbs than she intended.

By late afternoon, the investigations on the five new polio cases were done. Every case linked directly to Holly. Lacey's thoughts lingered on Holly's parents. She wondered if they'd ever be able to accept losing their daughter to a disease when she'd been given adequate prophylactic vaccines to ensure immunity. They'd done what they were supposed to. Made sure she had every immunization. But all their preventative care hadn't been enough to save their daughter. Why? Everything pointed to the vaccine. But how could so many different lot numbers be compromised? One bad batch of vaccine wasn't unreasonable. But forty-eight different batches were hard to fathom. Still, no matter how farfetched it seemed, she couldn't shake her gut feeling it indeed was a vaccine issue.

Lacey strode to the small lab where the vaccines were stored. She looked at the log sheet taped to the side of the refrigerator. Twice a day, the temperatures were recorded and initialed by the nurse who conducted the check. All were within the normal range. She opened the refrigerator door and pulled out the thermometer. Thirty-six degrees Celsius, right on the mark. She put the thermometer back and shut the door.

Lacey pulled the historic temperature log from the cabinet and flipped to the section where the temp of the incoming vaccine was documented. Everything good there, too.

She released a heavy sigh. It had to be something with the vaccines. But if the vaccines proved to be stable, then what?

Lacey's mind whirled, shooting out alternate possibilities, but nothing would hold up. That spark of hope she'd incubated earlier fizzled a little more with each passing minute.

"Looking for something?" Betty asked and Lacey jumped.

"No. I'm going over the temp logs."

"Why?" Betty walked to the refrigerator then ran her hand over the counter.

"Double-checking everything."

"I've already done that. More than once."

"Just making sure we didn't miss something."

Betty narrowed her eyes. "What, don't you trust

me?" She turned and walked out of the room.

Oh, good grief, Lacey thought. *Why is Betty so touchy?* Her mood plummeted. She left the lab feeling forlorn. Why couldn't she figure this out?

She walked across the building to the conference room and found Joe and Linda between calls.

"I'll be leaving in a few minutes," she said. "Please don't hesitate to call if you need anything. I'll have my cell with me this weekend whenever I'm not home."

"We should be fine, but we'll call if we need you," Joe said.

"Here's a key to the back door." Lacey handed it to Joe. "Feel free to come and go as you please."

"Thanks." He slipped it on his key ring and gave her a smile. "Try to enjoy your weekend. Maybe, just maybe, we'll have good news by Monday."

Lacey felt guilty leaving them, but they were right. There was nothing she could do until the tracking was done. As she exited the building, she offered up a silent

CHAPTER TWENTY-TWO

While Lacey worked around the house Saturday afternoon, she was happy Jake was finally getting around to painting the storage shed he'd bought several weekends ago at a yard sale. She knew his goal was to move all his tools to the shed, giving him the much-needed room in the garage for his two ladders that presently leaned against the outside of the house, taking the blunt of the weather.

Lacey stowed the vacuum cleaner in the hall closet and made her way to the kitchen, poured iced tea into a tall glass, squeezed in a generous amount of lemon, added two packs of pink sweetener, and plopped in ice cubes. She plodded into the family room and collapsed on the couch, restless. Couldn't get the polio and tetanus cases off her mind. Tried to figure where she had gone wrong. What she overlooked or, worse yet, completely missed.

Later, after Jake had come in from the backyard and showered, Lacey asked if he was up for dinner and a movie in Springfield. Both boys had plans with friends. Lacey felt antsy and wanted to get out for a while. Maybe it would help her focus on something other than her failure.

"Yeah?" Jake answered. He pulled his brows together. "Sure you're up to going to Springfield? Aren't you on call?"

"Uh-huh. I always need to be available, but an hour away is okay."

"Let's head to Springfield, then. It'll be good to catch a flick. What do you want to see?"

Lacey shrugged. "Whatever. I'll let you pick the movie if you let me pick the restaurant."

Jake shot her a grin. "Porter House, right?"

Lacey nodded. Porter House had the best prime rib she'd ever tasted, and her mouth had been watering for a big plate of excellent beef. She kissed the tip of his nose. "Is that okay with you?"

"Sounds great."

Lacey dashed up the stairs and changed into gray slacks and a pink and black button-down top with wide cuffs rolled back on the sleeves. Using the curling iron, she had her hair fixed in five minutes. After dabbing blush on her cheeks and going over her lips with light-pink gloss, she slipped into two-inch black heels and headed downstairs.

Jake whistled and winked his approval. She gave him a smile as she made sure her cell phone was tucked in her purse then walked with Jake to the car.

As they headed to the I-44 exit ramp, she wondered how things were going with the lot numbers and how long Joe and Linda planned to work. She said another silent prayer that they'd find something, anything, to help end this investigation. *Make this town a safe place for our kids once again.* She had confidence in the two specialists. If there was anything to find, they'd flesh it out.

"You're pretty quiet tonight," Jake said.

Lacey glanced out the window and noticed they were already halfway to Springfield. "Sorry. I guess my mind has been a million miles away."

"Thinking about work?"

She sighed. "Uh-huh."

Jake squeezed her hand. "It's a bad time for you, Lace. But don't blame yourself for everything that's happening."

"Who else am I gonna blame?"

"You don't have any control over this situation."

Lacey closed her eyes. Maybe he was right. She couldn't fix the whole world. *But right now, I'd settle for just one small county.*

Jake released his grip. "Are you hungry?"

"You have to ask?"

He laughed, and the deep, masculine sound rumbling in his chest made her go mushy. He knew her so well. What would she do without his constancy in her life? She leaned back against the padded headrest and watched the lights flickering past in the eastbound lane.

I-44 was busy, normal for a weekend. The closer they got to Springfield, the more congested the traffic became. Jake veered right onto the 65-bypass exit. After five miles, he made another right on Sunshine. The parking lot at Porter House was already full and they had to hunt for a space.

When they entered the restaurant, the hostess told them they'd have a forty-five-minute wait, which was fine with Lacey. The movie didn't start until nine. They sat at the bar and sipped sparkling water and cracked peanuts from their shells.

"Hey, you two!" Joan and her husband Sam stood behind them.

"Hi." Lacey was surprised to see a familiar face. Joan was her usual less-than-casual self in a navy Mizzou Tigers sweatshirt and faded mom jeans, but her expression looked uncharacteristically grim.

"Mind if we sit with you while we wait?" Joan asked.

"Not at all."

Joan scooted in beside Lacey, and Sam pulled out a stool beside Jake.

"I thought you were expecting company," Lacey said.

"Yeah. My brother Art and his wife Sara got in from Illinois late last night." Joan smiled but it didn't quite reach her eyes. "They went to Waynesville this afternoon to spend the night with his old college buddy. They'll be back in the morning."

"With their three grandkids." Sam sighed wearily and palmed a handful of peanuts.

"We had no idea the kids were coming with them," Joan said. "They never breathed a word."

Sam tossed a peanut into his mouth. "It's been interesting, to say the least."

"How old are the kids?" Lacey got the distinct feeling that Joan and Sam were ready for the weekend to be over.

"Four, five, and six." Joan arched a brow. "And they are pretty lively."

"That's an understatement!" Sam rolled his eyes. "It's like a circus."

Joan shot him a look, so he turned and asked Jake if he'd caught the game the previous night. Lacey remembered how Todd and Brian had been at that age. Never a dull moment. She missed those times. They were getting older, and things were different around their house. Not necessarily calmer but definitely quieter. Well, most of the time.

"When they left, we decided to take a breather and ended up here." Joan glanced around. "I should've figured we'd have a wait, being Saturday night and all."

"It's worth it though." Lacey reached for a peanut. "I love this place."

"Yeah, me, too," Joan said.

Joan was the backbone of the health department. She offered many years of wisdom and experience. So easy to work with and never one to complain. Lacey valued her, not only as a nurse but also a team player. She dreaded the day Joan would announce she was going to retire. Lacey hoped that would not be for many years to come.

A few minutes later, a table was ready. Lacey and Jake said good night to their friends and slipped off the barstools. A young waiter in a white coat threaded between tables packed with patrons who buzzed with laughter and conversation. The young man stopped at a table for two and held the chair for Lacey. He handed them large black menus with *Porter House* embossed in gold on the front then rattled off the specials. Lacey nodded as he talked, but she already had the taste of prime rib on her palate. She wasn't about to be talked into something different.

Jake ordered potato skins and fried cheese sticks for appetizers then looked at Lacey. "Anything else?"

"Not for me."

The waiter left to get their drinks. Jake opened his menu, but Lacey didn't. He shot her a look and shook his head.

"Hey, don't diss me," she said. "I know what I want. And I'm having the strawberry cheesecake for dessert."

By the time Lacey finished the entrée, she was stuffed. She asked for a go-box for the cheesecake. Jake confessed he was plenty full himself. He had polished off an entire order of barbeque ribs and as they headed to the front of the restaurant, he laughed about the bones he had mounded on his plate.

Once they were outside, Jake stopped short and groaned.

"What?" Lacey asked.

He pointed at the car. "A flat tire."

Jake was particular to a tee about both their cars. He always made sure the tires were in good condition. When any sign of wear showed up, he took care of it. He kept both cars in tip-top shape.

"Just what I need." He handed his jacket to Lacey and rolled up his sleeves as he headed to the car. "Must have picked up a nail."

Even Jake couldn't prevent that from happening.

CHAPTER TWENTY-THREE

The next morning, Jake surprised Lacey by announcing he was going to church. She tamped down the urge to do a flip, settling instead for a quick hug and a kiss to his cheek. Even the boys seemed pleased as they headed out thirty minutes early to practice for the fall festival program the youth group produced each year.

When Todd started driving, Lacey's life was a little less hectic. He saved her dozens of trips a week hauling himself and his brother to their various activities. Still, she wasn't completely comfortable with Todd driving all over creation. She guessed she would never quit worrying about her kids, no matter how old they were. She gave Todd last-minute drive-careful instructions as the boys dashed out the door.

~ ~ ~ ~ ~

Everyone at church was happy to see Jake, and the service was exceptionally uplifting. When he promised Pastor David he'd be seeing a lot more of him at the services, happy little flutters danced through Lacey's stomach and she felt a smile spread across her face.

After church, Lacey rode with Jake to the rear of Walmart. He'd dropped off the flat tire at the automotive department on the way to church. She scooted out of the car and hoisted her purse strap over one shoulder.

"I'm going to grab a gallon of milk," she said and headed toward the grocery section.

"It's only going to take a minute here. I'm just gonna pick up the tire."

"Okay." She gave him a promising smile. "Just the milk and I'm right back."

The store was packed. Lacey grabbed a jug of Hiland from the cooler and had to remind herself not to look at anything else as she headed to the checkout. She paid the clerk and walked back to automotive.

No Jake. She pushed through the door with her plastic sack and smiled at him sitting behind the wheel of his Camaro. His gaze was fixed forward.

"Just the milk. See?" She heaved the sack over the seat into the back.

Jake gave her a fleeting look and clicked on the ignition. He looked pale.

"What's wrong?"

"The flat tire." He finger-raked his hair and met her gaze. "We didn't pick up a nail. The tire was cut, slashed in the whitewall with something very sharp. Lacey, this was deliberate."

"Huh?" *Slashed?* Lacey's mind sputtered with confusion. "How did we make it to Springfield, then?"

"That's the thing. The repair guy said it had to have happened while we were in the restaurant. No way could it have been done any sooner. With such a large puncture, it would have gone flat pretty fast."

A fist of understanding jabbed Lacey's brain and her thinking cleared. "Either we are really unlucky and this was random vandalism, or someone followed us last night."

The grim look on Jake's face told Lacey he had deduced the same thing.

"I think someone followed us," he said.

Icy fingers grabbed Lacey's flesh and sent prickles up her spine.

Jake scratched his face. "Maybe I'm being paranoid, but this can't be a coincidence. Not with everything else that's going on."

"I agree." She pinched the bridge of her nose. Why was someone doing this to them?

"We've got to report it to the police." Jake pulled the gear into reverse and backed out of the parking space. He turned into light traffic and headed toward City Hall.

Ten minutes later, a middle-aged woman at the reception counter ushered them into Detective Prater's cubicle. He motioned them to a couple of maroon bucket chairs. The detective wore a wrinkled white button-down shirt open at the neck over gray dress pants. His eyebrows were thick and bushy with flecks of gray that punctuated kind, blue-gray eyes. Jake gave him a quick rundown of the incident.

"Since this appears to have happened in Springfield's jurisdiction," the detective said, "we'll need to get their police department involved."

He pulled open his drawer and fished out a form. "Start with this. The form I need for Greene County is up front."

As he stepped out of the cubicle, Jake looked over the form. He pulled a pen from a Chiefs mug floating in a clutter of papers.

"This could take some time, Lacey. Why don't you go home? I'll call when I'm done and Todd can come get me."

"Okay." Lacey sighed. "The kids will be wondering what's taking us so long. I'll see you afterwhile."

She tossed her bag over her shoulder and walked away, feeling confused. Angry. Frustrated.

Why is this happening to us? she wondered for the hundredth time as she slid under the wheel and drove home.

~ ~ ~ ~ ~

"Hey! Where's Dad?" Todd met her in the doorway.

Lacey took his arm and walked beside him into the kitchen. Brian sat at the counter drinking tea and working on a biology report due the next day.

"Guys," she said, "there's something we should discuss."

She scooted out a barstool next to Brian and sat. Todd stood, leaning on the counter, eyes wide. She pulled in a breath and told the story, start to finish. When she finished, the boys stared with wide eyes, faces pulled into frowns.

"Why would someone slash your tire, unless..." Brian didn't finish the thought, but Todd picked up the slack.

"You really are being harassed." Todd's eyes grew even wider. "That really stinks."

Lacey agreed. It smelled rotten through and through.

She let the boys vent several minutes before they got back to their studies, and she busied herself by pulling lettuce and vegetables from the refrigerator and tossing together a big bowl of salad. After checking the roast in the Crock-Pot, she whipped up a pan of cornbread and popped it in the oven. She stayed calm on the outside only because she didn't want to alarm her children. Inside, she was screaming and throwing one heck of a fit.

It was forty-five minutes before Jake called for a ride and another fifteen before he and Todd got back home. By that time, Lacey was close to screaming out loud. "Prater said he's not sure this incident was related to the note and phone calls," Jake said as he sat on a barstool, "but I could tell he thought it was. He said whoever's doing this is very familiar with our family activities. The person had to know where our vehicle would be and when."

Lacey shivered. She'd been doing that a lot lately. Where were the warm, toasty feelings she associated with her home? "Let's eat," she said, deflated, and dished up the food.

Lunch was tense and the food went cold. Everyone seemed lost in thought. Even the boys didn't seem to be taking this as lightly as they had the note. Lacey didn't want them to be worried or frightened, but they needed to be aware of the danger looming over the family.

When Jake's phone rang, Lacey jumped.

Jake dug his cell from his pocket.

"Detective Prater? What can I do for you?" He shot Lacey a look and covered the mouthpiece. "He wants to ask you a couple questions."

Lacey took the phone. The muscles in her neck tensed and she rubbed a hand over the knot.

"Lacey, I'm sorry to interrupt your Sunday afternoon," the detective said, "but I've got a quick question for you."

"No problem. I want to get this resolved. Just to be honest, it's scaring me to death."

"I can understand that." The detective's voice was deep yet had a calming tone. "Did you mention to anyone that you and Jacob had plans to go to Springfield last night?"

"No. It was a spur-of-the-moment deal. I asked Jake around four o'clock yesterday afternoon if he wanted to go out to eat and see a movie."

"Jake said you'd mentioned it about four, but he didn't know if you'd said anything about it to someone else. Maybe earlier in the day? Or even at work Friday?"

"Nope. I hadn't even considered it then. Like I said, it was a last-minute decision."

"All right. I'll let you get back to your family. Thanks for your help. If you or Jake think of anything else, feel free to call me. I gave him my cell number."

"Okay."

"Have a nice afternoon."

"You, too." Lacey hung up and looked at Jake. "He thinks this is a big deal, doesn't he?"

"Yeah, I got that impression at the station."

Jake pulled her against his chest. Lacey couldn't wrap her head around the idea that someone hated her family enough to follow them all the way to Springfield and slash their tire.

Jake gave her a final squeeze and brushed a stray hair from her forehead. A look of pain deepened the wrinkles on the bridge of his nose. "People don't just cut someone's tire unless they mean business."

Lacey grabbed his hand and held on. Her thoughts ran scared.

CHAPTER TWENTY-FOUR

The specialists' vehicle was parked in the back lot when Lacey arrived at work early Monday. They were really putting in the overtime. She crossed her fingers and prayed they would have a breakthrough to share with her this morning. God knew she needed some good news.

She stowed her purse in her desk drawer and hung her jacket behind the door. In the hall, she caught a whiff of freshly brewed coffee, so she headed to the break room where she found a full pot. Nice to have it made for a change. She filled the largest mug she could find and added a pink packet of sweetener and a big shake of Coffee Mate.

"I thought I heard someone." Joe peeked around the door.

"Hey, Joe. Thanks for making the coffee. It's delicious."

"Thank Linda. She made it." Joe laughed and retrieved a cup from the cabinet. "If I'd made it, it would be strong enough to choke a horse."

"I'm sure you're exaggerating but I can drink it strong."

Linda breezed into the break room and headed to

the cupboard.

"Great coffee. Thanks," Lacey said.

"No problem." Linda pulled a cup from the shelf and picked up the coffeepot. "I figured I may as well make myself useful."

"So." Lacey pretended she wasn't anxious. "Anything new to share?"

"Sorry, no. We traced the lot numbers, and no one reported any problems with the vaccines." Joe shook his head and sighed. "I didn't figure we would find anything."

Lacey's hopes deflated like a balloon. She had felt certain something had compromised the vaccine. *Now what?* They were running out of ideas.

Linda set her cup on the counter and crossed her arms. "The pharmaceutical companies were helpful. I got them started on it Friday, and by Saturday afternoon they had our information. Those lot numbers only went out to two states, Missouri and Illinois. That cut the search down a great deal."

"The drug companies faxed us a list of each entity that received a shipment," Joe said. "The list is quite lengthy but not as overwhelming as we first thought it would be."

"That's good." Lacey tried to keep disappointment from her voice. "You guys did a lot of work this weekend."

But apparently, it didn't do any good.

"Neither of the drug companies received any reports of problems with the vaccines," Linda said. "They are as bewildered as we are. Each company offered to help in any way they could."

Joe topped off his cup. "We contacted the facilities we knew would be open evenings and weekends, like hospitals and urgent cares. None of them have seen anything even remotely resembling polio or tetanus.

They promised to follow up on clients who received inoculations from the identified lot numbers and let us know if anything does show up."

Lacey didn't respond for a moment. Though she'd tried to prepare for bad news, the thumb of defeat pressed down on her.

"Something is wrong with the vaccines. That has to be it." She fumed. "It may have left the drug companies in good shape, but something, somewhere along the line had to have happened. What else would explain this?"

A perplexed look flickered across Joe's features. "Lacey, we rechecked your logs on incoming vaccines to eliminate the possibility of compromise during shipment. The temps of the vaccine were within normal limits on every receiving date, which ruled out the premise that the vaccine was not viable when it arrived at your office."

"Okay. So, let's think about this. We know for certain the shipments of vaccine left Sanofi and GSK in good condition." Lacey chewed the information and swallowed it like a bitter herb. "Our sign-in logs show normal temps on all the incoming vaccines. So, we can safely assume the vaccine wasn't damaged during shipment. And our refrigerator logs indicate a safe environment for the vaccines after we got them, no compromise there. So, what's going on, then? You tell me. Why is our county having polio and tetanus cases?"

If Joe or Linda had an answer, she'd pay any amount of money to hear it.

"We're as much at a loss as you are," Linda said.

"Have your staff follow up with the facilities we haven't contacted yet," Joe said. "Doctors' offices and other health departments on the list. But I'm betting you'll get the same answers. The hospitals and urgent cares would be the ones treating communicable diseases, and they haven't seen any cases of polio or tetanus."

Weariness creased his features. Lacey felt as worn out and disillusioned as he looked. Linda pushed a stray hair off her forehead and blew out a sigh that sounded like a blood pressure cuff deflating.

"Other than the cases in Lester County," Linda said, "there has not been one case of polio reported in the United States. Two tetanus cases have been reported in the past six months. Both from different states, and the individuals were adults over sixty that hadn't had a tetanus booster in forty years."

"What we can be reasonably sure of at this point," Joe said as he rubbed a hand over his jaw, "is that the vaccines used in the polio and tetanus cases were not compromised."

I still think it's the vaccine, Lacey thought, but bit her tongue. She'd made her point numerous times. No need to voice it again. "That puts us back to where we started. We've exhausted every available avenue and turned up nothing. A big zero. Not even a hint of a clue. What do we do now? Just sit back and watch our kids become paralyzed or die?"

"I'll talk to Darrell and see what he thinks." Joe patted her arm. "I've already faxed my report to him so he'll have a chance to look it over before I call. I'll let you know what he says."

"Thanks, guys. I do appreciate all your help."

They'd worked hard the entire weekend and had to feel as whipped as she did. She headed back to her office. It was close to eight thirty and everyone was settling into their daily routine. She needed to get a press release prepared. The media would be waiting like vultures.

"Lacey, you have a call on line two," the intercom

blared. Lacey picked up the phone, hit the blinking green light and identified herself.

"Hey, Lacey, it's Susan. Brace yourself."

She sucked in oxygen. "What now?"

"Two more polio cases." Anguish nicked her tone. "And a little boy, John Franklin, one of the last cases, died early this morning."

"Oh Lord." Lacey smacked her desk, sending papers flying to the floor. "When is this going to stop?"

"It can't be soon enough for me. Everyone over here is really freaking out. Even the ED docs are having a hard time dealing with it."

"Are the new cases of polio the same age as the others?"

"Uh-huh. Six-year-olds, Hoover Elementary."

"Fax me the reports."

"Will do."

Lacey ended the call and picked up the papers scattered on the floor, arranged them in order, and laid them on her desk. She walked to the fax and waited while the machine spat out the recent cases then hustled to her desk and prepared the press release. She hated that she had more depressing news to report to a community that was growing more restless with each passing day.

She faxed the press release then met her RNs at the nurses' station to update them on the results of Joe and Linda's long weekend. She spread the new polio case reports across the counter and told them about the little boy who had died that morning.

Ann swiped a hand across her eyes and said, "I'll get started on the investigations."

"Give me one." Betty held out her hand. "I can help."

Joan plucked some tissues from the box by her

phone and handed one to Ann. She met Lacey's gaze, shook her head then grabbed a chart from the clerk's cubicle before walking away.

Joe and Linda headed down the hall. Before they could turn down the corridor leading to the conference room, Lacey motioned them toward her office.

"Don't tell me," Joe said as he and Linda followed her through the doorway. "More bad news?"

Lacey nodded and filled them in. She passed out copies of the new polio cases and the file on the deceased child. After a few minutes of studying them, Joe gave Lacey a pained look.

"Are you okay?" Joe asked.

"I don't know what okay is anymore." She held tears at bay, wanting nothing more than to give in to a long cry. But she didn't have time for that. "Have you talked to Darrell?"

"Just got off the phone with him. He'd finished reading my report and his conclusion is the same as ours. The vaccines used in the cases were stable."

Maybe they were right. Lacey tucked her hair behind her ear, frustrated. Everything in Lester County was falling apart and she was helpless to stop it.

"What now?" she asked.

"We're going to head back to Springfield for a few days. We've done all we can do here for now."

She nodded. "I agree."

"Lacey, this isn't just your problem. It's a state problem, too. We aren't leaving you alone on this, and we will be back. Promise." Joe gave her a hint of a smile. "If you come up with anything, anything at all, call me. I mean it."

Lacey blinked away the moisture in her eyes.

"The CDC is working around the clock, too," Linda

said. "So don't think for one minute you're being abandoned."

"I know. I've got a lot of help." Lacey sniffed. "And I want to thank both of you for all your hard work. I know you've put many hours into this, and I appreciate it."

Joe and Linda stood. They both gave her a hug then were on their way. Lacey hoped they'd get some relaxation in the next few days. They needed it.

The remainder of the day flew by. Before Lacey knew it, the workday was over. Her nurses looked exhausted, and it was only Monday. What would the rest of the week dump in their laps?

CHAPTER TWENTY-FIVE

After work, she had to take a different route home. That, or get bogged down in the five o'clock traffic at the intersection of Jefferson and Elm where the crew from the city utilities department was working on a downed transformer. Instead of making her usual right on Jefferson, she made a wide left across four lanes and clicked on her headlights.

The days were definitely getting shorter; winter was just a breath away. She dreaded winter. Last year, ice-covered streets had made her periodic midnight runs a little difficult. But she'd managed to keep up with the incoming shipments and her scheme had advanced right on schedule.

Her plan couldn't be working out better. Her mouth turned up at the corners, and she patted herself on the back for putting together the perfect solution. The payback wouldn't be over in five minutes. Not like the spontaneous shootings by disgruntled boobs who didn't have the sense to think things through. Just yesterday, a fifty-year-old man who'd been fired from a post office in St. Louis had bombarded the office armed with a handgun. He'd killed two and injured half a dozen. All he'd get out of his revenge was a life sentence in some godforsaken prison. She would take out more lives, and no one would ever be able to point a finger at her.

She hit a red light and stopped behind a guy in a black leather jacket who leaned back on his Harley Davidson as if he'd driven straight off the set of a James Dean movie. She stared at the back of Mr. Macho's midnight-blue helmet and tapped impatient fingers on the steering wheel.

The light changed to green, and the motorcycle guy revved his ride. He busted through the intersection and plowed into a puppy that darted into the street. Mr. Macho veered left, never looking back.

The stupid freak. Didn't he know he'd hit an innocent animal? She'd always held a special place in her heart for animals. Unlike people, they loved you unconditionally and never stabbed you in the back.

She steered to the curb and raced to the pup. She fell to her knees and made a quick assessment. He was dead, poor little thing. Tears of rage sprang to her eyes, and she spewed words about the cyclist that shocked even her. She wished she'd paid attention to the license number. She gathered up the limp, lifeless body and was about to head for the owner's house when she noticed the name on the mailbox.

Margaret Weber. Lacey's mother.

She looked down at the puppy.

"Bandit!"

This was priceless. And she knew what she was going to do.

CHAPTER TWENTY-SIX

Lacey wiggled into her car early Tuesday morning ready for her run. It would be a great day to jog in the park. Although it wasn't quite daylight, the park would be well lit. Several other joggers would be there so she wouldn't be alone. And she'd keep an eye on her car. Surely it was too early for anyone with mischief on their mind to be out and about.

She backed out of the garage. A flash of red caught her eye, and she looked at the front door of the house. Sitting on her doorstep was a large package wrapped in red foil. A huge gold bow was tied on with wide gold ribbon that glittered in the headlights.

Intrigued, she slipped from the car and walked to the stoop. She pulled the small white envelope from under the ribbon and opened the flap. Her name had been typed in large bold print on a floral shop card. She gathered up the box and trudged through the garage into the kitchen.

Under the bright, shiny paper was a cardboard box secured with utility tape. *Get out or the next time this will be Todd* was scrawled in all capital letters across the top. A needle of apprehension pierced her chest, and she swallowed her breath as she sliced through the tape. When she pulled open the lid, her jaw unhinged.

She heard screaming. It took a second for her to realize it was coming from her voice box but she couldn't stop.

Between shrieks, she registered the sound of Jake's feet thundering down the stairs. He skidded into the kitchen with his hair disheveled, eyes circles of fear.

"Lacey! What is it?" He looked around the room and back to her.

Lacey couldn't speak. At least her screaming had ceased.

He grabbed her shoulders and met her gaze. "What, Lacey? What's wrong with you?"

She pointed at the package.

Jake stepped to the counter and looked in the box. He turned so pale Lacey thought he might hurl. She knew she was close.

"What sicko would do that?" He shut the lid and put his arm around her. "I'm so sorry."

Lacey let out a sob and nausea roiled up her throat. She pressed a hand to her mouth. Swiveling on one foot, she stumbled toward the half-bath off the utility room. She jerked open the door and fell to her knees in front of the commode. Just in time. She retched so hard she thought she'd lose the lining of her stomach.

Jake turned on the faucet and handed her a wet a rag. He cradled her, wiping her mouth and face with the damp washcloth. "I'm so sorry, baby," he whispered.

"Somebody killed Mom's puppy." Tears spilled down her cheeks. "Cut his poor little head off."

Nausea churned up again and she grabbed the rim of the stool. This time, all she had was dry heaves that left her shaking and weak. Jake rinsed the rag and wrung out the excess moisture.

"Anyone that'd do that is capable of doing anything," he said.

Lacey ran the rag over her face. The cool cloth felt good next to her skin.

"Did you see what was written on the top?"

"No." Jake's brows knit together. "What?"

When she told him, he lost it. Fury blazed in his eyes, and he shot up like a rocket. She'd never seen him so shaken, so out of control.

"I'm getting the police over here. Right now!"

He tore from the room like he was being chased by demons. In a sense, he was. Whoever had done that was driven by darkness.

Lacey made her way out of the bathroom and climbed the stairs. She lingered on the threshold to Todd's room, lost in thought. She tasted bile on her tongue and leaned against the doorjamb, trying to sort through her options. If Todd was in danger, she couldn't ignore it. But short of an armed guard 24/7, what could she do?

She looked at her son. He enjoyed the slumber of a teenager and her heart spilled over with love. Sprawled out with his legs and arms tangled in the covers and his head denting the pillow, he didn't look sixteen. He looked like the little boy she'd read stories to each night for more years than she could remember.

She padded to the bed and gently straightened his covers. He stretched and turned over then slid a hand under his cheek. All the commotion hadn't disturbed either child. She'd always said they could sleep through a tornado.

How was she going to keep her oldest child safe? She couldn't even take care of the polio and tetanus cases in the community. What if she failed her son, too?

Tears stung her eyes. He was so young. So innocent. Who would dare threaten him? And why?

CHAPTER TWENTY-SEVEN

Lacey slipped through the back door of her mother's house into a compact kitchen nestled comfortably behind a screened porch. A few months after Dad died, her mother sold the big colonial house where Lacey had grown up. Said she didn't need all those empty rooms. Lacey guessed it was the memories rather than the rooms that inspired the relocation.

"Hey, sweetie. How's my baby girl?"

Lacey gave her mother a smile she didn't feel and a thumbs-up gesture.

Her mom stood at the counter whisking eggs in a white Corelle bowl. She added a splash of milk, gave it another few whisks then poured the mixture into a Teflon skillet. Sizzling arose with the scent of eggs and butter.

"There's plenty. Stay for breakfast?"

Lacey had headed for her mom's house shortly after an officer from the local police department left her home. He'd taken the cardboard box and had promised to update Detective Prater as soon as he reported for duty. Though her stomach had settled somewhat, the taste of bile was only masked by the toothpaste.

"No, Mom, I'm not hungry."

"Not hungry?"

Her mother gave her one of those looks only a mother could conjure up as she tucked a strand of short, sandy-blonde hair behind an ear and wrinkled a brow. Dressed for work in a beige cardigan over black pants and sensible low-heeled black pumps, her mother didn't look her sixty-four years.

"What's wrong? You look sick. Are you not feeling well, honey?"

"I'm not sick, Mom."

Lacey dumped her jacket and purse on a chair and kissed her mother on the cheek. For a nanosecond, she considered not telling her about Bandit. Her mom had been overwrought the previous night when the puppy had clawed under the fence and gone missing. What harm would it do to let her think he'd just wandered off?

Her mother popped a piece of wheat bread into the toaster.

"I wish you'd let me fix you something." She raked the scrambled eggs onto a plate and looked at Lacey with narrowed eyes. "Sure you're not hungry?"

"I'm sure."

She struggled for equilibrium and glanced at her watch. If she was going to tell her mother about Bandit, she'd have to quit stalling. Mom would be heading to the library in a few minutes, where she'd taken the job at the circulation desk three years prior. It had kept her too busy during the day to dwell on the loss of her husband. Lacey and Jake had tried to fill the void at night.

The toaster ejected its bounty. Mom slathered fat-free strawberry cream cheese on the golden-brown bread. She took a bite of eggs and tasted the toast. She shot Lacey a wide smile as she filled two cups with coffee then motioned toward the refrigerator. "Half-and-Half's in there. Help yourself."

Lacey studied her mom and smiled. She was such a creature of habit. Since Dad had died, she never ate breakfast at the table. She'd sit on her little stepstool next to the sink so she could watch the early morning antics of the squirrels in her backyard.

Lacey walked to the fridge. The door was completely covered with school pictures of Todd and Brian. A handprint of Brian's from kindergarten still hung beside his recent school picture. Lacey poured cream in her cup and walked over to her mother.

"Sit down, Mom. I've got something to tell you."

Mom wiped her hands on a bright orange kitchen towel, left the steaming eggs on the counter, and pulled out a chair at the table. She met Lacey's gaze and pulled in an audible breath. "Tell me, what's going on?"

~ ~ ~ ~ ~

Lacey cruised through the light traffic down Jefferson Street toward the health department. Anger boiled inside her. She wiped away tears with the back of her hand as she flashed on her mother's face carved with pain. Mom had bawled like a baby. Her tears had turned to anger and back again to hurt before Lacey had to leave. As upset as she was, Mom didn't want to be late for work. People depended on her, she'd said, and she couldn't let them down.

That was her mother, always putting others first.

It's just not fair. New tears stung Lacey's swollen eyes. She dug a tissue from her purse and blew her nose. *Now Mom is worried about my family, too.* And she didn't need that. She was approaching retirement age, and this should be a time of kicking back, enjoying life, not fretting over stalkers and lifeless puppies.

Lacey parked in the health department's private lot and entered the building. She dragged herself through her coffee-making and fax-checking routine then plowed into her office to face another day of fighting communicable disease. Susan called first thing.

"The hospital is running over with flu cases." The nurse sounded frazzled. "We're sending new admissions to Springfield and Rolla. We're full. Can't take another patient."

"I've noticed several cases of flu reported. A lot more than this time last year." They'd had their flu clinic early, in August, with a huge turnout. That had been plenty of time for the antibodies to peak and provide maximum protection. "Have the cases you've seen had a flu shot?"

"Most of the cases, yes."

Of course they have. Lacey shook her head and gripped the warm mug. Suddenly she felt a chill she couldn't explain. She glanced over her shoulder, making sure the area remained empty and no one lurked behind her.

"Hold on. I'll check and see how many confirmed cases we've got in our county." Lacey booted up her computer. She sipped from her cup, feeling the hot liquid glide down her throat, and hoped it would stay in her stomach.

When Lester County popped up, Lacey's eyes grew round.

"Forty-eight. Wow, that's too many this early in the season."

"Way too many." Dismay defined Susan's tone. "And I bet there's really more than that. The number will double when all the cases are confirmed and entered into the system. I'm telling you, we've seen that many in the last couple of days. Last night, we admitted fifteen with flu-like symptoms and referred eighteen others to St. Luke's and Lakeside because we had no more beds available."

"Let me look at the stats state-wide." Lacey clicked on the flu graphs for Missouri, wondering if the entire state was seeing increased numbers. "If one more unusual thing happens this year, I'm gonna scream."

"Get a number!" Susan laughed, without mirth. "If screaming would help, I'd let it rip."

That made Lacey smile, despite her mood. Susan, usually so professional, had her moments. But didn't they all?

"Okay, I've got the graphs pulled up. All the counties except ours, of course, are reporting one to three percent of the population positive for influenza so far. Lester County is reporting thirty percent." Lacey scrolled through the graphs. Lester County stood out like an apple in a bowl of grapes. "We are way over the norm."

"That's unbelievable."

"Twenty-five percent are type A influenza, the other five, type B."

"Same strains that are in the vaccine this year."

"Yep. The vaccine was right on target."

"Percentages way too high, huh?"

"Looks like it." The wheels turned frantically in Lacey's head. She had an uneasy feeling that this was somehow tied to the polio and tetanus cases. But how?

Lacey ended the call with her eyes glued to the computer screen. Polio and tetanus. *And now influenza?* Sure, every year, even with the flu shots, a percent of the protected population contracted it—but a small percent, not thirty percent. Sheesh.

Lacey rubbed her eyes then focused on the morning

press release. Four more polio cases to add to the list and the flu numbers were jumping daily. She could almost taste the bitterness the community would swallow when they heard this turn of events.

CHAPTER TWENTY-EIGHT

The image of the beheaded puppy flashed through Jake's head for the umpteenth time. Then a worm of apprehension wiggled through his gut as Ms. Ames' face flashed across his mind.

What if it's Kimberly that is harassing Lacey? How far would she go to get to me?

Things were spinning out of control, and he was worried about Lacey and the boys. Just how far would this sadist actually go? The police had been no help. They were sorry, they'd said, but they had nothing concrete to build a case on.

A dog head seemed tangible enough to Jake, but he'd seen enough movies to know the cops needed a suspect, someone to go after. And no one fell into that category. The cop had taken the cardboard box and Jake prayed they could get an identifying fingerprint.

He grabbed his jacket from the coat tree and sprinted to his car. After a quick run to Subway, he plopped down on a bench at the park.

He scanned the view as he bit into the roast beef with provolone and popped the seal on his chips. The ground, hidden in a thick bedding of yellow, orange, and brown leaves, made him flash on his childhood.

He had a sudden urge to roll around—that always made him feel safe as a kid. He smiled as memories filtered through his head of the happy times he'd frolicked in his backyard while his dad had patiently tried to shoo him out of the way so he could rake the leaves into a pile and burn them.

He sighed. He really missed his dad. Especially in the fall. Maybe because it had been a brisk, sunny autumn day the last time he'd seen his father. Right before the car accident. Jake had been home from college for Thanksgiving break and had spent four days with his family. When he'd headed back to his dorm, he hadn't known that the next time he would see his dad would be in a casket.

Jake shook off long-ago memories and sank his teeth into the sandwich. His gaze shifted to the huge maple a few feet from his bench. He was surprised at the amount of leaves still hanging on. The early November sun winked through the branches and a faint breeze caressed his face. It wouldn't be long before the limbs were bare and the colorful dressing only a memory for another year.

He popped a chip into his mouth. Decibels of Lacey's screams squealed in his head as he opened his bottled water. A fire fanned through his gut. The flames of injustice kindled until the heat seared every neuron. He tipped up the bottle, but the cool gulp of water did nothing to relieve the sweltering waves.

Why would someone harass Lacey? She'd never done anything to anyone. She was the kindest person he'd ever come across and she wouldn't even think of trying to harm anybody. It had to be some lunatic. Slashing a tire was one thing, but no sane person would kill an innocent puppy. Surely, Kimberly would not resort to something this low.

He wondered how Lacey's mother was holding up.

She had a soft spot for animals and had bonded with Bandit right from the start. She must be devastated.

He took another swig of water and crammed the rest of his sandwich back in the bag. He wasn't hungry anymore, couldn't eat another bite. He slid from the bench, tossed the bag in the trash, and ten minutes later was back at his desk.

~ ~ ~ ~ ~

Jake's fingers darted across the calculator. He'd already picked up on two mistakes in the Wilson report that needed an overhaul. He had to make the numbers balance before he turned the file in to Brad, no later than five o'clock. He totaled another column and glanced up when he heard a muffled cough.

"Hey, Kimberly." He smiled. He was ready for a distraction. And from her actions that morning, it was obvious she was willing to interact professionally. That was a big relief.

She walked to the center of his office and twirled in a full degree circle, her hair billowing as she turned. She stopped and met his gaze. "Well?"

"Well, what?" Jake laughed, wondering if she was trying out for a ballet class.

"What do you think of my new haircut?"

Her hair had been cut, but not by more than an inch or so.

"Looks nice," he said. He had liked her hair before, and he still liked it.

"Do you think I should go a little shorter?"

What is it with her hair? "Whatever you think. Hey, I'm just a guy. What do I know? Ask the girls you work with."

"I'm not trying to impress the girls." She sauntered around his desk and stood a feather's width away.

He liked the way her hair smelled, too. He bet it felt all silky and smooth like the satin pillowcases Lacey had recently bought.

Stop it right now!

"You okay?" she asked. "You seem a little sad today."

"Sad. Mad." Jake sneered and rolled back about a foot to establish a safe distance. Then he told her about the events leading up to finding the dog. Kimberly's mouth hung open. She acted surprised, but he wondered if that was it, just an act. He couldn't imagine she would be capable of such heinous acts.

So why did his suspicion linger?

"Good grief. No wonder you're bumming." She stepped behind him and rubbed his shoulders with slow strokes. "Poor baby. Let me make it better."

Jake closed his eyes and breathed deeply. So much for the safe distance.

"You feel so tense, honey." Her hands glided from the nape of his neck to the top of his shoulders. Slowly and firmly, she kneaded his taut muscles.

Jake eased his head back and let his eyelids fall shut. It felt so good, and what could it hurt? She was just trying to console him.

She nuzzled his neck, and her lips nibbled his earlobe. A thousand goose bumps stood at attention on his body. Before he was even conscious of what she was doing, she pulled him up, turned him toward her, and snaked her arms around him.

Her lips felt soft and moist as she brushed them gently across his mouth. Lost in her taste and scent, he succumbed to everything he'd been aching to do for weeks. He pressed his body close, feeling every swell and curve, every line. His lips bore down hungrily, and his tongue darted into her mouth. She grabbed a handful of his hair and arched against him.

The ringing of the phone brought Jake to his senses. He pushed Kimberly back and shook his head. "We shouldn't have done that."

"You loved it as much as I did, stud."

When she placed a kiss on his cheek, a dose of realization slapped him across the face. He shuddered.

The phone rang again. He held up a hand. "No more. We can't do this."

She smiled and leaned close. He could feel her hot breath against his face. "Later," she whispered and left.

He grabbed the phone on the third ring and said "hello" to a client wanting an update on the boat company account. Jake didn't know how he finished the conversation, but somehow managed. He sank into his chair and dropped his head into his hands.

How could he have acted like that? And liked it so much?

Despite the guilt wracking him, he ached for more. He could still taste her. She had full, pouty lips that Jake had imagined on more than one occasion how kissing them would feel. *Now I know.* Only he wished he didn't.

He'd betrayed his wife. Made physical contact with another woman. How could Lacey ever forgive him? How could he ever forgive himself? He'd enjoyed it and if the phone had not interrupted, how far would he have gone?

Dear Lord, what have I done?

CHAPTER TWENTY-NINE

Lacey slid open the bottom desk drawer and pulled out the tetanus case folders. Technically they were closed, but she couldn't close the cases in her mind like they didn't matter anymore. They did. To her. To the families still rocking from the shock of losing a child so suddenly and so violently.

She started with Gregory Morris. Her eyes rolled over the information in his file. Something just didn't feel right. She couldn't shake the sensation that she was missing something vital. She was still stuck on the bad vaccine theory. However, she realized it wasn't feasible that both polio and tetanus vaccines would be unstable.

And now influenza?

Betty and Joan stepped through her doorway at noon.

"Wanna go to La Mexican Kitchen with us?" Betty asked.

"No. Diet day today. Sorry."

"Ugh! That's no fun."

After the pair left, Lacey grabbed a pack of peanut butter crackers, a blueberry Yoplait, and a diet soda from the break room. Not much of a lunch but only three hundred calories.

She filed the tetanus cases in her drawer and clicked on the state website. Under Influenza, she scrolled down to Lester County. The stats hadn't changed much since morning, but that didn't tell her anything. The new cases Susan had mentioned wouldn't be documented until the lab had confirmed the disease.

Lacey took a swig of soda and set the plastic bottle on the seashell coaster from her trip with Jake to Cancun two years ago. Things had been so right between them then. Five nights in a hotel that sat between a three-hundred-yard white sand beach, and Nichupte Lagoon had been the perfect place to celebrate their fifteenth wedding anniversary. They'd snorkeled, parasailed, and even tried their hand with a boogie board. But most of their time had been spent lazing on the beach, listening to the waves and soaking up the tropical sun.

Lacey opened the Yoplait and wondered for the gazillionth time why Jake wouldn't share his problems with her anymore. She thought of Betty and Joan at La Mexican Kitchen and swore she could smell enchiladas. Maybe she should have gone with them. But she had five pounds to shed. Besides, with so much on her mind, she would have been lousy company.

The office was deserted; everyone had disappeared over the lunch hour. The phones rang off the hook in the distance, and she spooned the last of the Yoplait into her mouth, disgusted. At noon and after office hours, incoming calls were diverted to voicemail. If someone wanted to talk to her, they could enter her three-digit code after the prompt to make the phone ring at her desk. It rarely happened; they always hung up before the options played.

Lacey rubbed her temples. The distant *brrringing* was getting on her nerves. Usually, it didn't bother her. Why was she letting it get to her today? She gobbled down the last of the crackers, finished her soda, and slid back from her desk. She had to get out of here for a while.

She pushed through the back door, stepped across the parking lot, and trekked down the sidewalk. The noonday sun peppered her face, and the breeze lifted the hair at the nape of her neck. Thoughts of the note, the slashed tire, and poor little Bandit flashed through her head. The note and tire had been bad enough. Killing her mother's puppy was unforgivable. And it scared her. What would this maniac do next?

She took a right turn at the corner and headed down the sidewalk past small houses nestled close together. Cars whizzed by in the street, no doubt rushing to make the best of the noon hour. Her Clinics—shoes that were almost but not quite as comfortable as her Reeboks—pounded the concrete as she power-walked.

She took another right on Lincoln and sidestepped a break in the cement. Then she heard a sound behind her and glanced over her shoulder. No one there. Was she hearing things? Unnerved, she made a U-turn before hitting the next intersection and headed back toward the health department.

She didn't hear anything, but she stopped mid-stride and wheeled around. No one.

Icy fingers squeezed her thoracic spine, sending a crisp jab to her chest. Why did she have the distinct feeling someone was following her? The wind caught the back of her neck, and she picked up her pace, pumped her legs forward and found herself at the back door of the building, breathing hard. So much for a relaxing walk.

She pushed through the door and let it fall shut, pulled two calming breaths, slow and deep, in through her nose, out through her mouth. What in the world was wrong with her? She had never been paranoid. But she'd never been threatened before. She sat at her desk and released a relieved sigh when she heard her coworkers return.

"Are you okay?" Betty pulled a chair close to Lacey's desk and flopped down on the seat.

Lacey put on a fake smile. "Just letting things get to me, I guess. But I'm okay." She shrugged. "Hey, don't worry. I'm fine."

"I'd say you have a few things to be concerned about." Her eyelids flickered and tension tightened her features. Lacey had kept the nurses updated about her recent hassles. They knew all about the threats and violence.

"I took a walk at noon and had the crazy feeling someone was following me. If that isn't paranoid, I don't know what is." She gave an artificial laugh, trying to make light of it. But she still couldn't shake the feeling.

Betty appeared to study her for a few seconds. She said, "It was probably just the wind. No one would bother you here. Not with us around." She flexed her biceps and cupped it with her hand. "I'd give 'em what for."

Lacey smiled, and this time it was real. She chided herself for being so jumpy. Betty was right. No one would stalk her in broad daylight. Yet that well-defined impression of someone tailing her crowded her mind, wouldn't let go.

"What did you get for lunch?" Lacey asked, changing the subject.

"The buffet, of course. It was good, even better than usual." The young nurse leaned back in the chair and patted her abdomen. "Too good. I'm going to pay this afternoon. A big meal makes me sluggish."

"I hear that," Lacey said. "Makes me want a nap."

Betty stood and scooted the chair back in place. "I better get to work before I nod off."

"I have faith you'll stay awake." Lacey chuckled. "Too much work to do."

"Remember, I'm here if you need to talk."

"I know. And I appreciate that. Thanks for caring."

Betty stopped in the threshold, turned, and gave Lacey a quick hug.

Tears stung Lacey's eyes as her friend went back to her workstation.

Her thoughts continued to tumble over one another as she pondered the creepy notion that someone was following her. It had felt so real. She swallowed the scary memory and directed her eyes to the computer screen.

Just since noon, fifteen more flu cases had been added to the Lester County influenza report. In a week, it'd probably be tripled. She shuddered, clicked off the site, and busied herself with the polio cases piled on her desk.

~ ~ ~ ~ ~

Midafternoon, when Lacey heard a commotion at the front office, she hustled to the clerical area. A young lady on the other side of the reception counter had tears streaming from red, swollen eyes. Her brown hair hung limp and tangled around a gaunt face.

"You didn't do anything to keep my little boy from getting polio. No one did, and now he's gone! Dead!"

Lacey stepped through the door separating the nursing station from the waiting room and laid a hand on the woman's arm.

"I'm the director of nursing." Lacey nudged her toward the open doorway. "Let's go to my office where we can talk."

"Get your hands off me. There's nothing to talk about." She wheeled around on tennis shoes and blundered past patrons in the waiting room. "It's too late!" she yelled over her shoulder as she bolted through the doorway.

Lacey's throat tightened. She could taste the young mother's pain. She could only imagine how she would react if she were to lose one of her boys.

Lacey threaded through the wide-eyed clients and burst through the front door. She found the girl sitting in a beat-up white Honda. She was draped over the steering wheel with her head buried under her arms. Her wracking sobs reached Lacey even before she opened the passenger's door and slipped inside.

The woman raised her head. "Why?" Tears and mucus ran down her face. "Why did it happen?"

Lacey shook her head. Empathy squeezed her heart, and she choked back her own tears. "I am so sorry for your loss. I know that must sound like empty words to you right now and it doesn't begin to help your pain. But please let me help you. Let me talk with you a while."

Fresh tears leaked from the girl's eyes. She hugged herself tightly as she rocked in the seat. Lacey gently patted her arm.

When her sobs ebbed into moans, she said, "It hurts so much. I can't stand it."

"You don't need to be alone right now." Lacey smoothed the girl's damp hair back from her eyes and gently turned the grieving face toward her. "Do you have anyone you can call? Family? Friends?"

She nodded. "My mom. She lives in St. Louis but

she's on her way down here. She'll be here before long."

"Okay. That's good." Lacey scooted out of the car and walked around to the driver's side. She opened the door and made shooing motions. "Scoot over. I'll drive you home and wait with you until your mom comes."

The girl looked at her with wide eyes. "Why? Why would you do that? You don't even know me."

"What's your name?"

"Beth. Beth Ramsey," she said as Lacey slid under the wheel.

"Now I know you, Beth." Lacey stuck out her hand. "I'm Lacey Bookman."

~ ~ ~ ~ ~

Lacey stayed with Beth until her mother, Sheila, arrived a little after four, and the two fell into each other's arms, sobbing and clutching each other. It broke Lacey's heart to watch the grieving mother and grandmother ask why they had lost their precious little Brandon.

Lacey slipped into the small bathroom off the living room to give them a few minutes of privacy. She took the time to phone the office and let the girls know where she was and when she'd be back. She splashed cool water on her face and wondered if Beth and Sheila would ever find their way through this tragedy.

She walked out of the bathroom and sat in a chair across from the sofa where the women huddled. Lacey wrote down the number of *Helping Hearts Heal*, a grief support group, and passed it to Beth.

"Do you have any questions about the group?" Lacey asked because she knew the pair needed to talk. In moments, they were off, tossing questions as fast as she could answer them.

~ ~ ~ ~ ~

Beth and her mom drove Lacey back to the health department.

"Promise me you'll call if you need anything," Lacey said.

"We will," Sheila said.

Beth nodded and gave Lacey a tearful smile.

Emotionally exhausted, Lacey trudged into her office with her nurses at her heels.

"Sheesh, Lacey," Joan said. "That had to be rough."

"Yeah. It was."

"You okay?" Ann asked. "You don't look too good."

"It's so sad. Beth's just a kid herself. I'm glad her mom's going to stay with her for a while." Lacey flipped through the polio files stacked on her desk and pulled out Brandon's.

"I'm worried about Beth. This little boy..." She held up the chart, fighting back emotion. "Should never have contracted polio. He had his immunizations on schedule. He should have been protected."

"This is so wrong." Irritation edged Betty's voice. She crossed her arms and arched a brow. "You know, sometimes I hate nursing."

Lacey flopped down into her chair. She opened Brandon's folder and scanned the file yet another time. She was familiar with all the charts. She'd been over them enough times she almost had them memorized.

"Good grief, Beth's just twenty-two," she said. "She was only sixteen when she had Brandon."

"What about Brandon's father?" Betty asked.

"Never in the picture. Beth's on her own."

"Bummer." Betty slipped into a chair beside the

desk. "Poor kid, she's been through a lot. Now this."

"She's getting financial help, right?" Joan asked.

Lacey shook her head and felt her heart break a little more. "She was on Medicaid until Brandon started kindergarten. Then she landed a job at Applebee's. For the past year, she's been working during the day and taking night classes at Drury College."

"Good for her," Joan said. "Sounds like she's got ambition."

"Yeah." *But a lot of good that did her.* Lacey closed the folder and wished she could make polio disappear and take all the bad memories with it. This was hitting too close to home. She hated what it was doing to the community.

"She said she wanted to give her son a better life," Lacey said. "She didn't want him having the stigma of being welfare dependent."

"Just when she's getting her life together and making a stable life for her son, this had to happen." Joan shook her head. "Sometimes life stinks."

"Like all the time lately, I'd say." Betty let out a huff.

"Well, I'm glad you were there for her, Lacey. I'm sure she appreciated you stepping in and comforting her." A flicker of something—was it pain?—flickered across Ann's eyes. "And, predictably, you're always there."

"Sometimes being there just isn't enough."

CHAPTER THIRTY

Jake finished the last page of the Benson audit and, satisfied, flipped shut the folder. A strong cup of coffee called his name, so he trekked down the hall toward the break room. He noticed the door to the storage closet stood ajar, so he stepped across the hall to shut it. A hand grabbed his arm and pulled him inside.

Kimberly had her lips on his even as she pushed the door closed with her foot. Her fingers grabbed a handful of hair, and she pulled his head backward, running her moist tongue up his neck. She stopped to take a mouthful of shivering flesh right under his jaw.

"No." Jake moaned and stepped back, stumbled when the back of his knees banged against a cardboard box. His pulse pounded in his ears, and he shook his head, silently repeating "no." But Kimberly was quick. She placed her palms on his chest and gave him a shove. He sat hard on the box of closed account folders.

In a flash, Kimberly straddled his lap and her mouth covered his. She sucked the air from his lungs and whispered, "Oh, yes."

He knew this was wrong. But at the moment, his

brain was not the organ directing his thinking. Heat flooded his body, sending waves of pleasure through his veins.

She found his lips again. Her mouth was hot and wet, and he couldn't get enough of her. Her scent, fruity and pungent with sweat, suffocated his resistance. His arms shot around her and he pulled her closer.

She let out a low groan, leaned back, and slid her hands down to his belt. When he heard the buckle click open, something snapped in his brain.

This was wrong. He couldn't do this. He didn't want to do this. He shook his head to clear it and determination kicked in. He pushed her back firmly and shot up off the box.

"You know you want me." Her eyes were clouded over and sensual. "Come on, it's not going to hurt anyone."

With all the strength he could muster, he grabbed the doorknob and blasted through the door. He had to put some distance between them so he could hang on to his control.

Thankfully no one was in the hall. He raced down the corridor like his life depended on it. It did. He didn't know how much more he could take and not give in to his desire.

Kimberly fell into step beside him, and they reached his office at the same time.

"Sit down," Jake said. "We've got some serious talking to do."

He walked behind his desk, putting the workspace between them like a moat around a castle. He didn't sit even though his knees trembled and felt like they might buckle.

Kimberly slunk into the chair and crossed her legs. She finger-combed her tangled hair, pushing it back from her face. She cocked her head to the side, tossed him a wink, and opened her mouth, but Jake held up a hand.

"Don't talk. Listen. This is over. It stops right here. Now."

"Ah, Jake." She shot him a pouty look. "Don't push me away."

"This isn't cute anymore, Kimberly. It's way out of control."

"Your point?"

"I told you. I'm a married man. I can't cheat on my wife." He laughed without mirth as the realization hit him. "And you know what? I don't *want* to cheat on her. Don't you get it? I love Lacey."

"You can love us both. I'd be willing to share."

"No. It doesn't work like that."

"You can protest all you want." The sides of her mouth turned up in a sneer. "But you wanted me. Still want me."

"I'm sorry that I led you on. But what just happened will never happen again. Never. And you need to get that through your head and back off."

Kimberly winced and shifted positions. "You can't tell me you don't like me, Jake." She smoothed down her navy-blue jacket, but it still looked like she'd slept in it. "You were all over me just now. Yesterday, too."

Jake couldn't deny it. He was attracted to her. But it wasn't love. He loved Lacey. And he wasn't going to risk his marriage for the sake of his raging hormones. No doubt, Lacey would be devastated. It just wasn't worth the pain it would cause his wife. Not worth the regret it would cause him. "I'm sorry. I've been way out of line, carried things too far. I should never have flirted with you. I thought I could handle it. But I was wrong." He pulled in a determined breath. "The game's over, Kimberly."

"We'll see."

"I intend to make sure nothing like this happens again. We have to work together, so we need to get along. But there will be no more physical contact between us. From now on, it's strictly professional. And if you cross the line again, I will take it up with Brad."

"You wouldn't dare." Kimberly's face reddened. She stood and sent him a bawdy look through narrowed eyes. Jake braced his hands on his desk, determined to stand by his decision. If she stepped toward him, he was prepared. She tugged at the hem of her jacket and barked out a laugh.

"Try me, and you'll find out."

"We'll see," she said again and turned toward the door.

"I'm telling you how it is if you want to keep your job. No more flirting. And definitely no more physical contact."

She stomped to the door and slammed it on her way out.

Jake slumped in his chair, wracked with guilt and remorse. He knew he'd crossed a line with his behavior. When Kimberly joined the firm, he'd had a choice. Flirt with her or brush off her flattery. He'd made the wrong choice and paid the price. He ran a hand across his forehead, pushing strands of limp hair aside. He must look as disheveled as Kimberly.

He should have backed off. Not only had he played Russian roulette with his life, he'd put Lacey's life in jeopardy. He finally admitted he needed help.

Jake opened his cell and tapped in a series of numbers. When the church secretary answered, he said, "I need to make an appointment with Pastor David. Today. I don't care how late. I've got to see him."

CHAPTER THIRTY-ONE

At three o'clock p.m., only a handful of cars were in the Calvary Heights Christian Church's parking lot. Jake grabbed a space near the side entrance and slipped through the double doors.

A smiling gray-haired woman in a simple tweed pantsuit sat behind a small desk sorting pamphlets and church fliers.

"Go on in." She motioned to the pastor's office. "He's expecting you."

Jake nodded, tapped on the door, and stepped inside.

"Welcome, Jacob." Pastor David grasped Jake's hand in a firm handshake.

The room smelled of furniture polish and fresh coffee. The pastor wore a short-sleeve reddish-yellow Polo over jeans and tennis shoes. His gray hair had been cut short and reading glasses perched on top of his head. Clear blue eyes punctuated with deep lines that extended to his thick brown-and-gray eyebrows radiated kindness.

The minister's office felt warm and inviting. Two overstuffed brown leather chairs clustered near a low coffee table. A large black Bible, various study guides, a concordance, and a closed laptop were spread across the top. This must be where he prepared his sermons.

"Have a seat." He motioned to one of the plush chairs. "I'll get us something to drink."

The pastor stepped to a small credenza set up with a coffeemaker, a bowl of sugar cubes, a tall container of Coffee Mate, and a small box of pink sweetener. "What do you take in your coffee?"

"Two sugars."

Now that he was here, face-to-face with the minister, he wasn't sure it had been such a good idea. He fidgeted with the gold band on his watch, pinching the skin on his wrist in the process. He shifted positions and glanced around the large, well-appointed office. A desk took up most of the west wall. It faced a window where light shimmered through the open blinds and made the glossy cherry finish sparkle. It was neat as a pin. His inbox was piled high with correspondence, and Jake felt a stab of guilt for disturbing his busy schedule.

"I'm sorry to come on such short notice," Jake said. "I hope I didn't interrupt anything."

"You didn't. I'm always happy to see you." The pastor smiled and set two mugs of coffee on the table. "Mine's the white one. I always did love my cream." He chuckled and lowered his weight into the other chair.

"Lacey takes lots of cream," Jake said for lack of something better. He picked up his cup and took a small sip.

"Wonderful weather we've been having. I love fall, don't you?" the pastor asked.

Jake nodded but fell silent.

After a few moments of the awkward silence, Pastor David said, "Whenever you're ready to talk, I'm here to listen. But I'm in no hurry. Take all the time you need."

Feeling foolish and not knowing where to begin, or even if he should begin, he blurted, "Actually, I've been having some, well, some problems at the office. But I probably should just work them out on my own."

"Sometimes talking about a problem can help." Pastor David picked up his mug and took a drink. "And you know anything you discuss with me is completely confidential."

"I know." Jake inhaled deeply then blew out through pursed lips. "Well, I guess I'll start at the beginning."

"The beginning is good."

Jake started with the first day Kimberly had walked into Brad's CPA office and how just her presence had made him feel young and alive again. The pastor listened patiently, nodding from time to time but never interrupted. When he finished his story, heat radiated up his neck and face. He should've known it would be humiliating to confess such intimate details, and to the pastor, no less.

"I'm glad you came to me, Jacob." He leaned forward and gave Jake a warm smile. "God knows the trials and struggles we go through. He knows all about our failures, and you know what? He loves us anyway, in spite of our downfalls."

"I've really messed up. I love my wife. For the life of me, I can't understand why I'd let myself get so carried away with another woman. Lacey has always been the love of my life."

"When you get out of sync with God, it's easy to wander down the wrong path. But now you've realized you've been treading on dangerous ground and you're willing to get back on the path God has planned for your life."

Jake shook his head. "I want that."

"We're all weak, Jake. Every single one of us. But when we confess our weaknesses to God, He is faithful to help us. The only way we can overcome the sinful desires of our human nature is to live day by day in the power of the Holy Spirit as He works through our spirit. Walking each moment by faith in God's word assures absolute victory over the desires of our sinful nature."

Jake sighed. He knew all this. Why hadn't he been applying it to his life?

The pastor reached for his well-worn Bible and opened it. "Let me share some scriptures with you."

Pastor's voice was soothing and knowing as he read and counseled Jake for the next hour. He gave Jake ample time to vent his feelings. And once he'd started, he found it easy to talk to the older man. He shared everything with his mentor, leaving out nothing and taking full responsibility for his actions.

"I'd like to see you and Lacey get involved in the *Renew Your Marriage* classes we offer. Do you think Lacey would agree to come?"

"Oh yeah. She's wanted me to get involved for quite a while, but I've balked. Thought our marriage was just fine. That's a laugh, huh?"

"Jake, not one couple I can think of has a marriage that is free from problems. A good marriage doesn't just happen. It takes work. Hard work to keep it fresh and healthy."

The meeting encouraged him. Voicing his dilemma to another human being brought things into perspective. He'd let the thing with Kimberly get out of hand. But felt certain he could get back on track. Get his heart and desires focused on Lacey.

"Just remember. When you become out of tune with God, it's hard for you to be in tune with any of the other things in your life." The reverend handed

Jake a card. "I'm just a phone call away. My cell number's on the back. Don't hesitate to call or text if you need me. And feel free to stop by anytime."

"I appreciate it." Jake scooted from his chair and stuck the card in his pocket. "You've helped me a lot."

"Before you go, I'd like to pray with you."

Jake bowed his head as the minister sent up a heartfelt prayer that Heaven surely heard.

"Thanks for everything," he said.

"Not a problem. My door's always open. Give Lacey and the boys my love."

The two men embraced in what felt to Jake like a paternal hug. Only then did he realize how much he missed those hugs from his dad.

Though the pastor had always been an inspiration to him over the years, Jake suddenly viewed him in a whole new light. He would definitely make a pretty good stand-in father.

~ ~ ~ ~ ~

Lacey paced back and forth in the kitchen, wringing her hands. She'd never felt uneasy being home alone. However, she'd never received random threats. That note had rattled her. But seeing Bandit's little head in that box was way too much to process.

All the doors and windows are locked. I double-checked. Absolutely nothing to worry about.

She pulled in a long breath, slipped onto a barstool, and chided herself into halfway believing she was making too much out of the threats. Why let a sicko get to her? If indeed it was just a sadistic joke, the perpetrator would be having a great time if he could see her now.

Maybe he can see me. A shiver raced through her body, and she tried to shake off the scary idea of eyes piercing through the walls of her home, stripping away all aspects of privacy.

Wrapping her arms around her chest, she walked to the bedroom and dug an old sweater from the closet, slipped it around her shoulders then headed back to the kitchen. She sat at the snack bar and thumbed through recipes, wishing she had something to do that would take her mind off thoughts of an empty house and puppy heads.

Dinner was ready. The boys would snack at the church, but she'd made sandwiches for later because no doubt in her mind, they'd be ready to eat again after youth group let out.

What was it with teenage boys? They never seemed to get enough to eat.

Lacey was starved. Funny how stress didn't diminish her appetite one bit. But she didn't want to eat until Jake got home.

Where was he anyway? She wished he'd hurry up. What was taking him so long? He should've been home an hour ago.

She walked to the refrigerator, opened the door, and peeked inside. She lifted the plastic wrap from the salad she'd made earlier, stole a cherry tomato, and popped it in her mouth. When Jake got home, she'd add ham and cheese cubes, slather it with ranch dressing, and the meal would be ready. Chef salad was one of Jake's favorites.

She walked back to the bar and plopped down. Why couldn't she relax? She'd never felt so antsy.

She glanced toward the window and caught a glimpse of...what? A shadow in the moonlight? A person? Fear froze her to the spot.

A pounding on the back door jolted her straight up from her seat. She almost knocked the barstool over.

She stepped quietly into the utility room. "Who's

there?"

"Mom! It's us," Todd said. "Open up."

Feeling a bit foolish, she turned the dead bolt, pushed open the door, and gave her sons a fleeting look.

"Why's the door locked?" Brian asked.

"Remember our talk last night?" She didn't mention she thought someone lurked outside. She didn't want to frighten her sons in case her imagination had played havoc on her raw emotions.

Her boys looked at her but remained silent.

Lacey raised a brow and met Brian's gaze.

"Oh!" Understanding slid across her youngest son's eyes.

"We can't take any chances. From now on, we lock doors."

"Gotcha." The reply came in unison.

"Do not forget." Lacey gave them her best *pay-attention-to-what-I'm-telling-you* look. "I want you guys to promise me you will be very careful."

They nodded, and Lacey tousled their heads then pulled them into a hug. "I love you guys."

"What's to eat?" Todd asked.

Lacey laughed. She hauled out the ham and cheese sandwiches and set the platter on the counter. Brian grabbed chips from the pantry while Todd retrieved soft drinks, popped the tops, and slid one across the bar to his brother.

"There's plenty of salad if anyone's interested."

"Naw." Brian took a swig from his soda can. "I'm good."

"None for me," Todd said. "I'll take some cheese cubes if there's extra."

"There's plenty, so eat up."

The teenagers finished a sandwich then gobbled down half a bag of chips, a tray of cubed cheddar cheese then headed upstairs.

With the boys in the house, Lacey finally relaxed to a degree. Still, her senses stayed sharp.

The muffled roar of Jake's Camaro entering the garage caught her attention.

Thank goodness, her husband was home.

~ ~ ~ ~ ~

Jake fished a flashlight from the drawer and headed outside to check around the window where Lacey indicated she may have seen movement. She was right. It was not just her imagination. Someone had been there.

He yanked the evidence tacked in place under the window. He walked inside with the bounty he'd found in his hand. "Someone was out there, Lacey. Just look."

He held up two ziplock bags. A dead bird in each slider, accompanied with a note. Bag one's note said *thanks for polio*. Bag two said *thanks for tetanus*.

"Whoever is doing this blames me for the outbreak," Lacey said. He saw her eyes fill with tears.

"I agree." Jake blew out a breath. "You are in danger, Lace. And that scares me to death."

CHAPTER THIRTY-TWO

The KY3 van from Springfield parked in front of the health department caught Lacey's attention.

She checked her watch, 7:25 a.m. She wondered how long the NBC affiliate had been camped in the parking lot. Since the first reported case of polio, the media either called or came to the health department daily, armed with cameras. Thank goodness Robert took care of the press. However, her boss was at a meeting in Jefferson City. Oh, joy. That left her to face the media. Radio was one thing, but TV made her cringe.

At least it will be taped, she thought as she parked at the rear of the building then hustled to the back door and pushed through the doorway. She tossed her jacket and purse on a chair then hustled to the break room. Minutes later, armed with caffeine, she slid behind her desk.

Her fingers raced across the keyboard, pounding out the day's press release. She proofread the hard copy, satisfied with her recitations of the latest facts. She would use the document when she talked to the reporters. The cold hard facts were in print. Twenty cases of polio, two resulting in death, two with permanent paralysis; two cases of tetanus, both resulting in death; and a 30 percent increase in influenza cases so far this year.

The public wanted the facts. Bleak though they were, she wouldn't try to fool them with false hope. People also wanted reassurance that everything would be okay, that an end to all this mayhem was in sight. As much as she ached to do so she couldn't set a timeframe. She wondered if she'd ever be able to report it was finally over.

She faxed the press release to the local media before the front doors opened. Walking to the front entrance, she pulled back her shoulders, schooled her features, and introduced herself to the TV news crew.

The two KY3 reporters were cordial and empathetic. They voiced concerns that polio would spread to their area, Greene County, only fifty miles south of Parkdale. So far, it didn't look like that would happen. The outbreak seemed confined to Lester County.

After a few minutes of discussing the situation off camera, the lead reporter held up a bubble microphone and mouthed, "Ready?"

Lacey nodded. She wished she had a sip of water to wash away the dryness in her mouth.

"This is Charles Hardy with KY3 TV reporting from Lester County Health Department in Parkdale, Missouri. I have here with me Mrs. Lacey Bookman, the Director of Nursing. Lacey, I understand the first case of polio was reported on the nineteenth of October."

"Yes, that is correct," Lacey said.

The reporter began a short overview about the seriousness of the disease and ended with a question regarding the specifics of the ailment. Lacey gave a quick synopsis of polio, including the reservoir, incubation period, mode of transmission, and period of communicability.

"Polio is a viral infection most often recognized by the acute onset of flaccid paralysis," she said. "The infection occurs in the GI tract and spreads to the regional lymph nodes. In a minority of cases, it progresses to the central nervous system."

"Can you comment on what is being done to control the spread of polio in your county?" The camera panned toward her as Charles stuck the microphone in front of her face again.

"As you probably know, we closed the elementary school where the polio started. We wanted to remove the children from an environment that could put them at an even higher risk for contracting the disease." Lacey gestured toward the building. "We've held special immunization clinics right here at the health department. Since October 20th, we've given over a hundred and fifty polio boosters."

"But." Charles looked into the camera. "Even with all your efforts, polio seems to keep spreading. Is that correct?"

"Yes." *Please don't ask me why.*

"What are you advising parents? Are there things they can do to lower the risk of their children getting this disease?"

"We encourage parents to keep their children home, away from public places, and especially away from any children who are sick. And like with any other illness, handwashing is very important. Wash your hands thoroughly and frequently. Sneeze or cough into the bend of your elbow or a tissue and throw away tissues as soon as possible. Keep your hands away from your eyes, nose, and mouth. And if your child becomes ill, call your physician immediately."

"Okay, Lacey. Now share with the viewers what is going on with the tetanus cases."

"Tetanus is not a communicable disease. That means, it is not spread from person to person. You don't catch it from anyone. Tetanus is caused by a bacterium found in soil and enters the body through breaks in the skin. Puncture wounds and wounds with a significant amount of tissue injury are more likely to promote germination. The two teens that contracted tetanus were adequately immunized and by all rights should have been protected from this disease."

"How many reported cases of polio and tetanus do you have in the county?" Charles asked.

Lacey moistened her lips and read the stats directly from her report. Most of the community was aware of the deaths and paralyses, but hearing it on TV would shock many of the residents. Some would panic and the phones at the health department would be jammed with incoming calls.

"Any ideas or insight why the polio and tetanus immunizations aren't protecting the kids like they are supposed to?" Charles asked.

"Nothing conclusive at this point." *Nothing inconclusive either,* she thought. "We are continuing to search for answers."

"Are any other agencies involved in the ongoing investigation?"

"Yes. The Missouri Department of Health and Senior Services and the Centers for Disease Control in Atlanta are actively involved." Lacey pulled in a breath. "We are in contact with them daily."

"Anything else you'd like to share with the public before we close?"

"I want to assure our community that everything possible is being done to control this outbreak. The

CDC is working around the clock. At the state level, we have epidemiology specialists working closely with us. So, I ask our community to please try to remain calm. We will continue to keep you updated daily with any information we have."

"Thank you, Lacey."

The TV crew packed their equipment and loaded it into the van. The reporter thanked her again and made his way through the parking lot that was jammed with cars. People stood outside the vehicles, talking in hushed tones.

The news van had brought out numerous spectators. Thankfully no issues occurred while the crowd observed the interview.

The rest of the day faded away in relative calm. No crisis with the clients. But KY3 wouldn't air the interview until the six p.m. edition.

~ ~ ~ ~ ~

After the first polio case, the health department boomed with activity, much busier than normal. Answering phone calls and calming the walk-ins kept the clerks hopping. Some of the questions couldn't be handled by the girls up front and were transferred to a nurse. The overflow calls and the increased number of walk-ins, coupled with the normal day-to-day business, was a strain on all the RNs.

For the past couple of weeks, Lacey looked forward to five o'clock roll around. Just getting away from all the questions—most of which had no answers—was a relief. Some days, Lacey wondered how she'd made it through all eight hours without pulling out her hair.

This was one of those days.

Blissful silence dominated her office after the front door locked behind the last client of the day. While the nursing staff finished paperwork, Lacey had one more call to make before heading home.

Beth's mother answered on the first ring and said Beth was resting. Sheila was convinced Beth would feel better once she got through the ordeal of the funeral which was scheduled for the following afternoon. Sheila thanked Lacey for checking on her daughter and said she'd be sure to let Beth know she called.

When Lacey hung up, she found herself alone in the building. The rest of the staff had slipped out while she'd been on the phone. She shut down her computer, eased into her jacket, and went to the back door. When she flipped off the light, the building became a blanket of darkness. She shivered and pushed open the door. It was much lighter outside than inside.

The chilly autumn evening felt refreshing even though the fingers of dusk had grabbed the sky. A fine mist sprinkled her face. The dark, overcast sky hinted at a full-blown thunderstorm.

No jogging tonight.

Thunder rolled in the distance, promising much-needed rain. A flash of lightning lit up the sky. The night felt ripe for tornados. *We do need the rain,* Lacey thought, but she hoped the storms passed over. *No tornados or hail, please.*

Lacey walked to her car, scooted under the wheel, and cranked the ignition. Backing out of the parking space, she felt a *thump, thump.* She pushed the gearshift into park, slid out of the car, and walked around her vehicle. She stopped with a jerk. Her startled breath rushed into her lungs like a cold wind. She hugged her jacket close to keep the chill away. Hot tears mixed with the fine mist and stung her eyes.

Her right front tire was completely flat.

CHAPTER THIRTY-THREE

Lacey pushed damp hair back from her face and stared at the flat tire. She stood rooted to the spot with feet like blocks of cement. The mist turned to a heavy drizzle, plopping on the hood of her car and dripping down in little splashes around her feet. She scanned the deserted parking lot and envisioned red-hot eyes burning into her back, watching, and ready to reel her in.

The hard fist of urgency punched her in the gut and uprooted her, and she leaped into her car and cut the engine. She raced to the back door, fumbling with keys that fell from her grip. Fighting for control, she snatched up the wet bundle and found the key she was looking for, twisted open the lock, and stumbled inside.

She flipped on the light switch, chasing away the dark shadows that hung like specters over the room, yanked the phone from her purse, and hurried into her office. Jake's voicemail made her moan. Her heart stampeded like a runaway herd of cattle as she left him a message then pounded in her home number. No answer there, either.

Eternal minutes ticked by. She paced around the

room, arms tight across her chest. Chills zigzagged between her shoulder blades. Again and again, she sidled over to the window to peer through half-closed blinds. She saw nothing unusual in the parking lot or the alley behind. She was glad the lot was so well lit. If someone was lurking out there, she'd be able to see them.

She glanced at her cell, willing it to ring. *Call me, Jake. Where are you?*

A loud clap of thunder vibrated the window, and she jumped. Her heartbeat raced. *I'm safe. Locked inside. No one can get in here. I'll just sit tight and try to hold onto my sanity until Jake calls.* She walked to her desk, plopped down, and strummed her fingers across the surface.

Once again, she tried Jake's cell and the house. No one answered and she didn't leave another message.

Too wired to stay put, she peeked through the blinds again. Rain rolled off the window in sheets, hindering her view, but the lot still appeared deserted. Her phone blared and she nearly tripped over her own feet as she dived for her cell.

"Jake," she shrieked. "Where are you?"

"He isn't coming," a muffled voice said, followed by a sadistic laugh. Then, "You're all alone...or are you? Maybe someone's watching your every move."

Lacey screamed and threw the phone down. Her fear grew claws, activating her fight or flight mode. She loped out of her office, skidded to the back door, and tore across the parking lot. Her Clinics squeaked as her feet pounded through puddles. Casey's was only six blocks away.

Rain battered her face; cold, blinding rain. She didn't care. All she could think of was getting to safety. She hit the street at a dead run. Not one car in sight, no one to flag down. Tears and rain mingled, and she could barely see two feet in front of her. Her breath came in ragged bursts. She ran, one block then the next, moist air filling her lungs, and her shoes splashed through ringlets of running water. When she made a right on Clark Street, she saw the lights of the convenience store.

Thank God. Only two more blocks.

Hang on.

She rounded the end of Clark and hit Jefferson at full speed. Her heart pumped frantically, her legs churned and though her nurse's shoes were soaked, she kept pace. Just one more block.

Almost there.

Air heaved from her in gasps, her heartbeats an earthquake in her chest. She flung terrorized glances over her shoulder, expecting someone to grab her any second.

She flew by two cars parked in front of the quick shop and fishtailed to the entrance. She shot through the glass doors like a warhead and met the suspicious eyes of a blonde, blue-eyed thirty-something clerk who wore a Yellowjacket's sweatshirt and too much makeup. She popped her gum as she eyed Lacey.

Lacey could only imagine how she must look with her hair wet and matted to her head. Her clothes clung to her body and rainwater dripped on the floor. She probably had raccoon eyes from her mascara and eyeliner unless it had completely washed off.

"Please," Lacey gasped, struggling for control. "Call me a cab."

The clerk just looked at her with narrowed eyes.

"I had a flat tire. I need a cab to get home." Lacey managed not to choke on the words.

The woman dragged a cell phone from behind the counter with an exaggerated sigh then punched in numbers. "I need a cab at 1222 North Jefferson," she said then looked at Lacey. "Where you going?"

Lacey rattled off the address.

The clerk repeated it into the phone then hung up. "Five minutes." She looked her up and down with a skeptical gaze. "He said he'll be here in five."

"Thank you." Lacey walked to the door and stood to the side, trying to make herself small and inconspicuous. A memory suddenly surfaced in her temporal lobe, and she realized she'd left the health department without her purse. She had no money or ID on her. If no one was home, how would she pay the cab driver?

Her head spun into rewind, pausing at the fifty dollars she kept stashed in her jewelry box for emergencies. This was an emergency, or as close to one as she'd ever want to get. She'd stashed ten five-dollar bills in there a couple of years ago. Every time she'd used some of the cash, she'd replaced it. That would be more than enough to pay the fare.

CHAPTER THIRTY-FOUR

Jake closed the Emerson folder and slid it into his briefcase. He'd fine-tune it that evening and turn it in to Brad first thing in the morning. If things had been different, he'd have gone over the file with Kimberly, explaining the escrow in detail, but she'd been steering clear of him.

Kimberly had gone out of her way to ignore him all day, even turning away when she met him in the hall. If that was how she wanted to play it, fine with him. He could deal with that kind of behavior. In fact, he preferred it to her sexy, come-and-get-me façade.

But he couldn't dump the entire gaffe on her. He'd been a willing participant until the flirtation had escalated to a code-red alert. After confessing everything to the pastor yesterday, he'd finally been able to put his feelings in perspective. Accept his share of the blame. Take responsibility for his bad choices and stop putting himself in a position that could ruin him, his marriage. He'd been too wrapped up in himself to see or even care where his infatuation with Kimberly was headed.

As he snapped shut the valise, the intercom buzzed. "Jake," Brad said. "I need to see you in my office for a few minutes."

Jake looked at his watch. Almost five. He sighed. "I'm on my way."

He headed down the hall, tapped on Brad's open door, and stepped inside. Brad looked up and plopped down his pen. His brows creased over troubled eyes. His desk was characteristically cluttered with papers, paper clips, folders, mail, and three almost-empty cups that looked like they were about to grow something funky.

"What's up?" Jake asked and sat down.

"Kimberly just paid me a little visit."

"Still pushing for a 'real client?'" Jake made air quotes and chuckled.

Brad snorted. "I *wish* it was that simple."

Jake's gut churned and he shifted in his chair. He didn't like the sound of Brad's tone.

"Kimberly has filed a sexual harassment complaint against you."

The words struck Jake like a blow to the gut. He shot up from his chair and Brad motioned him down. Nonplused, he submitted.

"She says you've been behaving a little too friendly, if you know what I mean." Brad coughed into his fist. "I don't have to remind you about the sexual harassment policy. You know we have a zero tolerance for any of that nonsense around here."

Jake's jaw dropped and he squeezed his eyes shut. His boss looked too solemn to be joking. Plus, Brad would never kid around about something so serious. He scooted to the edge of his chair, leaned forward, and pressed his hands on the desk.

"Listen, Brad, even the flirtation thing is over with now. There were, well, a couple recent incidents that got out of hand. But I let her know in no uncertain terms she had to back off."

"Kimberly's story is a bit different." Brad rubbed his chin. "In fact, a whole lot different."

Jake's cell phone vibrated but he ignored it. He was fuming. He'd like to strangle Kimberly. What in the world was she trying to prove? And how had he ever let himself get caught up in her games?

"I can't believe this." Jake shook his head. "You know me better than that. I'd never harass anyone."

Brad caught his lower lip between his teeth and eyed Jake. Silence hovered between them for several uncomfortable seconds.

"I've got to follow up on this. It's my job. You know that," Brad finally said. He sighed. "Kimberly says you have been pursuing her for weeks, insisting she see you after working hours. She alleges that when she finally had the courage to tell you she wasn't interested, you physically accosted her. You pushed her into the storage closet and had your hands all over her."

Heat rushed up Jake's neck and settled on his face. Blood boiled in his veins. "That's not true. Brad, she's lying."

"I don't doubt that." Brad scooted his chair back and walked around his desk. He squeezed Jake's shoulder. "Hey, I believe you. But I've got to follow up on any complaint I get. Fill out a report. You know the routine."

Jake nodded. "I know."

"You need to watch yourself around her. Don't ever, and I mean never, not even for one minute, be alone with her. And whatever you do, don't give her any ammunition to use against you. She's out for blood. I could see it in her eyes." Brad stepped back and leaned a hip against his desk. "She's a user, Jake. I know her type. I'm not stupid. I know she's lying through her teeth. I'd fire her right now, but she would scream I was messing with her constitutional rights."

Jake pulled in a breath. His indiscretions had caught up with him. Yes, Kimberly was lying, but she wouldn't have had anything to base her lie on if he'd behaved like a married man should have. He couldn't figure out who he was angrier with—her, or himself.

"You flirted with her way too much, but I know you'd never force yourself on her." Brad laughed without a hint of humor. "Or anyone else, for that matter."

"I let things go too far, I admit that. And I could kick myself for being so stupid."

"If it'd do any good, I'd kick your butt for you. I hate to say I told you so, but I did warn you."

"I know." Jake huffed out a disgusted breath. "And just so you know, there was a closet incident. But she pulled *me* in and kissed *me*. And yes, I did respond at first. But when I came to my senses, I got out of that closet as fast as I could. We went to my office, and I laid it on the line. I knew she was mad, but I never dreamed she'd pull something like this."

Brad slapped his ample thighs. "She's mad, all right. But she'll just have to get over it."

"Yeah. I hope so," he said, but the uneasy feeling in his gut told him she wasn't done making his life miserable.

"Listen to me, buddy." Brad pointed a warning finger at him. "Just keep away from her."

"Don't worry."

I've had it. I intend to stay as far away from her as I can.

Brad walked around his desk and let his weight fall into the chair. "Don't forget the meeting we have with Homestead Industries first thing in the morning."

Jake nodded.

"And Ms. Ames isn't sitting in on this one."

When Jake left Brad's office, Kimberly stood by the water fountain with a smirk plastered across her face. She must have stayed late, assuming they'd be talking about her accusation. Jake tamped down the urge to let her have it full force. Instead, he nodded politely then breezed by her.

He dragged his cell out of his pocket. Two missed calls from Lacey. He checked his voicemail.

And raced to his car.

CHAPTER THIRTY-FIVE

Ten minutes passed—not the five he'd promised—before the taxi driver pulled in front of Casey's. Relentless rain pummeled the night but it didn't matter. Lacey couldn't get any wetter if she tried.

Thunder rolled in the distance and a single streak of lightning broke into forks, zigzagging across the sky. She dashed to the cab, pulled open the back door, and plopped, wet and cold, onto the vinyl seat. Instantly, goose bumps stood at attention on her flesh.

A few minutes later, relieved to be home and thankful for her jewelry box stash, Lacey paid the driver and watched him drive away.

She pushed the door closed behind her and twisted the dead bolt then slammed the brass chain in place. All the lights were on, and the message light on the phone blinked green, but she ignored it. She picked up the handset and called Jake's cell. He answered, sounding flustered, on the first ring.

"Lacey, where are you? I got your message and went to the health department and found your car. I swung by the house and Todd and Brian said they hadn't seen you. We loaded up in my car and we've been driving around looking for you. Are you okay?"

Lacey blurted out her story in gasps. It didn't make much sense even to her. She was blubbering a mile a minute, trying to tell Jake everything at once and getting nowhere fast.

"Stay on the phone," he said. "Keep talking to me. I'm on my way home."

By the time she saw Jake's headlights, she had related most of what had happened. She flung herself through the garage door, dripping wet and still sobbing. He put his arms around her and pressed her against his chest. His leather jacket was reassuringly smooth and retained a rain-like aroma. She sank into the security of his embrace and breathed in the humid air mixed with a hint of lime.

Unspoken questions slipped across Todd's and Brian's faces, but she saw Jake motion for them to go inside.

"Did you recognize the voice on the phone?" Jake guided her into the kitchen. "Do you think you've heard it before?"

"No." Lacey thought a second. "I don't know. It was... Well, it sounded artificial. It could have been a man talking in a high-pitched voice. I'm just not sure. I was so scared, I couldn't think. I just wanted to get away from there."

"How about the phone number? Did you recognize it?"

"No. But I never really paid attention. I thought it was you, so I answered."

"You're trembling, Lace." He draped his arm around her. "You're so cold and wet. Let's get you out of these clothes and into a nice warm tub."

Lacey looked down at her dripping scrubs and muddy Clinics, thinking she must look even worse than she felt.

Jake nudged her up the stairs, stepped ahead of her

into the master bath and turned on the water. He dumped in a capful of bubble bath. "You're gonna feel a lot better when you warm up."

Lacey doubted she'd ever feel better, but she peeled off her clothes and slid into the foaming water. Jake pulled out his cell and called Captain D's. He ordered a large family meal with extra hush puppies. When he hung up, he phoned City Hall and asked for Detective Prater.

Lacey zoned out, only half hearing Jake relay the earlier events to the officer. She figured nothing could be done. Just like the other times. No one was ever around to see anything tangible.

Lacey had to admit she felt better after the soak in the tub, less chilled at least, and that was something. She slipped into sweats, stuffed her feet in her Camels, and plodded downstairs. Jake and the boys were setting Styrofoam containers of fish on the bar.

Lacey hoisted herself up on a stool.

"I'm sorry you couldn't get us when you called, Mom," Todd said. "I was on the phone."

"That's okay, honey."

"I heard the beep a couple times but never figured it'd be you. I should've clicked over and—"

"Don't worry about it. I'm fine. Really."

Todd looked a little pale. Lacey winced. She must have scared him with all her hysterics.

"Hey, I said it's okay." She tousled his hair. "I'm sorry I lost it in front of you guys. I didn't mean to upset you."

"No wonder you were freakin'," Brian said. "I would've lost it, too."

Jake dished food on paper plates and they ate around the snack bar. After dinner, Brian stayed with Lacey while Todd and Jake went to the health department, changed her tire, dropped the flat at

Walmart, and brought both cars home. They returned drenched.

"The rain's not let up any." Jake hung his raincoat on a peg in the utility room while Todd shed his shoes and headed toward the stairs.

"Was everything quiet at the office?" Lacey asked.

Jake nodded and kicked off his shoes. They landed with a thud in front of the dryer.

"I don't know what I expected you'd find..."

"Why would anyone want to be out getting into meanness on a night like this?" Jake pulled off his long-sleeved shirt and tossed it on the washer. "I'm hitting the shower."

Lacey stayed on his heels and plopped down on the commode lid. She wrapped her arms tight across her chest and waited while he showered. It would be the next day before they officially found out what had caused her flat. But she didn't need anyone to confirm it. In her heart, she knew it had been deliberate. Someone was out to get her.

"How could anyone slash my tire in the parking lot without someone seeing them?" Lacey asked and handed Jake a towel. "The others hadn't been gone that long by the time I headed to my car. Someone is watching me. Watching everything I do."

Jake rubbed the towel over his wavy hair. "It sure looks like it." He tossed the towel over the shower bar and gave her a fleeting look.

"What I can't figure out is why. Why you, Lace? It's got to be more than the polio outbreak."

CHAPTER THIRTY-SIX

She poured Asti Spumante from the half-empty bottle on the end table and took a long drink, letting the bubbles tease her nose. She leaned back on the sofa in front of the fifty-two-inch Sony, wiggled her arms into a bright-blue Snuggie, and stretched her legs on top of the coffee table. Rain pounded mercilessly on the windows. She tossed a handful of popcorn into her mouth and chewed as she absently watched *Survivor*.

Lacey thought she was a survivor, but she was dead wrong. Lacey wouldn't survive—she'd see to that. She laughed when she thought of the sopping-wet woman running in to Casey's like a lunatic.

Cutting her tire had been so easy this time. Easier than Jake's at the restaurant with all those people around. This time, she just walked by Lacey's car on the way to her own, bent down, and raked the box-cutter's blade along the whitewall.

Then she parked across the street and waited. She hadn't been able to see Lacey's face when she found the flat tire, but her body language spoke volumes. Poor little Lacey had been scared to death. She'd just about ripped the back door off the hinges trying to get inside.

Outside, the thunder crashed. She liked storms, enjoyed the thrill of wind-driven rain blowing hard across dark skies, whipping sheets of water against her plate glass windows while the branches on the oak trees in front of her house bent in the wind, genuflecting to a higher power. Nothing she relished more than a full-blown thunderstorm.

She palmed a handful of popcorn and tossed a fluffy kernel into her mouth. Yes, her plan was going beautifully. Polio, tetanus, and flu were on the rampage.

And, Robert, your precious Lacey is powerless to stop them.

Unlike Lacey running scared, she was the one calling the shots. Completely in control while Lacey freaked out.

CHAPTER THIRTY-SEVEN

The next morning, Lacey woke with a start. She turned on her side and felt for Jake. His side of the mattress was vacant. She rolled out of bed and pulled open the blinds to a clear sky. She blinked the brightness from her bleary eyes and headed downstairs.

Lacey padded into the kitchen in a white terrycloth robe and fuzzy yellow slippers and found Jake sitting at the bar with the *Parkdale Daily Record*.

"What are you doing up so early?" she asked.

"Couldn't sleep." Jake wore gray sweats and Nikes. He tossed her a smile. "Coffee's made."

"Good." Lacey pulled a cup from the cabinet, filled it, and topped off Jake's half-full mug. He gave her a thank-you wink.

"Doughnut?" Jake motioned toward a plate stacked with pastries.

"Oh yeah." She picked up a glazed doughnut and eyed her husband. "You've already been out this morning?"

"I figured you could use a sugar fix."

"You're sweet." Lacey grabbed a pastry and took a bite. "It's yummy. Thanks. It's nice to have such a thoughtful husband."

"No problem." He leaned over and swiped a finger across her jaw, capturing doughnut granules like a magnet. He slurped the sweetness from his fingertip and laughed. "Tasty."

That made Lacey chuckle. Despite her mood, Jake could always make her laugh. He was quite a cutup when he wanted to be, but he hadn't clowned around much lately. Not with her anyway. She wiped her mouth with a napkin and said, "I'm messy this morning, huh?"

"You're fine. Just enjoy."

Jake pushed aside the newspaper and they fell into a light banter, both hedging around the previous night's events and just enjoying the moment. She missed quiet mornings with him, but their conflicting schedules had put a stop to that a long time ago.

Two cups of coffee and two doughnuts later, Lacey glanced at the wall clock and hopped off the stool.

"I've gotta get ready for work. Thanks for the coffee and doughnuts." She kissed him full on the mouth. "And thanks for just being you. I love you, you know?"

"I love you, too, Lacey," he said a little too seriously and gave her a flinty look. "Don't ever doubt that."

Why would she doubt it? She looked into his troubled blue eyes and wondered for the umpteenth time what was bothering him and why he wouldn't open up to her. It was something more than the stalker, but she didn't have time to get into it. She was already late for work. Well, late for her.

She took a quick shower, blow-dried her hair, dabbed blush on her cheeks and gloss on her lips then dashed to her car. Ten minutes later, when she stepped into the break room at work, she found the coffee already made and it smelled scrumptious. She was ready for a third cup.

Ann filled a mug and offered it to her.

"Thanks," Lacey said. "You're early again this morning."

"No." Ann turned up her wrist and tapped the face of her Timex. "You're later than usual. Bad morning?"

"Actually, a good morning. Jake was up early, believe it or not, and had coffee and doughnuts waiting. We lingered over breakfast like we used to do pre-kids, pre-job, pre-life." Lacey laughed. "We never get a chance to do that through the week."

"What was the occasion?"

"Jake was just trying to make it a nice morning for me after what happened last night."

"What—"

Lacey threw up a hand. "I'll tell you and the other girls about it in a few minutes. I don't want to have to repeat the story a dozen times. Let me get the press release out first."

"Okay." Ann looked baffled but let it go.

A few minutes later, after Lacey faxed the press release, she cornered her nurses and shared the unnerving events of the previous night. When she finished, three sets of wide, shocked eyes stared at her.

Betty's brows knitted together. "Good grief! We shouldn't have bailed on you last night."

"That's not gonna happen again." Joan shook her head. "You'll never be the last one to leave. If you have to stay late, we stay, too."

"Who in their right mind would have the nerve to slash your tire in the parking lot?" Ann paced around the workstation. "In broad daylight, no less?"

"Well." Joan narrowed her eyes. "It's got to be the same weirdo that slashed Jake's tire in Springfield."

"I'm sorry we weren't here." Betty gathered Lacey into a hug.

That did it. The levee broke. Lacey buried her head in Betty's shoulder, which smelled of vanilla and hairspray, and sobbed until she had hiccups. When she regained some measure of control, she stepped back and wiped her eyes with the tissue Ann handed her.

She took a deep breath, trying to reclaim her professionalism and scolded herself for breaking down in front of her subordinates. She'd never done that before. They were her friends, but at work she stuck to her role as leader. She was their boss, after all, and they looked to her for strength. Guidance. Not a weepy, out-of-control woman who needed to be coddled.

"I hope you guys know this isn't going to interfere with my job," she said. "I'm still able to focus. I'm not gonna fall apart on you."

"Of course you're not," Betty said.

The other nurses nodded in agreement.

"Don't worry," Ann said. "No one's as good at her job as you are. We all know that."

Joan gave her a big smile. "You the woman."

Ann laughed and characteristically launched into a long monologue about her vision of Lacey's future. How she felt certain Lacey would get through this and come out shining, rise above all her trials. By the end of the lengthy and somewhat mundane exposition, Lacey felt herself smiling.

"You guys are the best." Lacey was thankful for their love and support. What would she do without her nurses? "Now, I've got work to do."

~ ~ ~ ~ ~

The morning flew by quickly. Despite what she'd said to her RNs, Lacey had trouble concentrating.

Couldn't focus. Could hardly think.

Jake called and said he'd picked up her tire on his way to work. Just as they'd suspected, it had been slashed, same as his. He'd taken the information to the police station and talked to Detective Prater. Still no leads.

Of course there weren't.

Just before lunch, Susan phoned from the hospital. She'd received confirmed lab reports on three new cases of polio. Each case fit the same scenario as the previous ones.

Lacey hung up and sighed. Twenty-three cases of polio. She dropped her face into the circle of her arms and wept yet again.

Would this ever end?

CHAPTER THIRTY-EIGHT

"Aren't you afraid you'll get your tire slashed hanging around with me?" Lacey said as she slid out of Amber's car Saturday afternoon at the mall.

"Hey! It's not funny, you know." Amber shot her a stern look over the top of her Accord.

Her friend looked classy in a brown leather jacket over tight Levis and a V-neck cardigan in muted hues of red, brown, and beige. The sweater complemented the new cherry-red FatBabys she'd bought the previous week at the Super Saturday Sidewalk Sale downtown. They'd stood in line for almost an hour, but Amber was determined not to let the forty-two-dollar boots get away even though she already had four pairs of FatBabys in her closet. Not counting her Lacers and Ropers. But who was counting? And she did look hot in her bargain boots.

Her friend tucked an unruly curl behind her ear. "Don't kid around. I'm worried about you."

"Who's kidding? Two slashings in two weeks?" Lacey lifted a shoulder. "Seems like my luck's bottomed out lately."

"I don't believe in luck. Neither do you."

"Well, my providence hasn't been going so well,

then."

Amber shook her head and chuckled. She hooked an arm through Lacey's as they trekked inside and made a beeline for JC Penney's.

"So, who's getting married?" Amber asked. "Remind me again."

"My cousin, Sue. Don't tell me you've forgotten her? Nobody forgets Sue. Tall, red hair, freckles, loud mouth."

"I think it's coming back to me." Amber looked thoughtful and tapped a finger against her temple, faking a sudden memory. "Oh yeah, she's the one that's marrying that gorgeous hunk from Joplin, right?"

"Yep. If you like the all-muscle, no-brain type," Lacey said, and Amber laughed.

The women sidestepped shoppers, hustled across JC Penney's threshold, and turned into the linen department. Lacey scanned the shelves for something perfect for Sue. There were so many choices with so many colors and patterns.

"Is Jake going to church with you again tomorrow?" Amber asked.

"Yeah." Lacey tugged out a set of sheets. "I feel like I'm getting my old Jake back again. Almost."

"Almost?"

"There's still something going on with him. I can feel it."

"Are you sure? You've been under a lot of stress lately. Maybe—"

"I'm not imagining it, Amb." Lacey sighed. "I can't explain it to you. I can't even figure it out myself. But something is bothering him and he's not sharing it with me. He used to be so open with me. It really galls me that he won't let me in."

"Just hang tight. I know Jake. He can't hold out on

you for long. Whatever it is, maybe he just doesn't want to worry you with all that's going on in your life right now."

"And maybe I'm making too much out of it. I don't know. I just hate it when he shuts me out. If he's got a problem, I want to know about it."

"You mean *fix* it."

"What can I say?" Lacey shrugged and traded the pack of sheets for another. "Nurses are fixers."

"They can't fix everything, you know."

"Yeah. That's what you keep telling me."

"Then pay attention. For once." Amber's mouth formed a smile.

Lacey rifled through the entire top shelf and started on the second, wondering if she was way too picky. About the sheets. About Jake.

"Here you go." Amber held up a set of matching light-beige sheets and pillowcases. Plain. No design. "These are perfect."

Lacey eyed the sheets skeptically and laughed. "Isn't that just a little bit too drab for a wedding gift?"

"Drab?" Amber raised a brow. "Since you don't know her colors, you're gonna have to go with something a little subdued. Trust me."

Lacey turned up the price tag and shook her head. "Why in the world would something you just lay on at night cost so much?"

"Penny pincher."

"Spendthrift."

"Me? No way!"

"Way." Lacey pointed at her red boots. "I rest my case."

"Touché." Amber chuckled and picked up a bright-orange throw pillow from a bin. "Get the sheets, toss in the pillow and viola! You've got color."

Lacey tossed the pillow back in the bin then tucked

the beige sheet set under her arm. "Come on. Let's get out of here so we can go do some fun stuff."

"Hey, don't buy it if you're not sure. I was just trying to be helpful."

"If you think it's appropriate, my friend, then it's appropriate. I'm sure Sue will love it. Mr. Muscle-bound will love it. I love it."

She aimed Amber toward the front of the store. The pair fell into step, matching the brand-new FatBabys to Lacey's well-worn Nikes.

At the counter, a young man in a crisp white button-down shirt and pressed black trousers scanned Lacey's Visa. His longish hair, a suspicious shade of black, covered his earlobes in a stylish feathered cut. He was reasonably handsome with smooth skin and no crow's-feet around bright hazel eyes. He handed the card back to Lacey with a nod.

"Do you gift wrap here?" she asked.

"Yes, ma'am. You can pick it up when you finish shopping if you'd like."

"Sounds like a plan."

"What's the occasion?"

"A wedding." Lacey smiled and slipped from the store with Amber.

"Ma'am?" Lacey rolled her eyes. "Sheesh, that makes me feel old."

"Naw. You shouldn't. He's just young."

"Either way, it's not much of a morale booster."

They strolled down a wide corridor with shiny tiles, chatting and checking out the window displays. Something suddenly dawned on Lacey, and she whirled around to face Amber.

"Look around you."

Amber's gaze scanned the area. A puzzled look crimped her brow. "What?"

"Look at all the kids that are here today." Lacey

counted a dozen children weaving among the teenagers and adults. She lifted her arms, palms up. "And we're in the middle of a polio outbreak."

"Yep. The parents lack good common sense if you ask me."

"Of all the places to keep your kid away from, it would be the mall, for pity's sake. And look at them. Running around like nothing's going on. Is the school closing a wasted attempt to protect the children? Why won't people listen?"

"I listen. I haven't taken Suzie anywhere. We've even skipped Sunday School the last two weeks."

"Yeah, but you don't count. If you didn't pay attention to me, I'd harm you." Lacey lifted a clenched fist for emphasis and Amber laughed. "Every day in my press release, I stress the importance of keeping kids away from crowds. That's where all the germs are. Maybe I didn't stress the *stay-at-home* part forcefully enough. In the press release, right?"

"Don't spaz—it's not your fault. It's up to you to get the word out, which you've done over and over. But it's up to them to follow the directions. You can lead a horse to water..."

"But you can't make him drink."

They burst into laughter at the old-fashioned phrase. The one Amber used more times than Lacey could count. They fell into step again and Amber sobered.

"It's the truth. You're not responsible for these people." She waved at the crowd. "I don't understand why you let it bother you. Good grief, Lacey, getting all bent out of shape doesn't help one bit. You need to relax, girlfriend."

"I guess I do get a little carried away sometimes."

"Uh, hello, ya think?"

Amber looked her straight in the eye in her up-front way that was second nature to her, and Lacey had to admit she had a point.

"Quit being so right."

"Can't. It's a curse. I'm always right."

Lacey gave her friend a playful nudge and smack in the ribs. They continued down the hall and before she knew it, Lacey found herself in front of Fudge Galore with a growling stomach.

"Now how'd we end up here?" She faked a frown, but Amber wasn't buying it.

"Oh, okay." Amber nudged her through the doorway. "Come on, sweet tooth, my treat."

The blissful smell of chocolate and peanut butter made Lacey salivate like one of Pavlov's dogs. She pretended she wasn't excited as she made a beeline to the counter.

An hour later, arms loaded with bags and the taste of fudge lingering on her tongue, Lacey walked with Amber across the parking lot. They both had a sugar high and giggled like carefree teenagers.

The good mood ended abruptly.

Someone had keyed Amber's car.

CHAPTER THIRTY-NINE

Jake almost skipped his workout at the gym Monday morning. He hated leaving Lacey at home. The boys were still in bed, so she wasn't alone. Still, he felt a little uneasy, but she'd insisted he go.

"You can't babysit me every second of the day," she'd said as she herded him out the door. He knew she was right. They needed to keep some sort of normalcy about their life and not give the stalker any more power over them.

Stalker. A knot of resentment tightened in Jake's chest. He hopped off the stair-stepper after thirty minutes of ascending to nowhere and pulled in a breath. Even the thought of someone stalking Lacey infuriated him. What kind of person would do that? And the lowlife was branching out. First, Lacey's mother then Amber. No matter what Detective Prater thought, he'd never be convinced the car-keying had been random.

And though he hated to admit it, even to himself, he was more convinced than ever that Kimberly was the stalker. No one else made sense. He worried that not only was Kimberly putting his wife in danger, but he was the reason why. If Lacey ever found out, she would never forgive him.

He would never forgive himself.

Lacey tried to hide it, but she was terrified. She'd been so jumpy lately, hadn't been herself in days. Fatigue was taking its toll. He'd noticed dark circles under her eyes that hadn't been there before.

He wasn't sleeping much better, but it wasn't entirely because of the stalker. He was torn between telling Lacey about Kimberly and putting the whole mess behind him. One part of him said he needed to come clean. Confess and ask her to forgive him. The other part, knowing how it would affect her, said to just forget it. After all, nothing really happened. It wasn't like he'd had an affair. Why hurt Lacey by admitting to something already resolved? Taken care of and filed in his *Stupid-Things-I've-Done* file.

When he finished lifting the free weights, he was hot, sweaty. He showered and dressed in the men's locker room then hustled out of the gym.

Still mulling over the idea of telling Lacey about Kimberly, he pulled into the office parking lot. With the harassment complaint hanging over his head, he might be forced to tell his wife everything.

The first person he saw when he slid out of his car was Kimberly. She waited for him in the middle of the parking lot, wearing a form-fitting lavender sweater over tan thigh-hugging pants and black spike heels. He wondered how her poor feet survived when she pranced around practically on tiptoe all day.

"Hey, Jake." She slipped her hand through the crook of his arm and smiled, like she hadn't been ignoring him. Like she hadn't told Brad a pack of lies. "How's it going?"

"Great." Jake gently yet firmly pulled his arm away. "Let's not start this stuff again."

"Stuff? What stuff?" she asked with ersatz

innocence, batting her thick lashes.

"No more games, Kimberly."

"I'm not playing games. I'm just trying to be friendly."

He stopped and faced her. "I want to be friendly, too. But that's all. No touching. No words with underlying meanings. If you can do that, then I'm all for being friendly."

She stepped closer and tipped her head to the side and gave him a crooked grin. "You can't be close to me without wanting to take me in your arms, can you, Jake? Remember how it felt? You liked it. A whole lot. And I know it's just a matter of time until I have you in my—"

"Stop it." He threw out one hand. Heat rushed up his neck and spread across his face. Why couldn't he make her understand he was through with this fantasy? "That's never going to happen. Never, with a capital N."

Her brows knit together over narrow eyes.

He walked away and left her staring after him.

~ ~ ~ ~ ~

Jake slipped into his chair and let his head fall into his hands. Kimberly's musky scent lingered in his mind. How easy to pick up where they'd left off, give in to the recently vetoed desire that pulsed through his veins. But her harassment claim doused the fire. No one liked being manipulated.

A throat clearing jarred him. Kimberly stood in the doorway, leg beveled, with a coy smile spread across her face. She winked seductively, caught her lower lip between her teeth then sashayed down the hall.

Fifteen minutes later, she returned. "Did you miss me? I missed you." She twisted a lock of hair between her fingers. "I could sure use some attention from my sweet, sexy man."

"Kimberly, I told you—"

He stopped mid-sentence when she disappeared down the hall. Disgusted with her shenanigans, he got down to business on a report he'd put off for over a week.

Twenty minutes in, Kimberly sauntered through the doorway and plopped down in front of his desk. She puckered her lips into a fake pout and fluttered her lashes.

"What do you want?" he asked.

"Why are you so mean to me?"

Jake looked away, rolled his eyes.

"I want us to be close again. I miss you."

"Apparently you aren't getting the message. There is no us."

She lifted a brow. "There is, too. And you know it as well as I do. Come on, you can't deny what's been happening between us. It's bigger than both of us. Why fight it?"

Jake clamped his teeth together. He could deal with her silent treatment—in fact had welcomed it. But this? She was acting like they were lovers who'd had a spat.

"I don't have time for this. Now if you don't mind, I've got work to do."

She didn't budge. Jake came close to losing his cool.

"Okay. I'm gonna ask you nicely. Please leave."

"Huh-uh." The hint of a smirk touched the corners of her lips. "No way."

Needles of apprehension pricked his gut. "I don't want you in here. Now take a hike." He picked up a random paper and pretended to read.

She strutted to his desk, grabbed his tie, and pulled

him toward her.

He pushed her back and said, "Get out of here, or I'm gonna call Brad."

She frowned. Grabbed at his tie again. He threw up a defensive hand and yanked up the phone with his other. He was through giving in to her.

Just then, Brad stepped through the doorway and Jake hung up. Thank goodness his boss happened to pop in at the exact moment he was needed.

Kimberly stiffened and stepped back. Brad pointed a beefy finger at her and said through tight lips, "I want to see you in my office. Now!"

She blanched and glared at Jake as she stomped out.

"I heard." Brad laid a hand on Jake's shoulder. "All of it. And she's outta here." He pivoted on a smooth sole and closed Jake's door behind him.

Things were spinning out of control again, and Jake had an uneasy feeling.

CHAPTER FORTY

Friday morning, Lacey plopped down at her desk armed with precisely nothing except impressions and guesses and a lot of trepidation. She was exhausted. Another week slipped by in a flurry of new polio cases, two more tetanus fatalities, and influenza at the all-time high in Lester County. She flipped through the flu reports piled high on her desk.

Halfway through, she noticed a trend, something she'd dismissed as not being prevalent before. She sucked in a gulp of air and thumbed through the reports one by one, checking every detail, her eyes racing over a specific line item.

Cold prickles crept across the back of her neck. Suddenly it all came together. The missing link. She was on to something; she could feel it deep in her gut. She felt certain something *was* happening to the vaccines. *In* the health department.

She snatched up the phone and frantically pounded in Darrell's number. When he answered, she blurted out, "I've got something, Darrell. I finally figured it out."

"Slow down." Darrell chuckled.

Lacey paused and took a deep breath.

"Tell me. What have you got?"

"All of our flu, polio, and tetanus cases received their immunizations at the health department. Most of the children in our community get their shots here, so it isn't unusual that all the cases of polio and tetanus were vaccinated here. But with the flu shots, that's a different story. Three-fourths of the clients receive the flu shot at the doctor's office or other community clinics. We only vaccinate about one-fourth of the population. Every case of influenza that's been reported received the flu shot right here at the health department. Every one, Darrell. People getting their shots elsewhere aren't coming down with the flu."

Lacey's words tumbled out faster than she could breathe. "Holly, our first case of polio, got her IPV booster here. Her parents got their boosters at the doctor's office. All three of them were in Nigeria around the same people, but Holly was the only one who came down with polio. I don't know what yet, but I'm telling you, something is happening to the vaccines in our office. That has to be it. Don't you see? Nothing else adds up."

Darrell fell silent and she gave him a moment to digest her words. When he finally spoke, he said, "Lacey, are you sure about the flu cases? No one who received a flu shot outside your office contracted influenza?"

"Nope. Not one single person."

"Are you serious?" Darrell's voice kicked up an octave. "Whoa."

"It's the flu cases that finally tipped me off."

"You know, I think you could be right."

"I know I am. This isn't a coincidence. I just know it. But now I have to figure out what's happening to the vaccines once we get them."

"Joe tells me you ruled out the compromised vaccine theory. The refrigerator checked out. The logs show no problem."

"Right." Lacey sighed. "But there must be a reason why we are the only county experiencing these diseases. I'm just going to have to dig deeper. It's occurring somehow in this office."

"If you need help, Joe and Linda are available to come back down."

"Thanks. I'll let you know if I need them."

Lacey clicked off the line and stared at her reports. What was happening in this office? Could there be a problem with the fridge even though it appeared to be working properly?

She pushed away from her desk and paced across her small office. She tapped her forehead with the heel of her hand. *Think. Think. Think.*

A light switched on in her head, chasing away the fog. Logic wormed its way into her brain. Of course nothing was wrong with the refrigerator. If that was the case, then all the vaccines would be compromised, not just the polio, tetanus, and influenza. It had to be something else. She slipped back in her chair and pored over the reports again.

Something was compromising just certain vaccines in the facility. Between the time they arrived until they were refrigerated. But what? Her nurses were careful about monitoring the vaccines, making sure they were taken care of properly from the time they arrived in the office until they were administered.

Human error could occur though. An isolated incident could happen with one vial of vaccine...it might accidently have been left out of the refrigerator overnight and put back in the next morning. But Lacey couldn't imagine one of her nurses being so careless. They'd never put a vial of vaccine back in the refrigerator if they found it sitting on the counter. Besides, she was looking at numerous vials, not just one isolated incident.

Lacey hustled to the nurses' station, cornered her RNs, and relayed her theory. "Think back, guys. Walk me through what you do, step by step, when a shipment of vaccine arrives."

Her three RNs shot her puzzled looks. Each nurse, in turn, described in detail the steps involved when she received a new batch of vaccine. All accounts were the same and everything had been handled properly when a vaccine shipment was received..

"Well, something is happening to the vaccines. More specifically, something is happening to the polio, tetanus, and influenza vaccines. We need to pick our brains. We've got to figure out what's going on."

"I don't understand what we could have done to mess up any of the vaccines." Ann's eyes formed blue slits. "And you're not talking about one shipment. Good grief, you're talking batch after batch."

"Even the flu vaccine came in three different shipments on three different days." Betty sounded flustered and her mouth pulled into a frown.

"I know. That's why it's so puzzling." Lacey scanned their icy expressions. "Sheesh, don't be so defensive. I'm not accusing anyone of anything. But something is happening and until I can figure out what, I'm going to keep looking. *You're* going to keep looking. We've got to figure out what's going on."

The nurses shared scorching looks then eyed Lacey. She could almost smell their simmering flesh. They formed a fortress against her; Ann and Betty in their cartoon-character scrubs and Joan in her solid blue plain-Janes.

"Hey, guys, don't balk on me now. Please."

Betty shrugged. "I don't know what you expect us to do."

"Help me brainstorm so we can stop these outbreaks."

"Lacey, I can't imagine we're doing something to the vaccines in the few minutes between checking it in and putting it away." Joan shook her head. "I think you're way off base. I know you're trying to get a handle on this, but I tell you, we aren't compromising the blasted vaccine."

"I'm not suggesting you are. Just keep an open mind and try to think of anything that could have happened."

The three nurses fell silent. They stared at her like she was crazy. She stared back, willing herself not to pull her hair out. She needed a little cooperation here.

"Well, if you come up with anything," she said, "let me know. Nothing is too small to bring to me. Now let's get back to work."

Lacey lingered at the nursing station, her mind spinning frantically. She'd made her nurses mad. She hadn't expected them to take it so personally. But dang it, she was getting close to something and she knew it.

Gooseflesh crept up her spine as she headed back to her office. She threw a glance over her shoulder and the nurses quickly turned away, but not before she caught the outrage that blazed in their eyes.

CHAPTER FORTY-ONE

She paced back and forth across the white-and-gold Berber carpet in her bedroom. Lacey, the nosy little witch, always had her nose stuck in someone's business.

But how could she ever figure out what was really going on? So she thought something was happening to the vaccines. She couldn't prove it. No way.

She had to get back to the office. The shipment of polio vaccine had arrived, a hundred and fifty doses— and she needed to snatch it so she could return it late Sunday or early Monday. Twenty-four hours at room temperature was more than enough time to degrade every last vial. Lacey thought she was on to something. If she only knew how far away from the truth she really was. She'd freak if she knew how long she'd administered placebos.

The phone rang and she jumped. She picked up the receiver and said hello.

"It's Kimberly. I need to talk to you. Now."

CHAPTER FORTY-TWO

Sunday after church, Lacey ordered her favorite at Applebee's. Grilled shrimp and spinach salad. Jake and the kids opted for steak. The meal sizzled with flavor but Lacey's mind wasn't on food for the first time she could remember. She just picked at her entrée.

"You're distracted." Jake paused midair with a forkful of garlic potatoes.

"Got my mind on work. As usual." She sighed. "Sorry."

"Aw, Lacey, ease up on yourself."

"*Moi?*" Lacey tapped her chest and tried to adopt a teasing tone.

"Yes, you! You can't even enjoy your meal."

"I'm on the verge of cracking this."

"How, exactly?"

"I don't know. But I'm close."

"And how do you know this?"

"Just a feeling."

"You're going to make yourself sick if you're not careful."

"Naw."

In truth, she was half sick with worry. Something

had been nagging her about the vaccine since Friday. She couldn't put her finger on what exactly, but she couldn't let it go. She wanted to go over the vaccine logs again after lunch. She'd never be able to sleep if she didn't.

Jake gave her a half grin, but his eyes were filled with concern. She hated that she was spoiling a nice family afternoon. She changed the subject, determined to think about things besides polio, tetanus, and influenza at least until after lunch. Then she'd go to the office and work a while. *But for now, I'll concentrate on my family.*

She turned to the boys and asked about the recent game. And they were off. She heard in graphic detail about every tackle and rush, punt, and touchdown.

The rest of the meal was pleasant, relaxing. And she did polish off her salad. When they left the restaurant, Jake dropped her and Brian at the health department and headed to the car wash.

Todd's face had dropped the minute he'd heard the dreaded C word. Lacey smiled because Jake would not just swing through a drive-through wash. No, not her picky husband. He would choose the do-it-yourself stall, the one where you washed it the old-fashioned way. Then he'd dry it by hand and finish with a wax job. She knew she had at least an hour in the office. Maybe more. Poor Todd.

Lacey pulled her keys from her purse, clicked open the lock, and stepped through the back door. She handed Brian change for a soda and booted up her computer. He could play games while she did her thing.

Lacey lined the disease cases across the raised countertop surrounding the nursing station. The U-shaped counter stretched eighteen feet long and four feet high with three separate desk areas behind it. It provided privacy for the nurses; it also doubled as a work area.

She pored over each polio case first, looking for a lead. All of them were similar—same age group, school, and exactly the same symptoms. She'd read the reports so many times she knew what they said by heart. Predictably, nothing new jumped out at her.

She tackled the tetanus cases next. Not as many of them to go over. All of the kids were up to date on their tetanus toxoid and had received a booster at the appropriate time. Every one of the teens had had a minor injury prior to onset. Two had received a second booster after the injury right here at the health department.

Right here at the health department.

Why hadn't those kids been protected? Frustrated, Lacey massaged her forehead. A headache was on its way. Again.

She stepped back and took a breath. The theory about bad batches of vaccine coming from the manufacturers hadn't panned out. So that left her with the theory that something was happening to the vaccines in the office.

But what? And how?

Lacey felt uneasy at some deep, intuitive level. Something about this whole thing was off. She thought about Holly, the first polio case. Holly had traveled to Nigeria with her parents, a country where polio was still prevalent. She'd become ill five days after returning to the States, indicating she'd been exposed to the virus sometime between her arrival in Lagos on September fifteenth and her departure on September twenty-ninth. Holly's parents were protected because they'd received their IPVs at their physician's office. She wished Holly had gotten a booster there. If she had, maybe all of this could have been avoided. Holly would still be alive. There would be no epidemic.

Lacey ignored the dull pulsing in her head and walked to the medication lab behind the nursing station. She pulled out the vaccine logs. Everything was in order, but she knew it would be. She had stood over Betty's shoulder on Friday while the young nurse checked in the latest shipment of polio vaccine. Betty, her lips pressed together in a tight line and her eyes narrow notches of blue, had resented the supervision and shot darts through Lacey the entire time.

It wasn't that she didn't trust Betty. She trusted all her nurses. She just had to figure out what possible mistake could occur during check-in that would seem harmless to them at the time but would compromise the vaccine. Betty did the check-in without hesitation. Nothing occurred that would indicate a problem.

Lacey opened the refrigerator, which purred like a contented kitten, maintaining a perfect temperature. She started to close the door then hesitated. Something was amiss; something didn't look quite right. The shelves weren't as full as they had been when she'd checked the vaccine for the final time on Friday.

The shelves were labeled, the name of each vaccine taped in place in front of the appropriate vials. Lacey's eyes scanned the entire stock. The vials behind the polio name tag looked sparse. She counted two vials, which was only twenty doses. They had received one-hundred-fifty doses of IPV Friday afternoon, so there should have been seventeen vials. Where were they?

She looked through the entire stock. Could they have been misplaced? She pawed through the vials shelf by shelf. Nope. The missing polio vials were nowhere in the fridge.

She closed the door and tried to process the

information. She had breathed down Betty's neck the entire time she'd done the check-in. She had personally witnessed Betty setting the fifteen incoming vials of polio vaccine directly behind the two vials already on the shelf.

She rubbed her eyes, confused. She opened the refrigerator door again and removed the two polio vials and checked them against the log. Both vials had been there before the new shipment arrived. All the vials from Friday's shipment were gone.

Gone?

Fifteen vials. One-hundred-fifty doses. Missing.

Missing?

She sighed. Vaccine just didn't go missing. That was absurd. Someone must have taken it. But why? Why would someone want to steal polio vaccine? That was way too weird to even contemplate.

She walked to the nursing station and sat in the first cubicle. She didn't know what to do. Should she call the police and report the vaccine stolen? Should she call Darrell and get his advice?

"Hey, Lace," Jake said, and Lacey jumped. Brian must have let him in the back door. She'd been so absorbed she hadn't heard a thing.

"I didn't mean to scare you... Hey, are you okay?"

"Oh, Jake." Lacey shot from the chair and pressed a hand to his arm. "I found something unbelievable."

"What? You look like you've seen a ghost."

Lacey blurted out her discovery, explaining how she knew exactly how many doses of polio were missing.

"Any signs of a break-in?" Jake's eyes scanned the area. "Anything missing besides the polio vaccine?"

"I haven't really checked, but everything else around here looks normal."

"If someone had broken in, what would you expect

him to take?"

"The computers, the TVs, something that could be sold on the street or to a pawnshop. Certainly not a hundred-fifty doses of polio vaccine."

"That does seem odd. Any reason someone might think it would be worth something on the street?"

"None that I can think of. I'd think if someone would go to the trouble of breaking in with the idea that the vaccines were street drugs, they would have cleaned out the entire stock, not just the polio. Jake, this is way too creepy."

"You're right. Beyond creepy. So, what are you going to do?"

Lacey looked at her watch—almost four p.m. on a Sunday afternoon. "I'm going to wait until morning before I decide what to do. I'll have my nurses here to help me figure this out. I'm not going to bother anyone today. Let them enjoy the rest of the weekend."

CHAPTER FORTY-THREE

A blanket of foreboding wrapped around Lacey as she stepped into her office Monday morning at seven o'clock. The hour was early even for her. She wanted to sort things out before the staff arrived, but that wasn't going to happen. She noticed Betty's car in the parking lot. Lacey wouldn't be alone.

She tossed her purse on her desk and strode to the break room. She figured Betty would have the coffee made but she didn't, so Lacey started a pot. She glanced around.

Where was Betty anyway?

Lacey poured a cup of coffee and pondered the missing vaccine. She'd have to make a decision this morning. Maybe her nurses would have an idea. She added powdered creamer and sweetener to her cup and headed down the hall, fixated on the disappearing shipment. Before she reached her office, she slipped into the lab and stared at the refrigerator, wondering who had pilfered it.

She pulled open the door to check the thermometer then jerked back, nearly spilling her hot brew.

The vaccines were back.

She blinked. It wasn't possible but there they sat,

arranged neatly on the appropriate shelf. She pulled the boxes out and checked the lot numbers against the log. Yes, definitely the missing one-hundred-fifty doses. She stacked the vials back in the fridge, confused.

She dragged to her office and shut the door. *What's going on here? Am I completely losing my sanity?* She slid into the chair and buried her head in her hands, trying to shake the confusion from her mind.

At 7:30 a.m., she left her office for a coffee refill. Everything remained quiet in the building and still no sign of Betty.

Why is Betty here so early? It's so unlike her.

She stepped into the break room and found Betty was pouring a brown arc of coffee into a cup.

"Good morning." Betty took a sip from her mug. "Coffee's good."

"You're early." Lacey picked up the carafe.

"Uh-huh." She looked at Lacey over the rim of her cup. "I had a couple dog bite reports to finish up before I turned them over to the sanitation department."

"Oh?"

"Yeah, I left them hanging Friday and wanted to get them taken care of first thing before we get swamped."

"Is that so?"

"Are you okay?" Betty cocked her head to the side.

Lacey shook powdered cream into her mug then dumped in a pink packet of sugar substitute. She stirred and tapped the spoon against the rim of the cup before placing it on a napkin beside the Bunn machine. "I'm fine."

She sidestepped Betty and headed down the hall. She made a detour to the sanitation department and checked their in-box before going to her office.

Befuddled, she flopped into her chair, trying to

decide what to do. The polio vaccine hadn't jumped back in the refrigerator on its own. Someone had put it back. The same someone who'd taken it out. Someone who had access to this building. Betty was here uncharacteristically early. She would have had plenty of time to do it.

The ramification of the unethical act hit her full force. She didn't like the conclusion that took shape in her mind. She picked up the phone and tapped in Darrell's number.

"Lacey. What's wrong?"

She kept her voice low. "Listen, Darrell, something very creepy is going on here."

"Like what, exactly?"

Lacey told him everything. "So, what do you make of it?" she asked.

"Good grief! Someone's tampering with your vaccine."

"Yeah, that's what I thought. But why?"

"To degrade it. Make it useless."

The words struck Lacey like a fist to the gut. It confirmed the eerie conclusion she'd come to but had tried to rationalize away. Her stomach churned and she felt a sudden urge for a Long John to calm her raw nerves.

"This is serious, Lacey."

"It's insane."

"If someone is deliberately tampering with your vaccine, they *are* insane."

Lacey pulled in oxygen and willed herself to think rationally. "That would explain our polio cases. Holly went to Nigeria unprotected. She came back after being exposed to the polio virus and not only does she come down with the disease, she also spreads it to a school full of kids immunized with the same degraded vaccine. This is unbelievable."

"So, you think Betty may be involved?"

"I don't want to accuse anyone, but she was the first one here this morning and that isn't normal for her. And no one else was around to put the vaccine in the refrigerator."

"Did you check the dog bite story?"

"Yep. There were two reports in the Environmental Sanitation intake box, both signed by Betty. But that doesn't mean she was actually working on them this morning. Or she could have put the vaccine back in the refrigerator and then worked on the reports. For cryin' out loud, I don't know. All I know is someone had to take the vaccine out of the refrigerator, and someone had to put it back. It was not in there yesterday afternoon, and it is there now."

"Whoever's doing this snatches the vaccine out of the refrigerator, letting it stand at room temperature long enough to destroy the potency. Then they put in back on the shelf and nobody's the wiser."

"Sick." Lacey glanced at the stack of disease case reports dominating her desk and wondered if all of them could have been prevented. Rage shot through her at the thought of someone deliberately causing mayhem.

"And there's no way to test for viability."

"Sheesh." Lacey pushed her hair back from her face. "This is worse than *Coma*. At least in *Coma*, kids weren't involved."

"What kind of person would want to hurt innocent kids? Bona fide scum does something like that."

"Yeah." But it was still hard for Lacey to believe someone she knew, someone she called a friend, would do such a heinous thing—deliberately causing deaths and intentionally crippling children.

"I'll update Joe and Linda and get them back to your county ASAP. And, Lacey, no more shots until we get this figured out. Don't give any shots of any kind under any circumstance until we get to the bottom of this. You can't risk giving damaged vaccine."

"How am I going to explain stopping shots? Won't that make whoever did this suspicious?"

"Say it's due to the investigation. Blame it on us."

Lacey's office wasn't hot, yet she wiped sweat from her forehead. "I'll need to do a press release, let the public know we won't be giving immunizations for a while."

"Sounds like a plan."

"Okay. As soon as I hang up, I'll call a staff meeting and drop the bomb on them."

"And, Lacey, be careful. You're dealing with a psycho. Most likely someone close to going over the edge. Say as little as possible about stopping shots and be vague. Remember, you can blame this on us."

"Will Joe and Linda be here today?"

"Yes. They should be there before noon."

"That's good." Lacey's throat tightened at the thought of the magnitude of this scenario. How could one of her own do something like this? Cold, calculated murder.

"Play it cool," Darrell said. "Don't take any chances."

"I won't. Thanks, Darrell. For everything."

She quickly typed a press release announcing the halt of all immunizations and when she walked to the front office, she was cold cocked by a wall of sound. Phones ringing, the fax working overtime; half a dozen clients crowded the counter vying for attention. The girls at the front desk trying to stay on top of phones that rang nonstop and a waiting room full of noisy people wanting answers. Lacey seethed. She could use a few answers herself.

She stepped to the front counter, pulled the clerks

aside, and quickly informed them all immunizations were on hold until further notice.

Then on to the nurses' station and announced, "We aren't going to give any shots per the orders of the State EPI's."

"You have got to be kidding!" Betty shook her head.

"But why?" Anger darted through Ann's eyes. "What is it going to accomplish?"

"Beats me." Lacey lifted a tense shoulder. "I think it's odd, too. But the decision came from the heads at the state level. Darrell's boss notified him late Friday and Darrell emailed me this morning."

Lacey hoped her words would ring true. Lying to her subordinates was something new for her, and it was hard to segue into deception mode.

"I think the state is making a bad decision," Joan said, and the other nurses nodded. "In the middle of a polio epidemic, we're supposed to quit giving polio shots? That makes sense, right?"

Betty huffed. "If we quit giving shots, we're going to end up with a lot more sick kids on our hands."

Lacey met her gaze. Betty looked and acted like a normal concerned human being, not some crazed killer. Could she have fooled Lacey so completely?

"Hopefully, this will only be for a week or so," she said. "Then we can get back to business as usual."

Lacey tried to keep her voice convincing. She had never been good at lying. And by the looks plastered on their faces, this time was no exception.

CHAPTER FORTY-FOUR

She pulled her cell from the pocket of her scrubs top and punched in Kimberly's number.

"Yeah?" Kimberly asked. "Whadda ya want?"

"My, aren't we in a good mood today?"

"You wouldn't be in a good mood, either, if you'd just lost your job. Thanks to you, I might add."

"There are other jobs. Don't be so melodramatic."

"I liked my job. I was all set to take that accountant test and get promoted."

"I told you! I'll help you find another job." She wished Kimberly would put a lid on her infernal sniveling.

"Whatever. So whadda ya want?"

"Have you taken care of that little matter I asked you to do?"

"I tried. I called Jake as soon as he got to work and asked him to meet me. He said no and hung up on me."

"Call him back. You've got to get him to meet you somewhere."

"Get a revelation. He loves his wife. He's not going to meet me anywhere."

"Then get over to his house while no one's home

and put your letter to Lacey in the box. If you can't lure him away from his office, at least you can spill the beans to Lacey."

"I'm getting really tired of your stupid little game. Give it a rest, will you? All you've accomplished so far is getting me canned."

"Shut up and quit your whining. If you pay attention and do what I tell you, it *will* work out."

Silence. Then an exaggerated sigh.

"I gotta go. I'm using my cell in the bathroom, so I don't want to stay in here too long. Might make them suspicious." She hit end and slid her phone into her pocket.

Kimberly was proving difficult to handle. When she'd showed up at her house Friday night, she was furious.

"It's your fault I lost my job," she'd yelled.

"So sue him. Turn the tables and say Jake was sexually harassing you."

"Are you nuts? I've already tried that. Besides, he has the boss as a witness."

She'd told Kimberly to quit bellyaching; she'd help her get another job. That calmed her down a little. By the time she'd left, she'd finally agreed to try to coax Jake into meeting her so she could record him admitting to the make-out sessions and convince him to say something incriminating that could be used against him with Lacey.

She was so close to destroying Lacey, she wasn't about to let this go!

She walked out of the bathroom and almost bumped into Lacey. She'd been acting funny all morning. And the news about no shots sounded fishy. Something more was going on than Lacey was admitting.

CHAPTER FORTY-FIVE

Lacey blew out a relieved sigh when Joe and Linda arrived shortly before noon. She grabbed her purse and hustled them out of her office so they could discuss the vaccine ordeal in private, away from prying eyes and suspicious nurses.

They piled into Joe's black SUV and drove to a Chinese place owned by a cute little Asian man and his wife. Lacey and the two EPIs found a booth at the rear of Magic Chef and ordered the luncheon special.

"There is no way to test the vaccine for viability," Joe said in a hushed tone as he stabbed a chunk of cashew chicken. "I called the CDC and they referred me to Sanofi. CDC said the manufacturer would be the only entity that would have the cumulative data to determine if the vaccine is viable following a temperature excursion. Sanofi determines viability by how long the vaccine has been in an uncontrolled environment. So, there is no way to prove the vaccine was tampered with."

Lacey nodded, numb. "Apparently the culprit knows just how long to leave vaccines at room temperature to degrade them."

She opened a packet of mustard sauce and

squeezed the contents onto her plate beside a steaming crab Rangoon.

"This is the most incredible thing I've ever heard of." Linda sat across the table. "If the polio has been debased, think of the implications. Number one, we're talking premeditated murder. Number two, this person has to be mentally deranged."

Lacey laid down the fork and crossed her arms over her chest to ward off a sudden chill. She tried to wrap her mind around the notion that one of her nurses—Betty, to be specific—could actually be involved in such a grisly crime.

Joe said, "Whoever's doing this is dangerous. A threat to all of us."

"And no matter how hard I try," Lacey said, "I can't imagine any of the people I work with fitting that bill."

Linda took a pull from her Diet Pepsi and set it down. "Is there anyone in your office we can trust beyond a shadow of a doubt?"

"Before today, I'd have said every one of them. Now I just don't know."

"Well, don't trust anyone." Joe pressed his lips together. "At this point, you can't chance it. Someone in your office tampered with the polio vaccine. It couldn't have come from outside."

"I know," Lacey agreed. "It's just so far-fetched I can't quite accept it. If I've been working with someone capable of something like this and never once picked up on it, what does that say about my perception of people?"

"Don't sell yourself short." Joe dabbed his napkin at the condensation around his glass. "We're dealing with a sick individual here, mentally and emotionally. And she's very smooth at fooling everyone around her. Look at Ted Bundy. He shocked the shoes off his peers. No one could believe he was capable of murder, much less, multiple murders."

Lacey felt cold prickles pop up along her neck. "This is something you just read about or hear about on the news. It doesn't happen in real life."

"Do you think whoever's tampering with the vaccine could also be your stalker?" Joe asked.

Lacey shuddered. "Good grief! I never thought of that."

"It's a possibility you need to consider. She could be out to get you personally."

Rattled to her foundation, Lacey flashed on Bandit. Would Betty do that to a poor little animal? Did Betty put the dead birds at her house?

She's been hurting innocent kids. Her gut churned and she felt vaguely nauseated.

"You need to watch your back," Linda said.

Joe touched Lacey's arm. "Be very careful."

They fell silent throughout the rest of the meal, which they just picked at. When lunch was over, the three headed back to Lacey's office and huddled over the same polio reports they'd pored over numerous times, plus two new ones that had been faxed over lunch.

Lacey shifted her gaze to the window, trying to make some sense out of it all. Her thoughts drifted to the tetanus cases, and she jumped to her feet.

"What?" Joe and Linda said as Lacey rushed to her door and pushed it closed.

"The tetanus!" Lacey flinched and tamped down her voice. She didn't want it to carry to the nurses' station. "I bet the tetanus has been tampered with. And, good grief, the flu, too."

"Oh my gosh, you're right," Linda said.

"We have totally been sabotaged." Lacey pulled her hair back from her face. "Unbelievable!"

Joe and Linda turned silent, but they nodded in

unison. Joe pulled open the door and they both left her office.

Lacey stepped across the threshold. Her three nurses shot her questioning looks. She ignored them and threaded through the workstation into the lab. She could just imagine what darted through their minds. They must think she'd finally lost it.

They'd been shocked to hear no shots would be given. Had stared at her with disbelief. Or had it been guilt? All three of her nurses couldn't be involved in the vaccine tampering, could they? If so, there was a conspiracy. She shook off the thought, unwilling to let it take root. Maybe it wasn't even a nurse who was involved.

But Betty was looking pretty guilty.

CHAPTER FORTY-SIX

Jake felt extremely thankful as he pulled into the garage. Thankful he had his life back together. With Kimberly gone, the office felt peaceful. Just like it had before she had bombarded it with her domineering presence.

He turned off the motor, grabbed his briefcase, and slid out of the Camaro, wondering how he managed to get into such a mess in the first place. But truth be known, he knew exactly how it happened. His poor choices and high-school behavior had almost cost him his self-respect. It had cost Kimberly her job.

Well, it's over now.

He was relieved he'd finally come to his senses. If only he'd ignored the flirty signals in the first place, she wouldn't have ended up losing her job. He hated the thought of anyone being out of work. Jobs were hard to come by with the deflated economy at an all-time low. A twinge of regret shot through him when he thought how close Kimberly was to nailing the accountant certificate and he hoped she'd pursue it, not give up.

Rebuking himself for allowing his feelings to spin so far out of control, Jake walked through the utility room into the kitchen. Lacey was sitting at the snack bar with her head tucked down. He could see her red, swollen eyes.

"What's wrong, Lace?" He touched her arm. "You okay?"

When she looked up, he saw hurt in her guarded expression. He raked fingers through his hair and braced himself to hear of yet another stalker incident.

"This is what's wrong." She held up a crinkled letter, waving it so he couldn't see what it said. "This was in the mailbox when I got home."

Jake's gut did a flip as he took the letter, understanding punching him in the face. Kimberly's familiar writing, small and neat, made him sick to his stomach. He read it quickly and all his good feelings swept away on a tsunami of guilt. He shook his head, defeated, and said, "I can explain."

"Oh, you can, can you?" Fresh tears leaked from her puffy eyes. "I was fool enough to hope you would tell me it was all a bunch of lies. But I can see I was wrong."

"There was never an affair, Lacey. I was never unfaithful to you."

"So that's supposed to make me feel better?"

"Parts of the letter are lies."

"Suppose you tell me which part?" She let out a snort and her eyes narrowed. She jumped off the stool and shoved it under the counter. "Is it the part where you made out with her in your office? Or maybe it's the part where you pulled her into the closet and made out with her?"

"Yes." Jake shook his head, his thoughts a jigsaw of mismatched pieces. "I mean, no. It didn't happen like that. She pulled *me* into the closet, Lace, I swear. And at first, I did respond but I thought of you, our marriage, and I knew it was wrong. Very wrong. Now she's turning it around, telling Brad I'm harassing her, when she's the one doing the harassment."

Jake was rambling; he knew it but couldn't stop. He had to somehow make Lacey understand. "I'm so sorry, Lacey. Sorry that I kissed her, sorry that I hurt you. I'm...so sorry."

Lacey stared at him, pain carving her forehead. "You kissed her. How could you?"

"I don't know..." Remorse clawed his chest and stole his air.

"You don't know, huh? Well, that's original." She paced to the refrigerator and yanked out a bottle of water.

"I know. I'm—"

"Sorry?" She slammed the bottle onto the counter. "You've got that right. You are one sorry excuse for a human being."

"I never meant to hurt you, Lacey. Never."

"She's a lot younger than me." Lacey picked up a picture of Kimberly from the counter and aimed it at him. "And much prettier."

Her tone sounded poignant and when she gulped, it ripped his own throat. He couldn't believe Kimberly included a picture. And it looked like one of those glamour photos.

What have I done to my wife?

"Lacey, don't." Regret sliced his heart. He touched her arm, but she jerked away.

"Don't touch me."

He folded his hands together in front of him and resisted the urge to grab her, hold on tight, and not let go until she could find it in her heart to forgive him because he wasn't sure he could forgive himself. "Please, just hear me out."

She looked down and ran her fingers over the face in the picture. Jake wanted to grab it and rip it to shreds. He wished he'd never laid eyes on that woman.

"Lacey, will you listen to me?" He unclasped his hands and took a step toward her. "Please?"

She wadded up the picture and shoved it down on the counter. "I think I've heard enough."

"At least come see Pastor David with me. He'll tell you how he's been helping me work through this."

"Oh, my Lord! Our pastor knows about this?"

Jake nodded. "I needed help. I knew I was in over my head."

"Too bad you didn't see him sooner, before your lust got the best of you." She laughed without mirth and looked at him with disgusted eyes. "I begged you for weeks to see the pastor. But no, you refused. Now I know why. You had the hots for your little office tart."

He shook his head. "If I could take back what happened, I would. But I can't. I can only plead for your forgiveness and promise you that nothing like this will ever happen again. I love you, Lacey. You're my life. Don't you know that?"

"No. I don't know that. Not after what you've done."

"Will you give me a chance—"

"I'm too numb to even think right now. Just leave me alone."

"Lace, I..." He reached out but she threw up a palm and glared at him. He dropped his hand.

"I said don't touch me. I mean it." She took a step back. "Order something for the boys for dinner. They'll be home from practice at seven or so. I'm not hungry."

She walked with slumped shoulders out of the kitchen. He was afraid she might be walking out of his life.

CHAPTER FORTY-SEVEN

Lacey looked at the clock on the nightstand. Ten o'clock. She sighed, exasperated. There was no use even trying to go to bed. She'd never get to sleep. She pulled a jacket from the closet, shoved her arms through the sleeves, and grabbed her purse on her way out the door.

Ten minutes later, she pulled into Amber's driveway and cut the engine. A light shone through the kitchen window, so she trudged to the back door and rapped gently. The blinds parted and Amber's dark, curly head peeked through the slit. She threw open the door.

"You're out late." She wore hot-pink stretch pants under a gray T-shirt with KC CHIEFS flanked boldly across the chest. "Get in here, girl."

Lacey stepped into the large, eat-in Americana kitchen. Subtle red, white, and blue wallpaper dominated the stainless-steel appliances. She tossed her jacket and purse in a chair. Amber immediately went to the counter to start a pot of coffee.

Lacey slid wearily into a chair beside the one holding her toss-offs. She was just like them. Tossed away like yesterday's headlines. Used and discarded.

As Amber worked, she didn't ask Lacey what was wrong. That meant she was on to her. She knew something big was going on and characteristically she wasn't pushing. Thank goodness because Lacey didn't know if she could talk about it, even with her best friend.

"Where's Dan and Suzie?" Lacey felt like an intruder popping in so late. "In bed?"

"Suzie is." Amber switched on the brew button. "Dan's watching the news."

"I'm sorry." Lacey had a sudden urge to dart out the back door, which would make her look even more pathetic than she felt. "I shouldn't have stopped by so late."

"Nonsense." Amber pulled out a chair and sat down. "Something's on your mind, right?"

Lacey nodded.

"Ready to talk about it?"

"That's just it. I don't know if I'll ever be ready to talk about this."

"That bad, huh?"

"Worse." Lacey met Amber's concerned gaze. In that instant, she knew she could tell her anything. Always could. "Oh, Amb. It's Jake."

"Jake? My heaven, what's happened? Has he been in an accident?"

Lacey shook her head. "No. Nothing like that."

"What, then?"

"He cheated on me."

"Jake?" Amber's lips tightened, as if she were debating whether to continue. She touched Lacey's arm. "Not Jake. You've got to be mistaken."

"Well, he didn't have a full-fledged affair but he might as well have." The words tasted as bitter as bile. Anger boiled inside her at the memory of his confession. The confession that'd ripped out her heart, shattering any belief she'd had in him.

Amber closed her eyes and shook her head. "Oh, Lacey, I'm so sorry." She filled two mugs with steaming coffee and set them on the table. "Tell me everything. What happened?"

Lacey took a long drink then set the cup down. She told the story start to finish, beginning with pulling Kimberly's letter from the mailbox. Amber listened the careful way she always did, nodding from time to time while she kept her eyes focused on Lacey. By the time she'd finished, Amber's forehead had sprouted deep worry lines.

"I told you Jake's been different lately. Acting weird. Pulling back from me." Lacey blinked away the tears stinging her eyes. "But I never dreamed it was because he had the hots for another woman."

Amber looked at her thoughtfully. "Like he said, Lacey, he wasn't really unfaithful."

"Oh, ya think?" A fist of pain smacked her in the chest. She couldn't believe what she was hearing. Not from Amber, who was always so in tune with her feelings. "Well, what would you do if Daniel pawed around on another woman?"

"Before or after I castrated him?"

Amber chuckled but Lacey didn't. She couldn't.

Amber sobered and cleared her throat. "I'd be mad. Hurt. Probably want to kill him. Hurt him back. But, Lacey, can you honestly tell me you are ready to throw your marriage away because of this one slip?"

"One slip! It was a heck of a lot more than one slip. He betrayed me. He fondled and kissed someone besides me. And you should have seen her picture. She's gorgeous. No wonder he was willing to forget about the vows he made to me."

"Lacey, listen to me. I'm not trying to minimize what Jake did. I know you're cut to the quick. And, sweetie, I feel your pain." Amber took her hand and gave it a gentle squeeze. "Jake messed up, you're right. Big-time. And believe me, I'd like to give him a piece of my mind right now! But he loves you. You have to know that."

"I don't know what I know, much less how to feel. I haven't processed it yet."

"Can't you find it in your heart to give him a little slack? Try to understand?"

"What's there to understand?"

"That he's human, and humans make mistakes. Great big ugly ones sometimes."

I responded at first, he'd admitted.

"I don't think I can."

"Talk to him at least. Hear him out. You haven't even given him a chance."

"A chance to what? To tell me he didn't mean to rip my heart out? That he'll never do it again?"

"Why is that so farfetched?"

He put his arms around her and kissed her.

"Because I don't want to hear any more of his flimsy excuses."

"What are you afraid he'll say?"

"That he'll talk me into believing in him again and I can't do that. I hate him."

Amber shook her head. "You don't mean that. You're just hurting right now."

"Yes. I do. When I picture him with her, it makes me physically sick. If he really loved me, he wouldn't have been tempted by someone else."

"So, what are you going to do? Leave him?"

"I haven't thought that far ahead. But, yes, I can't stay with someone I can't trust."

"But you love him. You can't look me in the eye and tell me you don't. And he loves you." Amber took a sip of coffee and looked at her over the rim of her cup.

"Don't you think your marriage is worth fighting for?"

Lacey shook her head. "It's too late. He's the one who put our marriage in jeopardy, so why should I fight?"

"You know not everything is black and white, girlfriend. There are all kinds of shades of gray in the world."

Lacey studied the one person in her universe she'd thought would understand. She and Amber weren't on the same page, not even the same chapter. She was treating this like Jake forgot to take out the trash. Well, it was more than that. Much more. He'd *wallowed* in trash. And she couldn't just forget about it and act like it didn't matter. She wouldn't.

"You're upset—" Amber began.

"Yeah, you've got that part right. I'm upset. You're supposed to be my best friend and you just don't get it."

"Get what?"

"Why I can't forgive him. He's made me feel like garbage."

Amber walked to the counter and refilled their mugs. "I'm on your side, you know. I just don't want you to make a hasty decision, one that you'll later regret."

"I don't see that it's my decision to make. *Jake* made the choice when he decided to cheat."

"Oh, honey. I know you're hurt. And I hurt for you, honest. But Jake isn't a bad person. You know that. Please, can't you at least pray about this?"

"Yeah? Well, how about, *Dear Lord, bless Jake and his hot little heifer.*"

"Lacey, listen to me. He doesn't want her. You've always been the one Jacob Bookman wanted. He's loved you since you were sixteen." Amber leaned back and smiled. "I used to be so envious of you, having someone like Jake."

"Well, now the table's turned. I'm envious of you."

Amber lifted a brow.

"Daniel would never do this to you."

Amber sighed. "We never know what the future holds. But, Lacey, one thing is certain. We can't always be in control of everything around us. Jake's hurt you and you're disillusioned with him right now. And I don't blame you, but don't let one indiscretion destroy what you and Jake have. You could at least try to talk to him, try to work through this."

I responded at first.

"Adultery is grounds for divorce."

"Lacey!" Amber narrowed her eyes. "Jake didn't have sex with that woman."

"He did in his heart. He wanted her. He had me. Right in his home, in his bed. But obviously that wasn't enough. He'd rather pant after someone half his age." Fresh tears stung her eyes, but she blinked them away. She didn't want to cry anymore. "I guess I failed at marriage, too. I can't seem to get anything right."

"You didn't fail at anything." Amber stroked Lacey's arm. "You're *way* too hard on yourself. You won't give Jake a break because you can't even give yourself one."

Lacey knew it was time to go. She guessed she'd lost her best friend, too. Amber couldn't see how she felt about this. They'd disagreed before but never over an issue as important as this. Well, she couldn't change how Amber felt, so why bother to try?

She took her cup to the sink then said goodbye.

CHAPTER FORTY-EIGHT

Lacey rolled out of bed at five o'clock, exhausted and stiff from a sleepless night. She threw on the sweats she'd worn to Amber's then trudged downstairs and headed outside into the dark morning. Maybe a run would clear some of the fog from her brain.

She almost hoped someone would be lurking outside waiting for her. She was ready to take on the world. She was tired of people walking all over her.

The morning was crisp. Frozen dew hung on the trees and glistened on the grass. She picked up speed and ran down the middle of the street lit by lampposts. Her lungs gasped at the cool air as she pumped her arms and plowed forward faster. Faster. Her heartbeat thudded in her ears, *Lub-dub, lub-dub.* Her pulse escalated to a speed that might have been dangerous if someone cared. She didn't.

She was so mad at Jake. Furious with him. How could he have betrayed her? How could he say he loved her when for weeks he'd been harboring a secret passion for another woman? One who looked like Angelina Jolie? Part of her wanted to scream at him to get out of the house, stay out, and never come back. He'd hurt her beyond measure, and she would never get over it. Never. How could she ever let him touch her again without thinking of his lips on that other woman? All those times he'd acted so distant and indifferent toward her, he'd been panting after that pretty young thing.

I'll kick his sorry butt out.

The thought of Jake not being a part of her life anymore caught in her chest like a cold fist of iron and stole her air. She wondered how she'd ever make it without him. Another part of her wanted to pretend nothing happened. Just ignore all of it. Run home and crawl into bed with him, snuggle down into his warm arms, let him hold her and make the pain go away. Like only he could. The indecision felt like a knife stabbing her heart, twisting and cutting the very life out of her.

Finally, after forty-five minutes of labored running, she stopped on a street several blocks from home. Her breaths came in gasps, and she wasn't sure she would ever breathe at a normal rate again. She plopped down in the cold, crisp grass of a stranger's yard. Pulling one leg up to her chest, she rested her chin on her knee. She sucked in oxygen until her respiration was nearly normal.

The run cleared her head somewhat but had done nothing to assuage the smarting in her raw heart. Hot, salty tears streamed down her cheeks. Only then did she realize she was crying again. She wiped her face on her sleeve and wondered if she'd ever feel like smiling. She pulled herself up, swiped her hands down the back of her wet sweats, and headed down the street.

I hate you, Jacob Bookman. I hate you for doing this to me. You were supposed to be someone I could depend on. Someone I could trust. Hah! What a laugh!

Only she was lying to herself. She didn't hate Jake, not really. She didn't know how to *not* love Jake. She'd loved him for so long and with a passion so strong it sometimes scared her.

Two blocks from her house, she sat down on the curb, not yet ready to face a cheating husband. She pondered the things Amber had said. Was her friend right? Did she owe it to Jake and herself to try to work through this? And if she did try, could she actually let go of the hurt and pain? Could she forgive and forget?

The early morning sun peeked through the clouds, scaring away the moon and announcing a new day. She looked up and down the block. She was alone. She buried her head in her hands as sobs wracked her body.

God, please help me. I can't stand this. I want to love Jake and trust him again. I do. But I can't do this within myself. I'm so hurt but I can't stand the thought of losing him. Can I believe him when he says nothing like this will ever happen again? Do I dare trust him again?

She dropped her hands as her heart fell to her toes. All at once, a startling insight jolted her. The safe predictable world she'd created for herself, the one she guarded so fiercely, the one in which she controlled the variables, hadn't simply vanished leaving her exposed and vulnerable. It had always been a fallacy.

She closed her eyes and opened her heart. She flashed on Jake taking her hand and gently leading her upstairs to a bath he'd lovingly prepared after a day of hell at work. In that split second, she swallowed her fear and made a life-changing decision. A decision that might very well leave her wide open and more vulnerable but one that was grounded on seventeen years of solidity.

She knew what she had to do. Tenacity catapulted up her spine. She shoved to her feet and headed home. To Jake.

Somehow, they would get through this. They had to. She couldn't let him walk out of her life.

Her footfalls pelted on the sidewalk as she picked up speed. In no time, she saw her house. Her home. Her life. Past and future. She started up her drive. Jake stood at the window, watching.

She jerked open the door and slammed it behind her then scurried into the living room, skidding to a stop in front of Jake. His face drawn and his eyelids drooping, he looked totally wiped out. His forehead creased with guilt and his pained eyes focused completely on her. She felt her heart break for what he'd done but she wanted to move past it.

Lacey choked out a sob and took a step forward. Jake reached for her and gathered her in his arms. She leaned against him as tears spilled from her eyes. She sucked in a breath as he buried his head in her hair. He smelled faintly of the lime-scented aftershave he always wore. They clung to each other, pulling each other closer, tighter, as if by trying hard enough, they could enter the other and truly become one flesh.

Lacey let go of her hostility and drew comfort from his strong arms in a way she never had before. The pain that squeezed her heart relaxed just a little, and she let herself feel how very omnipotent was something so simple yet so intense as a husband's love.

Even when he'd made a mistake.

Lacey's face was wet with her own tears and with his. When she could speak, she said, "I love you, Jake. And I don't want to lose you. I'll go to counseling with you, whatever it takes to fix this between us."

"Oh, Lace, I thought I'd lost you. I am sorry, so

sorry, a million times over sorry." Jake released her and brushed a stray hair from her forehead. Regret deepened his crow's feet. "I can't undo what I've done, but I swear I'll never let anything come between us again. You have my word."

CHAPTER FORTY-NINE

Lacey hit the shower and let the warm water caress her fatigued muscles, but not for long. She had to be quick if she didn't want to be late for work. She toweled herself dry and grabbed the blow dryer, quickly shaping her short hair. After a few strokes of makeup to cover her puffy eyes, she raced downstairs and, ten minutes later, darted into the health department.

After she fetched a cup of coffee and settled at her desk, she made a mental note to call Amber at noon and apologize to her wise and true friend, who, as always, had been right.

Though she was tired from a sleepless night, she felt confident. She could face anything, all her home and work problems and even the stalker, as long as she had Jake by her side. She would fight with everything she could muster to save her marriage. She was not a failure.

She pulled up Word and started a letter to Kimberly. She knew exactly what she wanted to say, so it took her only five minutes. The letter made it clear that she was standing by her husband and did not want any more interference. Ever. She hit print and stuffed the letter into the outgoing mail before anyone else arrived.

From what Jake had told her last night, Kimberly's actions bordered on harassment. At the time, Lacey had been too hurt to believe it. *Now I do.* She knew Brad wouldn't have fired Kimberly if he didn't have the goods to stand behind his decision. It wasn't easy to fire an employee nowadays because they could sue, and most likely win, if the facts weren't documented.

"Good morning." Joe sauntered in with an oversized Break Stop Styrofoam cup.

"Hi, Joe. Have a seat." She noticed he looked drained. "Bad night?"

"Yes and no. I couldn't get to sleep thinking about what we might find with the polio vaccine. Then around two this morning, I had a brainstorm. If someone is taking the vaccine, we've got to prove *who.* Not just that it's being tampered with. Let's order more polio vaccine today and watch the office to see who takes it."

"That's a great idea."

"What's a great idea?" Linda asked as she stuck her head around the door.

Lacey closed the door while Joe updated Linda.

"Won't that look suspicious?" Linda asked as she slid into a chair. "You already have plenty of polio vaccine here. If you ordered more, especially since you're withholding shots, that's gonna look like a setup."

"Not if we play it right." Lacey propped a hip on her desk and gave her co-conspirators a grin. "I'll say Clayton County needs to borrow our stock of polio ASAP for today's shots since their order won't arrive until late this afternoon. Then I'll order a shipment from the distributor. When it's delivered, I'll say it's Clayton County's payback."

"I like how your mind works," Joe said. "What are you going to do with the vaccine you supposedly transfer to Clayton County?"

"That's where you come in. We'll pretend you are going to deliver the shipment to Clayton. But in reality, you'll take it to my house and store it in my fridge."

"Sounds like a plan." Joe crumpled his cup and tossed it in the trash.

Lacey phoned the distributor and placed an order for one-hundred-fifty doses of IPV. She was assured the shipment would arrive the next day.

"Now." Lacey pushed back from her desk. "To make the perpetrator act quickly when the vaccine arrives tomorrow, I'll start dropping hints about opening back up for immunizations. I'll say I'm complaining to the state, trying to get an okay to resume shots. So, if she wants to ruin the new shipment, she'll have to move tomorrow night."

Joe and Linda agreed that the plan sounded full-scale. At the nurses' station, Lacey told Ann to pack the polio vaccine in a cooler. It wasn't unusual to transfer vaccine between counties. It happened all the time.

Lacey slipped Joe her house key along with directions and told him to watch *The Price Is Right* before coming back to the office. That would be the right timeframe required for a round trip to Clayton County Health Department.

Later that afternoon, sixty-five more flu cases came through the fax. Lacey checked the stats on the website. Lester County remained the only county with an outbreak. She printed out the sheet and strode to the conference room where Joe and Linda had polio cases fanned out in front of them.

"We may never be able to prove it," Lacey said,

laying the paper in front of the two EPIs, "but I know in my heart the flu vaccine was tampered with, too. Just look at the numbers. Whoever is responsible for this is beyond insane. Innocent people are getting sick. And to save my life, I can't understand why someone would do such a malicious thing. What in the world does she think she's proving?"

Joe shrugged. "We're not dealing with someone capable of rational thinking."

Understanding took root in her head. Tiny prickles of ice brushed the back of her neck.

This person is a serial killer.

CHAPTER FIFTY

She couldn't believe her eyes when she saw a letter addressed to Kimberly in the out-mail slot. It didn't have a return address, but she recognized Lacey's oh-so-perfect penmanship. She snatched the envelope from the slot and tucked it into her scrubs pocket.

She slipped into the bathroom and opened the dispatch. From the sounds of the note, Lacey wasn't the least bit upset with Jake. In fact, she defended him. Standing by her man and all that crap. No doubt he'd lied to Lacey. He must have denied his part in the heavy make-out sessions and Lacey had swallowed it whole.

No way could she allow Kimberly to see this letter. She was still upset about losing her stinking job, not worrying about catching Jake up in a tryst. Kimberly, no doubt, hadn't acted out her part very well. Why else would Jake have refused her advances? Well, he certainly hadn't refused them at first, according to Kimberly, and not long ago seemed more than ready to make reservations at the nearest motel.

So why was Lacey still with Jake? Why hadn't she kicked him out?

She would need to do some serious thinking about

what steps to take next. And she'd handle it herself. She didn't want to push Kimberly too far and risk her getting fed up and blabbing everything. Everything she was savvy to. Kimberly knew only about the plot to split up Jake and Lacey.

When she'd found out that her second cousin landed a job in Jake's office, the wheels started spinning. Her plan to debase the vaccine had already been well underway when the new opportunity had fallen into her lap like a gift from Fate.

She thought back to the night she'd invited her cuz for dinner and asked for her help.

"Why would you want to break up their marriage?" Kimberly had asked in her whiney little voice. As gorgeous as she was, she was a twit, always had been. Book smart. Street dumb.

"To get back at her for all the rotten things she's done to me. She's been a thorn in my side for years."

"What's she done that's so bad?"

"Everything. You name it, she's done it. Lacey was always prettier and more popular than me in school. She thought she was smarter, too, but she wasn't. She always made me feel second-class. All through school, I had to take a back seat to little Lacey who always managed to get whatever she wanted. She beat me out of the lead in the school play in my sophomore year. She was a high-and-mighty senior, so they gave the part to her. I should have had it. I was the best. But the teacher had an eye for Lacey and he gave it to her."

"You didn't get any part in the play?"

"Oh, I got a part all right, because, like I told you, I was good. Better than Lacey by a long shot. And the real kicker is Lacey asked for my help all through the play. Can you believe her nerve?"

"So, you guys were friends? Ran together?"

"Oh no. Heaven forbid. Lacey was too good for

someone like me. She had her own group of friends, the popular kids. The in-crowd. But she wasn't above using me when she needed something."

"Then there was Jake. My Jake, until Lacey got her hooks into him. I'd had my sights set on him long before she came into the picture. He was my first love. I'd been in love with him since I was twelve."

"Lacey broke you guys up?"

"In a sense, yeah. I was totally head over heels in love with him even though he treated me like a kid sister. He was beginning to come around though. I could feel it. It was just a matter of time. Before that could happen, he met Lacey, and I was just a castoff. Once again, Lacey had outdone me. And I've never loved anyone like I love Jacob Bookman."

"What about your husband? You married him."

"Nothing could ever make me forget about Jake."

"You're still in love with Jake!"

"I'll never *not* be in love with him."

"Bummer."

"And it wasn't good enough that Lacey stole Jake. Five years ago, she beat me out of the nursing supervisor position that should have been mine. But that's another story."

She was next in line at the health department for Director of Nursing and had seniority over Lacey. After everything she and Robert had meant to each other, he'd bypassed her. They'd had a short affair a few years back that ended with good feelings for both of them. Or so she'd thought. He had told her they couldn't be together because he couldn't leave his wife, but he swore she would always have a special place in his heart. Apparently, that meant nothing to him since he chose Lacey over her. So, it was time for him to pay for the oversight. The health department would go under with Lacey in charge, and she would be on the sideline waiting to take over. With Lacey gone and Robert at wit's end, he'd have to ask her to step up and take charge. And when he did, voila, the polio problem would vanish. They would see what an asset she was.

"You really hate her, don't you?"

"You've got that right, and I'm going to bring her down if it kills me trying."

The feelings she had for Lacey raised hatred to a new level. She despised Robert for inflicting Lacey on the health department, and she intended to show Robert he'd made the biggest mistake of his life when he'd picked Lacey over her. *No one uses me and then tosses me aside like a piece of garbage.*

"So, what I want you to do is seduce Jake. Can you do it?"

"Of course, I can do it. But I don't want to lose my job. I like it there."

"You won't lose your job."

"How can you be so sure?"

"Trust me, you'll never get fired. Jake wouldn't dare let on he's involved with you."

"I don't know."

"I'll make it worth your time."

"No." Kimberly shook her head. "Jake seems like such a nice guy."

"You're buried in student loans. If you'll do this, I'll give you Grandma's diamond ring."

"Wow! That's worth a mint."

"You could sell it, pay off your loans, and still have some left."

"That's really tempting."

"When there's proof that Jake slept with you, I'll give you the ring."

She thought it over then high-fived her cousin and said, "Okay, you've got a deal."

She shook her head, ending her reverie. She crumpled the letter and stuck it in her pocket then concentrated on the odd events of the day. The polio vaccine was on its way to Clayton County. They'd get one-hundred-fifty worthless doses, but that would be okay. That shouldn't cause them a problem. One placebo dose per child shouldn't make much difference in the overall protection. The seroconversion rate should be around 85 percent for each child vaccinated. She wasn't trying to hurt anyone in Clayton County. Nobody there had shafted her.

She had added tampering with the flu vaccine this year to stir the pot even more. Get everyone on their toes. Flu wouldn't do damage like polio and tetanus, but still it caused plenty of grief for the health department. And people did die from influenza.

Lacey had been acting so strange today, even for her. Surely it was due to the revelation she'd received the previous night about her wander-lusting husband. No matter what she'd said in the letter, she had to wonder just how far her husband had really gone.

Good! Let her squirm. Yet another situation the control freak couldn't control. She deserved everything she'd be getting and more.

She hadn't meant to, or at least it wasn't her intention, to kill innocent people, but she'd known in this case it couldn't be helped.

CHAPTER FIFTY-ONE

Pastor David's car was parked in the driveway when Lacey got home from work. She pulled into the garage then trekked inside. Jake and the minister were at the snack bar with steaming cups of hot chocolate. Pastor David greeted her with a warm hug.

"Surprised to see you." Lacey returned the embrace. "But your visits are always welcome."

"I asked him to come by this evening," Jake said. "The boys are spending the night with your mom, so we'll have some privacy."

Lacey was glad the kids were gone. Those guys were pretty perceptive, and it wouldn't have taken them long to pick up on why the pastor dropped by. And they certainly didn't need any more shockers dropped in their laps.

"I called The Great Wall," Jake said. "Dinner should be here in a few minutes."

"Mmm. Sounds good."

"Cocoa?" Jake nodded at a steaming mug piled high with miniature marshmallows, one of his specialties.

Lacey smiled and scooted onto a barstool. The cocoa was thick with flavor and yummy, as usual.

"I let the pastor read the letter from Kimberly so he's up to date on what's going on. Lace, he knows everything. I've been completely honest with him."

"Thanks for coming over, Pastor David," she said. "Jake and I can sure use a dose of your wisdom."

"Well, I don't know about that." He chuckled and his eyes crinkled at the corners. "But I hope you both know I'm always here for you."

"I know that. And I appreciate it." Lacey ran her fingertip around the rim of her mug and glanced at the men. "I wrote a note to Kimberly and mailed it this morning."

Her husband and her pastor nodded but she couldn't gauge their reactions. She directed her focus to Jake.

"I told her I'm aware of everything that's been going on. That you apologized, and I accepted the apology. I let her know I was aware of her harassing you after you asked her to back off. And I made it clear that neither one of us will tolerate any more contact from her, whether it be by phone, mail, or in person."

"Let's hope that will put an end to this." Pastor David set his cup down. "You've both been firm with her. Laid it on the line."

"She called me at work this morning. Wanted me to meet her at Waffle House just to 'straighten things out.'" Jake made air quotes. "I hung up on her, Lacey, and told the clerks not to put any more of her calls through to me."

"Well, that was certainly thoughtful of you." Frustration nipped Lacey's words as resentment pulsed through her veins. She shot Jake a look. "The woman is persistent, but she doesn't know who she's up against."

Pastor David cleared his throat. "Before the food

arrives and we begin our discussion, I'd like to pray with both of you."

The three of them formed a small circle and joined hands. The pastor prayed for their marriage, for both of them individually, and for the family. The beautiful prayer touched Lacey deep in her soul. She knew Pastor David cared, really cared, and that warmed her as much as the hot chocolate. Maybe more. When the prayer ended, she grabbed a box of tissues and wiped her eyes.

A short time later, the food arrived. The smell of General Pao chicken made her stomach growl. Lacey poured iced tea all around and the conversation flowed freely throughout dinner. The pastor gently turned the discussion toward issues that needed to be addressed. He was so good at what he'd been trained to do, Lacey had to admire him. He reminded her of her father—honest to a fault, sensitive, with ethical standards straight as an arrow.

"We offer anger management classes at the church," he said. "It's human, and entirely normal, for you to feel a great deal of anger about all of this. I know you love Jake, and I know you have forgiven him, but now you need to let go of the anger. All of it. If you don't, it's going to eat away at you. And your anger isn't going to faze Kimberly one iota. It's you it'll hurt."

"I do love Jake." Lacey pursed her lips and looked into the minister's kind eyes. "But deep down, I am mad. Furious. At her. At Jake. Even at myself. When I think about..."

She cut her gaze to Jake. "Well, when I think about you and her together, the anger starts boiling up and I feel like I'm going to lose it."

Hurt creased Jake's face. "I get that. But, Lacey, we can work through this. I'm willing to do whatever it takes to get us back on track."

"I know. And I'm going to try, too." She looked at the pastor. "I'll sign up for the anger management classes."

"And we'll both attend the marriage classes." Jake squeezed Lacey's hand.

"Good." Pastor David smiled. "Be honest and open with each other about your feelings. Don't try to sugarcoat them. And keep God as the center of your relationship. That's what it takes to keep a strong marriage."

Jake pressed Lacey's arm. "I won't let you down, Lace. From now on, our marriage will come first, I promise."

Lacey felt a knot of guilt tighten her chest. She laid her hand over his. "I know how I am, Jake. I tend to get sidetracked with my work. And if I've ever made you feel that you aren't important to me, I haven't meant to. Because you are important to me. Very important. And I'm sorry if I haven't always put you first in my life."

"Aw, Lacey." Jake cupped her face. "None of this was your fault. It was never you. It was me. Always me. Totally my fault and I don't want you taking the blame for any of this, you hear me?"

Lacey nodded, unable to speak even though she had a thousand things she wanted to say.

"The important thing to remember," Pastor David said, "is how much you love each other and how much God loves you both. With a team like that, with God as the captain, you can't lose."

Jake gave Lacey's shoulder a squeeze.

"Well," the pastor said. "I need to get going. Still have a couple of things I need to wind up at my office before I head home."

"Thanks for coming over, I know you're busy," Jake

said.

"Never too busy for you two," Pastor David said as he headed to the door.

They said their goodbyes then Lacey and Jake tidied up the kitchen and made their way to the family room. They settled on the oversized sofa and talked, really talked, like they hadn't in a long time. And Lacey didn't say one word about the health department.

Jake's gaze swept her face as his fingers traced the outline of her jaw. "This has made me realize how important you are to me, Lace. Not only are you the love of my life, you're my best friend."

"I feel the same about you, Jake." Lacey pulled in a long breath and let it out. "I guess that's why it's so hard for me to understand how you could have done this. Why would anyone treat their best friend with such disrespect?"

Jake dropped his head and fell silent. When he looked at her, his eyes were shadowed. "I've been asking myself that question every day. I let the flirting get way out of control. I never meant for it to go that far. But what I've come to realize is there's no such thing as innocent flirtation when you're committed to someone else. I was way out of line, I admit that. And I know I keep repeating myself, but I am sorry."

Lacey saw the regret in his eyes and heard the pain in his voice. "I'm not trying to hurt you. I'm just telling you how I feel."

"I know."

"I don't want to keep everything pent up inside. I've got to get it out."

"We'll talk about things until we work through it."

"I'm sure the anger management classes will help. And I need that. When I think about it, I get so mad I can't think straight."

"I hate myself for putting you in the middle of something like this. You deserve a lot better than what I've dealt you."

"Let me ask you one thing, and please be honest. I need to know. Has anything like this ever happened before? With someone else?"

Jake sat upright. "No. Absolutely not. Never. I swear."

Lacey looked deep into his eyes and believed him. She was beginning to feel she would be able to trust him again. Exhaustion rolled over her and she rested her head on his shoulder.

"Just hold me a while," she said.

Jake gathered her into his arms and held her tight. "We are going to get through this. You've got to believe it."

"When you say it, I do."

He whispered soothing words as he pushed her hair behind her ear. Feeling loved and so safe, she wished she could always feel like that. She was where she wanted to be, safe in her husband's arms. The last thing she remembered before the shadows of sleep pulled her under was Jake gently rocking her with his chin pressed to the top of her head, ever so quietly repeating, "Everything's going to be okay."

CHAPTER FIFTY-TWO

The polio vaccine arrived at two o'clock in the afternoon. Lacey leaned against the lab door beside Joe and Linda while Betty checked in the shipment. Joan and Ann sat in front of their computers at the nursing station, entering data on five new polio cases.

"I am this close," Lacey said, measuring a quarter of an inch between her thumb and forefinger, "to opening the clinic for immunizations."

"It's too late to start this afternoon," Joe said. "Wait until morning. That way, you can get a press release out."

"Yeah, you're probably right. But come morning, we are going to be back in the shot business." Lacey hoped she and Joe sounded convincing. She wanted the culprit stopped. *Tonight.*

Betty shut the refrigerator with a dull thud. She walked around the corner and eyed Lacey. "The vaccine's checked in."

"Good," Lacey said and put on an enthusiastic face. "First thing in the morning, we'll be giving shots again."

Betty nodded and walked to the nurses' station. Lacey was on her heels and made her announcement to the rest of the nurses for the third time that afternoon.

"That's a relief." Joan snorted. "I'm even getting calls at home asking why we've stopped giving shots with so much disease in the county."

"I know the girls up front are worn out with the flak they're getting." Ann's mouth twisted down, and she plopped a hand on her hip. "And I never could figure out the rationale behind withholding shots to start with."

"Me either," Betty said. "If you ask me, it was stupid right from the start."

"Well, you know how the state people are." Ann hitched up a shoulder and her eyes narrowed. "Impossible to know how they think."

"Yeah," Betty mumbled but it didn't get by Lacey. Betty had been acting nervous all afternoon. Or was Lacey just imagining it?

Lacey walked into her office and motioned Joe and Linda to scoot their chairs closer. "I don't want anyone to hear us, but I don't want to close the door and arouse suspicion."

The EPIs pushed the chairs over to her desk and sat.

"We need a plan for tonight."

Lacey angled toward the doorway. In this position, she could see if anyone approached her office before they were within earshot. Linda scooted to the end of her chair and smoothed her watermelon-green ribbed top.

"Do you think we should call the police?" Linda asked. "Let them in on our plan?"

"No. They'd never come. We don't have anything concrete to tell them, just a lot of suspicions. They won't be any help at this point. We're on our own."

"So how are we going to pull this off?" Joe glanced

toward the door.

"Well, I think we need to be inside tonight when she gets here." Lacey thought how surprised Betty would be when they caught her red-handed. "If we park anywhere within two blocks of the health department, we run the risk of her spotting our vehicles. That would definitely scare her off."

"You're right." Joe scratched his chin and arched a brow.

"Okay," Lacey said. "Here's what we'll do. We all leave tonight as usual. You guys park in my garage so your cars can't be seen from the street. Then Jake brings us back and drops us off so there won't be any cars in the parking lot. Then we sit tight and wait to see who comes."

"What if no one comes?" Linda asked.

"Then we go to Plan B."

"Which is?" Joe asked.

Lacey shrugged. "Haven't thought of it yet."

"Let's just hope she shows," Joe said and chuckled.

"Yeah, I'm counting on getting this nightmare over with."

Joe nodded. "I hear that. Well, we better get some work done. But don't worry, we'll stay close. We'll keep an eye on you."

She watched the two EPIs head to the nurses' station to help with the polio investigations while she caught up on paperwork.

~ ~ ~ ~ ~

Lacey received four more polio cases late that afternoon. She rubbed her temples, frustrated. She prayed they could wind this up and put an end to the mayhem. When the nurses were busy and out of earshot, Lacey phoned Jake and told him about the plan.

"No way." Jake's voice kicked up an octave. "It's too dangerous. This is a police matter, not something for you to be handling. Good grief, you're a nurse, not a cop."

"Jake, be reasonable. We don't have enough evidence to go to the police. Besides, look how they're taking care of my stalker." Lacey snorted. "Plus, Joe's gonna be with us. We'll be fine."

"No, Lacey. It's too risky."

"Please. Try and relax. This will not be dangerous."

"I won't take a chance on something happening to you. This person has to be mentally unstable. No telling what she might do if she's cornered."

"There will be three of us, for Pete's sake. We'll be just fine." Lacey tried to insert firmness in her tone. "I'm going to do this. I have to. And we've got to act tonight."

"The only way I'll agree to this high-risk scheme you've cooked up is if I'm in on it with you. I mean it. I'm not taking a chance with your life."

"Fine." Lacey sighed in relief. For a minute, she had wondered if their plan would bomb before it had a chance to work.

"Todd can drop us off," Jake said. "I'll let him know what's going on. Then I'll call your mom and okay an overnight for the boys."

"I'm sure it will be fine with Mom. Gotta go now. Love you."

"I love you, too. I'll see you at five."

Lacey hung up and had a sudden craving for something dipped in chocolate, and lots of it. She opened her drawer and eyed the bag of Snickers bars that were begging to be eaten. Her mouth watered and she wanted chocolate, bad.

Or did she?

No. She didn't think so.

What she really wanted was to stop the maniac terrorizing her county and put an end to all the useless disease and death. It was time to quit looking at herself as a failure and step up to the plate. She had to take charge of her life. Take charge over the bingeing. Over the self-criticism.

And in that instant, Lacey knew she wasn't a loser. Never had been, except in her own mind.

She picked up the bag of candy bars, smiled to herself, and tossed it in the trash.

CHAPTER FIFTY-THREE

At 5:30 p.m., Lacey ushered her husband and Joe and Linda through the back door of the health department. She stood for a moment, watching Todd's Escort disappear around the corner before she tugged the door shut.

"Wow, it's dark in here," Joe whispered.

Lacey clicked on a penlight that was great for looking down throats but almost useless in cavernous places or deserted buildings. She treaded cautiously through the large clerical workspace with everyone on her heels. She turned into her office and opened the blinds an inch so the outside security lights could illuminate the room.

"That's better. For a minute I thought I'd gone blind." Joe chuckled and flopped down in a chair. "You're sure she'll come in the back?"

"She has to. All the employees have keys to that door. No other way she could get in. And once she's in, she'll have to walk right past my office to get to the lab."

"Okay." Linda gulped audibly. "Let's go over this one more time. When we see headlights pull in the parking lot, you and Jake will go to the door at the far

DELIBERATE MALICE

side of the lab. And Joe calls 911, right?"

"Yeah. Jake and I will be in place before she gets in the back door. And Joe will have more than enough time to make the call."

"Sounds good," Jake said as he finger-raked his hair and scooted into a chair. "I just hope the police are in the parking lot by the time she runs out that back door."

"They should be. We're not that far from City Hall." Lacey wondered how hard it could be for two men and two women to physically detain one female for a few minutes.

It is a woman, isn't it? She wasn't up for any surprises at this late date.

Lacey and Linda sat beside Jake and Joe. Four sets of eyes watched diligently out the window as time ticked by. Headlights entering the alley from either direction would be spotted instantly, so there would be ample time to get into position.

After a while, Lacey's eyes burned from staring so hard. She rubbed them and looked at her watch. Almost nine.

Where is she?

"She should've been here by now." Joe fidgeted with his smart phone that he'd put on mute. Then he stuck it in his pocket. "What if she doesn't come?"

"She will." Lacey knew the saboteur would have to act soon if she wanted to get her hands on the new batch of vaccine. And apparently her modus operandi was to debase the vaccine as soon as it came in.

Linda squirmed in her chair. "If she doesn't show, we're messed up, big-time."

"Not really." Lacey's gaze wandered out the window and back again. "Remember, I found vaccine missing, and then returned, in the refrigerator."

"Yeah?" Joe arched a brow. "Well, proving the

vaccine has been tampered with isn't going to tell us who did it. And if we don't catch her in the act, I'd say she's home free."

A bolt of panic flashed through Lacey's chest. She couldn't let herself think about the possibility they wouldn't catch her. They couldn't let her get away with this. So much depended on their success. She leaned back and tried to relax as the night stretched endlessly on.

Nine o'clock became ten o'clock. Jake touched Lacey's arm and asked, "You okay?"

"Yeah." She stifled a yawn.

"Tired?"

"Exhausted. This sitting around is worse than working."

"I could use some caffeine." Joe pushed up from the chair. "I'm gonna raid the break room. Anybody else want anything?"

Lacey passed Joe the penlight. "Grab a six-pack of Coke out of the fridge. And make it quick, will you? I'll yell if I see anything."

Lacey stood at the window, wringing her hands.

When Joe headed down the hall, she reminded him again to hurry. Linda peered through the blinds while Jake stood in the doorway for the few minutes it took Joe to make his run.

Joe set the six-pack on the desk and passed around sodas. He swallowed a quarter of his in one gulp then sighed. "I needed that."

Lacey popped the metal top and took a fizzy sip. The bubbles tickled the back of her throat. It had been a long, restless night, and she felt the effects. She needed a few jolts of caffeine to jump-start her brain. She set the can down and riveted her attention on the window.

The night dragged on; chatter and speculation

about the disease cases grew intense. They couldn't begin to plan their next step until they'd identified the perpetrator. By eleven o'clock, Joe and Linda were ready to abort the stakeout, but Lacey convinced them to give it another hour.

"She has to come tonight," Lacey said. "She thinks we'll start giving shots again tomorrow."

"I think if she was coming, she'd have already been here." Joe massaged the corners of his eyes. "Maybe it's not one of the nurses. If it's someone else, they wouldn't know about the new shipment that came in this afternoon."

"But why was Betty here so early Monday?"

"Just a coincidence?" Linda's eyelids looked heavy. "We're all jumping to conclusions, and we don't really have any proof."

Jake paced the room. "It might be Joan. She was at the restaurant the night our tire was slashed."

"Yeah, but her husband was with her," Lacey said. "He wouldn't just stand by while his wife took a box cutter to a tire."

"You wouldn't think. But this is a pretty crazy case." Jake fell silent. Everyone watched the window for telltale lights.

A sudden yawn sneaked up on Lacey and she stifled it with a palm. She looked at her watch for the hundredth time. Almost midnight. Even she had to agree they were wasting their time. She walked to Jake, who was leaning against the wall with his arms crossed. She pushed a stray strand of hair off his forehead and he smiled.

Linda snapped upright. "Did you hear that?" she whispered.

They all went dead-still.

"What? I didn't hear anything." Lacey grabbed Jake's arm. It couldn't be her. How could they have missed her headlights?

Jake stared at her and his mouth formed an O. He put his hand over hers and turned toward the door.

Grrinnd. This time she distinctly heard the familiar sound of a key turning in the back door's lock; it always made a loud grinding sound.

They were trapped. There wasn't enough time to get to the other side of the lab without being spotted.

The door squeaked open then slowly thudded shut. Joe flew to the blinds and shut them, leaving them in inky shadows. It had to be even darker in the clerical office. Lacey waited for the overhead light to come on. It didn't. Then a beam of light swept the hall in front of her door.

A dark outline moved slowly behind the circle of light, threading through the nursing station and creeping, almost slithering, toward the lab. When the silhouette entered the lab, Lacey heard the door slam shut. The flashlight's glow disappeared.

"Close the door and call the police," Lacey whispered. She stepped over the threshold and clicked on the pathetic penlight. "Jake and I will get into position."

Joe pulled shut the door, leaving Jake and Lacey exposed in the hallway. Every hair on Lacey's neck and arms stood straight up.

This is it, she thought and braced herself. *Time to get this over with.*

Lacey blinked. Her eyes slowly adjusted to the darkness as she headed down the hall with Jake on her like a second skin. She felt the pressure of each step on the bottoms of her feet and Jake's warm breath on the top of her head. They skulked down to the exam room that butted up against the lab. She stopped and listened. All she could hear was her heart pounding like a jackhammer.

She slinked past the exam room and turned left. A hint of light sifted under the lab door. It was open just a crack. They'd have to move fast. It wouldn't take her long to load up the vaccines and make a run for it. Lacey needed to witness her taking the vaccine out of the refrigerator and absconding with it. That way, she couldn't lie her way out of this.

Lacey flattened her back against the wall. Blood whooshed in her ears. She knew she'd show up like a neon sign if she was caught peeking around the door. But she'd have to chance it. She had to catch her in the act. This had to stop. *Here and now. Tonight.*

She sidestepped one foot at a time down to the lab's west doorway. Her heart hammered against her ribs and nauseating spurts of adrenaline coursed through her veins. Her feet felt clumsy as her toes curled tightly in her shoes.

She pressed her ear to the wall and listened. The refrigerator kicked on and hummed its competence. She sidled two more soundless steps along the wall. Her hand reached for the knob. Praying the hinges wouldn't creak, she pulled back the door an inch. Sweat droplets beaded on her forehead. She wormed her head forward and peered through the gap.

She felt her eyes go wide and her jaw dropped.

She jerked back and leveled the back of her head against the wall, trembling.

She grabbed her throat with one hand and clamped the other over her mouth, barely suppressing a scream.

CHAPTER FIFTY-FOUR

She crammed the last vial of polio vaccine into her bag and saw a slight shadow of movement out of the corner of her eye. Her head darted back and forth looking around the long, narrow lab. Nothing. Just her imagination. She lambasted herself for being so jumpy and zipped up her tote bag.

She closed the refrigerator door, wiped a drop of perspiration from her brow, and leaned against the opposite wall. Her heart thudded in her chest, and she pulled in a breath to calm her nerves. She needed another drink.

Pulling herself together, she clicked the flashlight on and turned off the overhead light. She opened both of the lab's doors. Leveling the beam in front of her, she followed the luminance through the doorway.

She tossed a look over her shoulder. Was that a noise? She twirled around, shining her light in a wide arc around the room. She saw nothing and heard nothing.

What in the world was wrong with her? She'd not felt this much anxiety during her previous raids, not even the first one.

CHAPTER FIFTY-FIVE

Lacey felt Jake squeeze her trembling arm. His face, creased with confusion, was inches from hers. She cupped her hand over his ear and whispered, "It's Ann."

Disbelief clouded Jake's shadowed features.

Lacey couldn't believe it, either. Of all the people in the workplace, Lacey never would have suspected Ann.

He opened his mouth, but Lacey raised a finger to her lips. His jaw closed, but she saw the conflict on his face as the wheels turned behind his eyes. She held Jake's gaze a beat then turned toward Ann, still unable to believe her eyes.

Why was she just standing there?

Not able to see her face from this angle, Lacey could only guess she was deep in thought. But why? *What do psychopaths even think about?*

She thought of Betty and felt a twinge of regret, sorry she'd been so quick to put the blame on an innocent person.

The silence in the health department was unnatural, and the tingle of unease at the base of her spine suddenly zipped to every nerve. She could almost smell Ann's evil.

Jake tapped her arm. When she turned, he mouthed, "What's she doing?"

Lacey shrugged. She had no idea but wished Ann would hurry up. It was imperative that they stop her. But why wouldn't she move? The eerie hush was getting to Lacey, making her half crazy and totally frightened. As if Jake could sense her feelings, he squeezed her taut shoulder. It relaxed a fraction as soon as she felt his touch.

Finally, Ann turned the light off and pushed the door back. Lacey prayed she wouldn't step through the doorway at this end of the lab. She didn't.

It was too dark to see anything except the tunnel of light from Ann's flashlight. Lacey tailed her as closely as she dared, cringing at the thought that she'd turn and scan the flashlight beam directly on her.

Ann walked out of the room and turned left. Lacey moved quietly across the lab and stuck her head around the door as Ann passed through the nurses' station and hesitated in Lacey's office doorway. Lacey wondered if Joe and Linda were still in there.

Oh my gosh, she thought. *I hope she can't see them.*

Ann stood in the archway for a few seconds, shining her light all around the office. She was mumbling something unintelligible, her voice gravelly. Unexpectedly, she spewed out obscenities against Lacey that echoed through the building. Lacey felt a quiver of trepidation flash through her body, and her knees went weak. Jake reached for her hand.

Ann grunted and walked away.

Jake held her hand while they trailed Ann down the hall. He pulled her close and squeezed her shoulder. She knew Ann had reached the back door when a glimmer of light seeped in and a cool breeze whipped across Lacey's hot face. She was happy Jake had insisted on joining them. He motioned over his shoulder at Joe and Linda's dim outlines. Everyone was ready and in place. Just a couple more minutes and this nightmare would finally be over.

Just as fast as Ann shut the door, Jake and Joe pushed it open and lunged through. In an instant, they were each holding her arms.

"That's far enough," Joe said.

With a full moon overhead and the security lights glowing under the eaves, the parking lot was lit up. Ann's eyes filled with shock as she scanned the four of them. She pulled viciously against the men's grip, kicking and squirming. She was muscular but no match for the guys.

"Let me go!" She screeched and twisted against the men. "Get your hands off me. What do you think you're doing?"

Headlights turned into the parking lot and blinded Lacey for a second. A police car pulled to a stop and two uniformed officers jumped out. Lacey silently thanked God for their prompt arrival.

Her ears pricked as Ann hurled profanities at Jake and Joe, accusing them of assault and threatening a list of lawsuits.

"You can't do this to me. I have my rights!"

Ann screamed at the top of her lungs between bouts of foul language. She calmed down somewhat when the tall, young officer with a Southern accent read the Miranda and the older officer cuffed her.

Lacey stepped closer and looked into the eyes of the woman who, until a few minutes ago, she'd considered a good friend. "Can you just tell me why?"

Ann spit in her face.

CHAPTER FIFTY-SIX

"Get down, Lady." Lacey raced to the golden retriever who pawed the fern in the family room. She was just a baby and didn't know the rules around their house yet.

Jake had surprised Lacey and her mom with two adorable puppies, brother and sister, on Mother's Day. He'd even named them Lady and Tramp. Corny but sweet, and so predictably Jake.

Lady cocked her head and made a beeline for her. Tail wagging frantically, innocently. Lacey dropped to her knees and Lady planted her paws on Lacey's chest then gave her wet puppy kisses with her rough little tongue.

Lacey ran her hands over Lady's thick, taffy-colored coat. She had a few white hairs on her chest and looked a lot like Sophie. Surprisingly, that didn't upset Lacey. Sophie had enjoyed a good, long life filled with love and had definitely made the Bookman's lives richer.

"You're such a good girl, you know that?" She scratched Lady's ear and the puppy gave her a warm doggie smile. "Yes, you are. A very good girl."

"Hey. I wondered where my sweeties were." Jake

strode into the room and patted Lady's wiggly head.

"You got a letter." He held out an envelope. "It's from the jail."

"The jail?" Lacey ripped open the letter, puzzled. She scanned the page and said, "It's from Ann. She wants me to come visit her."

"Why?"

"Says she wants to 'explain things to me.'" Lacey made air quotes and sighed.

"She's probably going stir-crazy. I can't imagine she's had any visitors since she was arrested. Richard didn't even go see her before he took a hike."

Lacey nodded. Richard was devastated the night he'd stopped over to apologize for his wife's erratic behavior. He told them that he'd quit his job and planned to leave town. Said he couldn't support someone who was capable of hurting innocent kids. Lacey suspected their marriage had never been all that stable to start with.

"She's up to something." Jake eyed the letter suspiciously. "She's been in county six months and now all of a sudden she wants to see you?"

"What could she be up to?"

"I don't know. But I sure don't trust her." Jake narrowed his eyes. "Are you going?"

"Yeah, I guess. She's behind bars. She can't hurt me anymore."

"Still, you need to be careful."

"I will."

"This is the woman that—"

"I know. I'll be careful."

She gathered her purse and left the house. She headed to the courthouse under the warm spring sun.

Lacey reeled when her thoughts turned to all Ann had put them through. She had to remind herself it was over. No new cases of polio reported in the past five months, and Lacey was only barely beginning to breathe a sigh of relief. The disease had finally run its course—the nightmare was over.

But the incident would live for years to come. Thirty-six children ended up with the dreaded disease, thanks to Ann's sick scheme. Eight children lost their lives and six had permanent paralysis. Not counting the four teens who died from tetanus. Todd might have been number five if she hadn't insisted on a Td booster at Dr. James's office—a viable dose of tetanus, not one that had been rendered useless. Lacey shivered. She suspected Ann was disappointed Todd hadn't been one of the victims.

Lacey had heard rumors that Ann's attorney was planning to use the insanity plea. Word had it she stood a good chance of getting off with a lighter sentence—ten to twenty years rather than life. Lacey shook her head at the thought and reluctantly made her way to the jail.

Ann wore an orange jumpsuit and sat across from Lacey in the visiting area. A thick, fingerprint-smeared glass partition separated them, so they had to speak through phones.

Ann's hair hung limp and stringy around her face and needed a cut and style. A shampoo wouldn't hurt, either. She was pale and appeared ten pounds lighter and ten years older.

"Hello, Ann." Lacey was the first to speak.

"Lacey. It's so good to see you."

"How are you?" she asked, then immediately knew how lame that sounded.

"As good as can be expected. Considering..." Ann gestured at the glass barrier and barked out a laugh.

Her chuckle had no glee and Lacey tried to conjure up a morsel of sympathy.

"Have you heard when the trial will start?"

"Sometime in June, my lawyer said. Of course, there will be a change of venue because everyone in this town is out to crucify me. I wouldn't stand a chance."

"Hold on, Ann." Lacey struggled for composure. "You have to consider the magnitude of your actions. The vicious crimes you committed. Children are dead. Children are physically disabled." Lacey tamped down her tone but not her message.

"You're right. It was terrible."

"And talk about pre-meditation. You tampered with the vaccine for years!"

"I don't know what I was thinking. You know, to do all that I did. It just wasn't me."

Then who was it, if not you?

Lacey knew Ann was lying or completely delusional. What she did wasn't a whim; she'd planned and plotted for years. Very methodical in her madness.

"I never meant for it to go as far as it did," Ann said. Lacey shook her head, not able to believe one word uttered from that woman's mouth.

That was what Jake had said to her about Kimberly. He hadn't meant for it to go that far. Even though things were good between her and Jake, what he'd let happen left a scar on her heart. Yes, she'd forgiven him. And yes, she loved him. More than life. But there was still a little something deep down that festered on occasion.

Pastor David assured her in time it would feel as though it had never happened. "Just hang in there," he'd told her on more than one of her down days. That was exactly what she'd been doing. Jake was worth it.

Lacey looked at the shell of a person she'd once admired, the depressing cubicle, and the haggard woman sitting across from her. The woman she'd shared intimate dreams with since high school, although Ann hadn't seen it that way. She'd thought of her as the enemy. This was the woman who'd tried to ruin her career and her marriage and drive her over the edge. And almost succeeded.

"Have you heard from Richard?" Ann asked.

Lacey shook her head. "Not since right before he left town."

"He left town!" Her jaw dropped and a frantic look slid across her face. "He's gone? Where did he go?"

Ann's shaky hands gripped the handset and Lacey wondered if she was getting any medication for withdrawal symptoms. Richard confessed he was aware of her abuse of alcohol and drugs over the years; she'd mixed prescription Xanax and wine on a daily basis.

Lacey sighed. "I'm sorry, Ann, to just blurt that out. But I thought you knew Richard moved away. And no, I don't know where he went. Even he wasn't sure where he'd end up when he left town."

"Oh well." Ann shrugged. "Maybe it's for the best."

Ann fidgeted with the phone cord and shifted on the small stool. Tears welled up in her eyes then spilled over. She wiped the back of her hand across her face.

"Lacey, I've done a lot of terrible things. To a lot of people. And I know I don't have the right to even ask you. But I am asking. For your forgiveness. I'm sorry. Can you find it in your heart to forgive me?"

"I've already forgiven you." She would never forget the horror of Ann's actions and certainly would never condone the horrible things she'd done. But she'd learned that holding on to anger would hurt only herself. "And I'm praying for you."

"Oh, thank you. But no need to pray. I've found God. I'm a better person now. Really."

Lacey sighed. Somehow, she couldn't buy that. She heard the words, but they sounded phony, rehearsed, and just didn't ring true. Even the slight smirk on her face revealed deceit personified.

"For your sake, Ann, I sure hope so."

"Well, I'm trying." Ann glared through the dirty glass. "You always were a know-it-all. Always!" She spoke through gritted teeth then, just as quickly, her expression changed, and her lips turned up into a tight smile that didn't quite make it to her eyes. "Just kidding, Lacey, about you being a know-it-all. Sorry. And I am trying. Really trying. To make peace with God, you know?"

Her glib response left Lacey doubtful. "I could have my pastor come and talk with you."

"Oh, would you?" Her voice dripped with saccharine sweetness and oozed phoniness personified.

Lacey flinched, wondering why she'd come here. Ann wasn't just cruel. She was ill. A sociopath. She needed intense psychological therapy, and that was beyond Lacey's professional scope.

"I'll be happy to," Lacey said. Maybe a visit from Pastor David would help her. After all, God was still in the healing business. "Well, I need to go. Is there anything else I can do for you?"

"Just pray my trial goes well and that I don't have to go to prison. I really miss nursing. I want to get out of here and get back to work."

Lacey stared at her. Cold prickles crept across the back of her neck and pulled up the hair on her arms.

Ann free to work again?

The thought terrified her.

ABOUT THE AUTHOR

Born in Arkansas, Lois Curran spent most of her childhood in Salem, Oregon before her family moved to Missouri when she was fifteen. She now considers the Ozarks her home.

An avid reader, writing has always been her passion. Lois decided to become a full-time writer after she retired from her position as Director of Nursing at her local health department. As a Registered Nurse, she uses real world details to create believable characters.

Cruising and traveling are high on Curran's list of favorite things to do. She also enjoys taking pictures of her many adventures and sharing them on social media. She spends the remainder of her time doing what she loves best – writing.

When Lois is not writing or reading, you will find her working out at the gym, or drinking a latte at her favorite coffee café near her home.

Curran is a member of Sleuths' Ink Mystery Writers, Ozark Romance Authors, and American Christian Fiction Writers.

Made in the USA
Monee, IL
03 January 2024

51021406R00177